Laura, The Tycoon's Daughter

RAILWAY ROMANCE SERIES, BOOK 1

SARA R. TURNQUIST

MOUNTAIN
SUMMIT PRESS

If you would like to stay up-to-date on this and other series from Sara and receive a free ebook, sign up for her newsletter:

https://saraturnquist.com/list

For the memory of Casey Jones

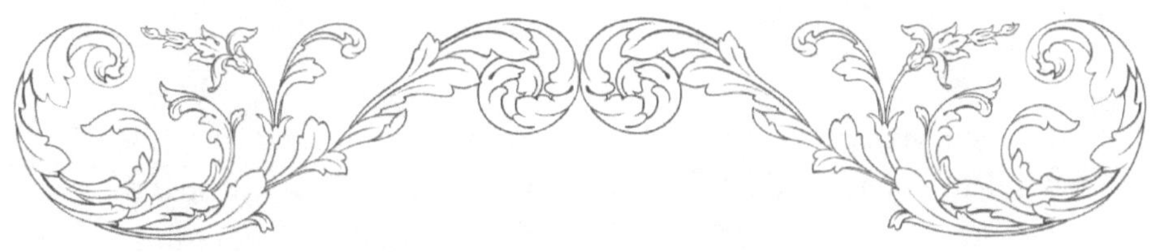

CHAPTER 1
Celebration

New Southern Hotel
Jackson, TN
March 3, 1899

Laura Millington released a sigh and wished to be anywhere but at a banquet with her father. Why did he insist on her presence at these things? She would much rather flee the social arena altogether and run off to find her next story.

She frowned. My, wouldn't Father find that amusing. But one day... one day he would see her stories for what they truly were. Setting her jaw at that thought, she determined that it would be so.

Maybe then he would take her seriously and regret forcing her into the mold she had come to know, but despise, so well.

Laura smiled at a gentleman passing on her left. He gave a slight bow. She dipped briefly then moved on. She did not wish to give the man any room to perceive interest from her.

Was it rude? Did she care?

Father would balk at her shunning attention from a man who appeared to be of certain means. But his objections didn't matter. Laura had much greater aspirations. Though the fire for writing filled her bones, Father had made it clear her future would not be invested thusly.

"There you are, darling," Father's unmistakable booming voice called from off to her right. Could she not escape the man, even in this crowd?

She shifted her focus and found him, as usual, amid men who were no doubt important. To him.

Still, she put on her best grin and strolled toward him. "I do apologize for my tardiness, Father. I was—"

"Never mind that." His words were sharp—more so than she imagined he would risk at a gathering of this nature. "I have people I would like you to meet."

Pressing her lips together, she longed to speak further but swallowed her words and put on her dutiful daughter mask. Yes, that would best please Father.

He made quick introductions around the circle.

She worked to commit the names to memory as she greeted each one. Father had certain expectations about her engaging with men of note.

"This is my daughter, Laura Millington, the gem in my crown."

Her face warmed slightly. She appreciated his rare compliment, but his behavior wore thin. Nothing about his recent treatment gave any indication she was precious to him. But how could she blame him? What with all the trouble and heartache she caused. But she buried her uneasiness so she might smile and thank him.

"My father is too kind." She didn't intend for her words to come out tightly, but they were past her lips before she could stop them. Easing the tension in her shoulders, she tried again. "He is gracious indeed."

The women in the small group batted their eyes, and the men returned their focus to her father, all but dismissing her. Just as her experience had taught her to expect of these pointless interactions.

She had naught to do but stand about, her father's work of art to be admired but not taken seriously.

The few women about excused themselves and moved off in a smaller cluster. Could she follow? As much as she would wish to do so, it would be of little use. There was no more real acceptance for her in their company either. Naught remained but to resign herself into her role—one she played rather unevenly.

After some moments, a hush came over the crowd. Had the guest of honor arrived? Laura turned to the main entryway. This gathering was for the sake of a man who had neither position nor accolades to his name. But Casey Jones had become quite the renowned engineer for the Illinois Railroad Company. The songs that the workers sang about Casey had reached her ears, but she had put most of the details out of mind. For they were surely embellishments.

Soon enough, a figure no less than six feet tall entered with a timid woman on his arm.

A great cheer roared about the room.

The man jerked back. Did he not know? His reaction belied that he had not expected such an affair.

A chorus of "He's a Jolly Good Fellow" filled the space.

Laura joined in, although her knowledge of the man was limited at best.

Casey Jones, man of the hour, had assuredly become the most well-regarded engineer in all of the company. Today was about him.

Her father grabbed for her hand and set it on his arm.

Laura fought the urge to pull back. He was only playing his part. She must play hers.

Did he wish to keep her close? Or to appease his own sense of vanity? As much as she wanted to believe the former, her heart tugged toward the reality of the latter. The truth remained. She was merely a pawn he would play at some point when he might gain the most advantage.

Those about Casey Jones and his wife pushed and shuffled them to the front of the room and the head table.

Her father stiffened. As one of the railroad owners, he anticipated being the center of attention. Not today. And he bristled at the attention lavished upon Casey, a man so far beneath him.

A few kind words were spoken by a stockier man—a greeting and invitation for everyone to take their seats. The crowd responded, bustling to find their tables.

Father leaned close and spoke in his firm, directive tone. "I was not able to secure you a seat at my table."

Why would he have made such an effort? He made no secret of how tiresome he found her. "But your table shouldn't be far."

She nodded and held back a sigh. Her father was rather important and would be placed where he could have the most advantageous conversations. Not something she relished being a party to.

Laura pulled back her hand as he did the same. Was he so ready to be rid of her? But what use was there in pondering that further? She moved about the tables, searching for her place. Although, as she glanced about for place cards, she noted that only a few seats were assigned. Trading her hunt from one form to another, she sought a familiar face, or at least somewhere she might have pleasant conversation.

A table to the left boasted a good mix of young women and their husbands. She maneuvered through the pressing crowd and grasped the back of the only available chair.

Her hand collided with another, larger one.

She jerked away.

A gentleman, tall and solidly built, stood nearby. And he drew back his own hand. "Pardon me—"

"I apologize, I didn't realize—"

They spoke at the same time.

He grinned. A smile that traveled into his brown eyes, both pleasant and warm.

Heat rose up her face as he stared.

"Please," he said, a kindness to his words, "Take the seat. I'll find somewhere else."

She scanned the room. Most of the available spots had been claimed.

"Sir, are you and your wife looking to sit together?" a voice from the right interjected. "We can move and make space."

Then the ladies and gentlemen around the table shifted.

Laura spotted a vacant chair across the table. "Oh, please, don't go to any trouble. We aren't together."

"I thank you," the brown-eyed man said to those at the table. "But it is wholly unnecessary. The lady and I are not acquainted, much less attached." His gaze warmed her once more. "Though should I hold such a prize, I would not keep it secret."

A general mumbling surrounded her, with only few words discernible.

"Perhaps, then, sir," a dark-haired woman directly to the stranger's right said, "you can make good use of this opportunity."

The temperature of Laura's cheeks rose again. Could she hope they weren't as deeply red as the extent of the heat she felt?

"I thank you," the gentleman said, tossing a genial look in Laura's direction before turning back to the woman of raven hair. "Though I might hope, I would not dare presume the lady is unaccompanied." He glanced about her as if to ascertain the truth of his statement.

Laura offered a small smile. "I am here with my father, although he is engaged elsewhere for the meal." She met his gaze again. His very presence exuded a strength and calm. And perhaps a hint of joviality. If only she could shy away. But that wasn't possible, so she said, "I would welcome the conversation."

He nodded and pulled out the chair, gesturing for her to sit.

She settled onto the red velvet cushioned surface and watched as he took a seat as well.

His shoulder brushed hers, and her uneven smile widened.

Such nonsense. How was she so out of place? She had been in the presence of other, perhaps even more handsome, men without faltering. But there was something about him that drew her in and set her at ease.

He turned, now facing her. No doubt the embarrassment was easily discerned upon her features. She had always done poorly at hiding her feelings.

"John Patterson." He leaned closer.

Her breath caught. "Pardon?"

"My name...John Patterson." His smile quirked. Did he find this amusing? "Though only my mother calls me John. To everyone else, I am Jack."

"Laura Millington." She offered her gloved hand—an action she quickly regretted. As his fingers enclosed hers, a tingling sensation spread up her arm.

She pulled back faster than was necessary. Could he see how he affected her? She prayed not. "It is...good...to meet you." No matter how she attempted to rein in her reaction to the myriad of sensations, it was for naught.

The couple to Mr. Patterson's right spoke, and he turned his attention on them.

She looked about, hoping to find someone else at the table with whom to make conversation. But as she leaned away from Mr. Patterson, her elbow bumped into the outstretched arm of the man beside her. An arm that had reached for his glass of wine. A glass of wine that now splattered over his stark white shirt.

JACK COULD NOT DETERMINE IF THE CONVERSATION HE HAD broached with the couple to his right would amount to anything. Not that it needed to. Sometimes social gatherings were just that—social. But he struggled with a reason to be attentive to something that was a means to no end. Not in his world. Everything added up...or should. Such was the life of a man who spent much time with calculations.

Everything had a purpose. For one, this benign conversation distracted him from the woman in the fine green gown to his left. She had made him linger at this table instead of seeking another available vacant seat. More so, it pressed him to allow those around the table to upset their arrangement and make a space for him beside her. Which he now regretted, because her presence had become magnetic. So, he focused on the couple to his right.

That was until the fair creature to his left rose abruptly. He barely had a moment to register her movement before the man to her left seethed.

What had happened to bring about such a reaction toward a lady?

The red-faced man struggled to his feet, arms waving. And he bore evidence on his shirt of a glass of red wine gone awry.

"Look what you've done." The man's nostrils flared.

"My apologies, sir," Miss Millington said, her face awash with embarrassment. She gripped her cloth napkin and appeared as if she might attempt to blot the stain. Then she hesitated. As well she should.

The man took a step back and his companion, perhaps his wife, came into the fray. Her features paled at the man's vehemence. She took the proffered napkin and, pressing between the man and Miss Millington, spoke soothingly to the irate man while dabbing in vain at his shirt.

"You've ruined it." His voice rose all the more, and he pushed away his wife's hands.

"Sir, I promise I will make this right." Miss Millington's concession sounded genuine.

The man glared at her and maneuvered closer until he stood far too near. "How?"

Miss Millington gripped the chair as if fearful she would fall over.

Jack could stand it no longer. He stood and moved to Miss Millington's side. "I say here, this is nothing that allows you to speak to a lady so harshly."

The man's eyes widened as he set his gaze on Jack. "Are you speaking for her?"

Jack pressed his hands downward between them as if such an indication would calm the man. "This was clearly an accident. Of the most unfortunate kind, I agree. But an accident all the same. Shaming the lady will not solve anything."

Miss Millington took a sharp and loud intake of breath, although Jack stood directly beside her. Did his presence not dissipate her fear?

"Come, Frederick," the timid woman beside the man said and set tentative hands on his arm. "Let's make the best of—"

He shook her off.

The woman shrank back, all but raising an arm to shield herself. What would this man's anger come to?

Jack would like nothing more than to set him straight. Or at least rescue the man's wife in some way. That would be a futile effort. However, Jack stepped forward and between the angry man and Miss Millington. While he may not be able to correct the man's behavior toward his wife, Jack would not allow this man to press the worst of his ire onto the helpless Miss Millington.

"I beg you, sir," Miss Millington's voice had more strength than expected. "I can replace whatever has been spoiled."

The urge to turn and determine if her features shown her feelings as completely as her voice did overwhelmed him. But he kept his gaze leveled on the man before him. For certain, he would assure that this man did not become violent while in his company. Toward anyone... least of all Miss Millington. The muscles in Jack's arms tensed in preparation to defend either or both of the women.

"See here." Jack's voice was tight. "As the lady said, the spill was not intentional. Perhaps it is best if we all part company."

"Am I to take my seat and go about the evening as if I haven't a spoiled shirt?"

"Frederick," the wife said, her voice small and hesitant, "We don't have to stay. It would be nothing for us to slip out."

"Listen to your wife. Her words are the most sense spoken in these last several moments," Jack said. Rather than dispel the heat of the situation, the words deepened the color upon the man's face. So Jack pressed on. "Either way, I will thank you to calm yourself. Miss Millington does not deserve your irate words."

The man paused. "Millington?" He craned his neck as if to look around Jack.

Jack leaned to the left to block his glare, lest he seek to intimidate the lady. "Yes...Millington. A good strong name, is it not?"

The man—Frederick—swallowed hard. Then he looked to his wife. "Perhaps it is best."

"Yes." The woman set a hand to his shoulder. "I do tire."

Frederick's eyebrows lifted and he considered the woman at his side. And, at length, nodded. "Very well."

For whatever reason—of which Jack told himself mattered not—the man allowed his wife to lead him away.

Jack turned to face the lady he had protected.

Her features were wane. The way her lips parted slightly before sealing, called to him. She was so vulnerable, so in need of his strength.

He put a hand to her elbow.

She jerked away from his touch. "I thank you for your assistance, Mr. Patterson. But I assure you, it was not needed."

Was not needed? Jack looked at the retreating forms. Not needed? The man had been prepared to give Miss Millington a piece of his mind before Jack stepped in.

Miss Millington's gaze caught his as she squared her shoulders. "Is this what you think? That a lone woman is not capable of holding her own?"

He balked. She would accuse him of such? Him? The man who came to her aid? Jack narrowed his gaze. How could she dismiss his efforts? It wasn't as if she had been managing the situation well. "Only when said woman falls victim."

As soon as the words were out, he wanted them back. Flames of gold flashed in her eyes even as her features stiffened.

"Victim am I? Well, I never..." She glanced back in the direction of the table. Perhaps only then aware of the audience they had enraptured.

Had they, indeed, become the spectacle he suspected? But he refused to back down from her glare.

"Come now," he softened his tone, "I only intended to lend aid."

A fire sparked in the amber depths of her eyes, bringing a light to the chestnut that made them fairly shine. "Aid that I neither requested nor required."

There would be no winning here. Still, a part of him wanted to push harder in his own defense. Perhaps because she was striking when angry, perhaps because the interaction gave rise to an excitement that coursed through his core.

Either way, one of them had to diffuse this situation.

"I apologize, Miss Millington. I was...unaware." He wanted to speak further but doused that desire with a dose of reality. This was neither the time nor the place to continue their discussion. And while he may find enjoyment in the rise of her emotions, that, too, bordered on inappropriate.

She settled back into herself and her eyes dimmed to a calmer, softer brown. It was a shame the fire in her waned, but probably best. He found it a bit too alluring.

Jerking her chin upward as if that would gain her inches to her height, she met his gaze for a long moment before looking away.

"May I, miss?" He reached for her chair. If they could be seated, all else would resume its due course.

She jerked the chair away from his grasp and settled in it without his assistance.

"It is indeed a pity," he said, letting the word stretch as far as he dared, "that something so fine should be spoiled."

Her gaze flew to his. And hardened. Did she discern his reference to more than the man's shirt?

He bit back a smile and took his own chair. And turned to the couple on his right again. "Now, where were we?"

The dark-haired woman offered a wide-eyed glance and gripped her husband's hand.

This was going to be a long night.

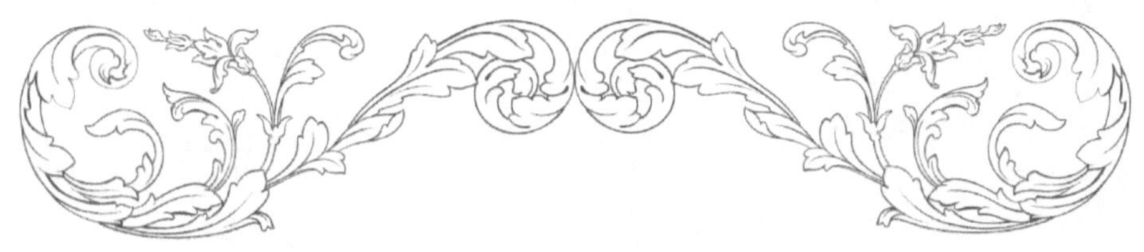

CHAPTER 2
New Acquaintance

Why had that man insisted on sitting beside her? Laura tightened her lips and forced her attention opposite. Only, no one sat there anymore. The wait staff cleaned any remnants of the spilled wine. The only remaining evidence of her gaff was a splotch on the tablecloth.

Seeing as she refused to speak to Mr. John Patterson, there was no one to talk with. No matter. She would be fine. It wasn't the first time she had been left to her own devices to entertain herself.

At that moment, a man stood and continued his accolades for Mr. Casey Jones. Perhaps one of his friends...at least the man spoke with such familiarity. Before finishing, he introduced the next man to speak. Laura recognized Mr. Bose Lashley as he stood. Laura noted his kind, soft way of speaking, but there was real metal in his words. All listening applauded his words of praise.

On and on, several stood and spoke of Mr. Jones and his adventures on the railroad.

Laura's fingers itched for paper and pencil with which to memorialize her observations and the words spoken. What would be the use? No one would publish such an article. Not from her. At least, not yet.

She squared her shoulders. One day. She was determined that it would be so.

As her attention shifted back to the speaker, she noticed one of her father's friends, Major E.S. Hosford. As he finished his longer speech, the Master of Ceremonies stood again, mist about his eyes. What a testament to the impact of Mr. Jones. At last, he called the guest of honor to his feet.

Laura's focus pinned on the exceedingly tall man as he rose. So far back from the head table, her view was somewhat obscured by all who sat between. Even from her vantage point, she could best describe his hesitation in speaking as emotional. He appeared somewhat hardened by a life on the railroad, still she glimpsed vulnerability in his affect.

He reached for the smaller woman beside him. While Laura wagered that any woman would seem petite next to him, the woman—his wife, she decided—appeared dwarfed by his size.

Mr. Jones tugged at her to stand up beside him. And then he spoke, his words both timid and wavering...and brief. He expressed, or at least attempted to, how this moment and the honor of the celebration touched his heart.

The responding thunderous applause filled the hall.

Laura glanced to either side, gauging the response of those around her. It was just natural—the writer in her wanting to gather as much information as possible.

It took a moment for her to realize Mr. Patterson had disappeared. More, it bothered her that it mattered. While she couldn't help the slight pang in her chest due to his absence, she could control how she responded. So she firmed her posture and turned her attention to the front of the room as Mr. Jones embraced his wife and shook hands with those around him.

All in all, he seemed rather moved—the mark of a good, humble man.

Laura was glad for it...for him. For all she had heard of him in the snatches of conversation about her this evening, she believed him deserving.

She scanned the room, seeking out someone familiar with whom to pass the time. Was she so desperate to be out in society, away from home, that she would jump at such an affair and consign herself to a lonely evening?

Sighing, she released some of the tension in her shoulders. Perhaps she should rejoin Father. Catching sight of him across the space, she maneuvered around and through those between them. As she neared, her father looked in her direction.

"Ah, dearest, there is someone I want you to meet." Her father waved her over.

Was this better than being alone, surrounded by strangers? At this late moment, she decided naught. But the time to hide had gone.

She offered her father a simple smile and nod as she picked up her step. If only she didn't have to watch her footing in this dreadful elegant gown. If not for that, she might get a better view of whomever Father had deemed important enough to concern her with.

Perhaps she should be thankful he considered *her* important enough.

She closed the distance and halted. The man from earlier—John Patterson—stood beside her father, waving a dismissive hand as he glanced her way. Was he trying to convince her father he did not wish to be better acquainted with her?

The viper.

As much as she wanted avoid him, she would not give him that satisfaction. Gripping her skirt, she marched to them with more gusto than she'd believed possible.

"Yes, Father?" She put on her sweetest smile.

Mr. Patterson watched her...maybe a little too closely. It made her uneasy.

"This is Mr. John Patterson, one of the designers working for the Pullman Company. You know, darling, the passenger car company. He is a fine railway engineer." He slapped Mr. Patterson on the back.

What that had to do with her, she did not know. Why should it matter to her that a man working on the passenger cars had come? But the investigator in her did pause, and she kept a smile plastered on. "Yes, Father, we have met."

Father's eyebrows gathered. "You have?"

Mr. Patterson found his voice before she could. "At the meal. It was my privilege to sit with your daughter."

She nodded, not wishing to extend their acquaintance for even one more moment or bother her father with the tale of the wine mishap.

Again, Mr. Patterson found his voice first. "If you will excuse me, Mr. Millington, Miss Millington, there are others whom I need to speak with—"

"Nonsense," Father said, his voice carrying farther than Laura would like. "This fine evening calls for dancing." He held out a hand in the direction of the open space where several couples already swirled about. He set his gaze on Mr. Patterson. "Would you leave a fine lady to her own devices when she should be dancing?"

"Father, really, I—"

"I will have you enjoy yourself." Father beamed, his brightness more put on than he could disguise. At least not from her. He had ulterior motives. That much was clear. Though what that might be, she did not know.

Either way, she had little desire to extend this interaction with Mr. Patterson, who was clearly put off by the very suggestion he take her hand. For her part, she wanted even less to be her father's pawn.

"It would give me great pleasure, Miss Millington," Mr. Patterson said, surprising her as he bowed slightly, "if you would do me the honor." He held out a hand, but the glint in his eye issued a challenge.

She would be remiss if she let on that it bothered her. That would be intolerable. So she slid a hand into his and widened her smile. "I thank you, sir. That would be delightful."

To say Jack was taken aback by Miss Millington's response would be putting it mildly. Who was this woman, rising to his unspoken challenge? It caused something to shift in the pit of his stomach. Regardless, he would not reveal the inner workings of his mind. He led her toward the other couples, keeping a firm grip on her hand. In fact, he had to remind himself not to hold her too tightly.

He spun her to face him and pressed his other hand gently to her back. Then she was in his arms. Moving to the rhythm of the music, he led her, swaying this way and that, stepping in time to the beat.

She kept in sync with him gracefully, her gaze averted to the side, her arms stiff as if to guard her space. Her lashes lifted and her gaze swept his.

He looked away. Why that should bother him, he didn't know. It wasn't as if he had done anything wrong—quite the opposite. Hadn't he been the perfect gentleman? How else was he to behave? It was difficult to think clearly with the scent of lilac filling his senses. Did she have some oil or perfume that made her smell so heavenly? It intoxicated him. And the warmth of her body, so close to his, reminded him that there was more to life than holding grudges.

Perhaps he had acted too quickly before and rushed to her defense unnecessarily. In as much, perhaps he had offended. But, again, it was difficult to order his thoughts with her so near—something that shouldn't affect him so. He was a man of science, of math. Things *always* fell in line. The sum made sense. The outcome ever a predictable thing.

Then why did his heart thunder in his chest? He could not refrain from looking at her any longer.

She had, however, averted her eyes again. It allowed him to admire her profile. Her smooth skin appeared creamy as porcelain. Would it be as soft as the whole of her seemed to be? Something in him wanted to reach up and graze her cheek. Would he discover it was warm as her closeness made him? Did he affect her the same way?

Amber eyes jerked to his.

Could he act as if he hadn't been staring? He held back from such pretense. Would he even be able to feign disinterest successfully? His heart tugged at him. "Miss Millington, I wanted to say—"

She shook her head. "It is not necessary to fill these silences. Certainly not in this case."

Her glare pinned him. Though it wasn't as if he wanted to escape it. How were her eyes so full of light, as if they burned from within?

"Please, Miss Millington..." His words sounded more strained than he'd have liked. "Let me apologize."

One of her perfect brows lifted. Was that permission for him to continue?

He sucked in a breath, wishing his preoccupation with her wasn't so obvious. "I am sorry for any offense I may have caused."

Her tight-lipped glare became a frown. "Any offense you *may* have caused?"

He forced himself to breathe in and out before responding. "Clearly, I have offended. Though I admit, I am not certain how. My efforts were meant to aid." He paused to lick his lips. Why was his mouth so dry? "I apologize all the same."

The hardness of her gaze softened, if only just. She drew in a breath herself. Was this a struggle for her as well?

"Perhaps..." she said before biting at her lip. "Perhaps I was a bit rash..."

The way she hitched her breath, causing her chest to jerk upward, gave way to a flush of heat within him. Dare he continue to tempt himself? For the sake of his own preservation, he might need to give himself a reprieve from her gaze. Attempting to disguise his distraction, he pulled her slightly closer.

She resisted at first, but then eased into his movement. Would she relent? Give up her spite?

A flash of red caught his eye. A young woman, dressed brilliantly in a ruby-colored gown, laughed loud enough to fill the whole of the large room. She was on the arm of Mr. Casey Jones, clearly delighted as he twirled her about.

That wasn't his wife. Who could it be? A sister? Jack did remember mention of a rather gregarious sister of noted beauty.

Laura stiffened.

He jerked his regard from the other woman and back to Laura. A bit too late.

She had clearly followed his gaze a moment ago. And now her face was a mask of repulsion. Halting her movements, she almost caused him to stumble.

"Pardon *me*, Mr. Patterson. I didn't realize I was keeping you." She pulled against him.

He tried to maintain his gentle hold on her but realized that might be misinterpreted.

Indeed, her eyes gleamed as if on fire as he did so.

"Unhand me," she retorted as she jerked free.

"Miss Millington, I—"

She stepped back. "I believe, Mr. Patterson, that our dance has ended. I bid you good evening."

He stepped toward her, wanting desperately to make amends for his stupidity.

She whirled around to face him again. "And I will thank you to leave me be. I could not be less interested in anything you have to say."

As she turned away once more, it seemed her gaze caught on the lovely woman on Casey Jones's arm. But she kept moving off as if it did nothing to faze her.

And left him there, the perfect fool.

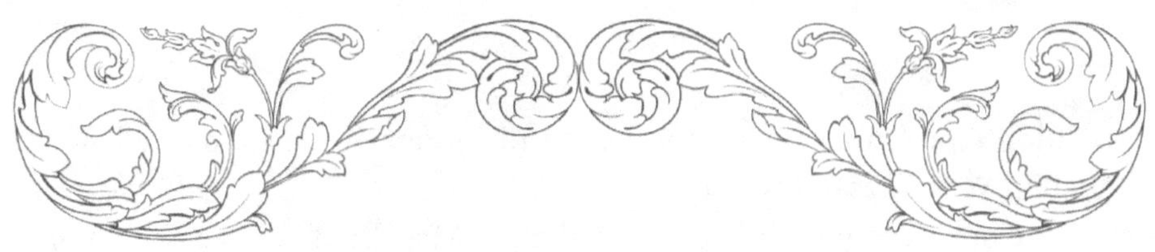

CHAPTER 3
In the Night

Brady Family Boarding House
Jackson, TN
March 3, 1899

With the weight of her father's condescension upon her, Laura forced her shoulders not to slump as she settled into her room at the nearby boarding house. A younger man with a shock of rusty red hair brought her things to her room for the evening as a gray-haired woman, who had introduced herself as Mrs. Brady, freshened the bed and closed the drapes. The gentle blue of the quilt, threaded through with yellows, introduced some calm to Laura's worn spirit.

Though Laura wanted to speak, to exchange pleasantries, she was weary from words exchanged with her father. He had been none too thrilled with the way she had treated Mr. Patterson and had much to say on the matter. Still, she wouldn't feel bad about that. She shouldn't. After all, he had been the one who misstepped.

She didn't need his aid. As if that had not offended enough, he couldn't peel his eyes off the beautiful blonde while he danced with Laura. What was in his head?

"I hope everything is to your liking." Mrs. Brady closed the coverings on the final window in the room.

Laura swallowed her trepidation, lingering from her exchange with Father. "I have no doubt it will be." She looked about the room. The soft colors and warm toned wood proved cozy enough. While Father preferred the elegance of a hotel stay, Laura wished for more private, comfortable accommodations. Yet another thing they disagreed on.

The younger red-haired man looked to Mrs. Brady.

She nodded and said, "Our other incoming guest may need your assistance."

Laura offered a smile of gratitude as he quit the room.

"Do you need anything before you retire, Miss Millington?" Mrs. Brady paused in the middle of the room. "The dinner hour has passed, but I could find something in the kitchen if you'd like."

Laura waved a hand. "I thank you, but that won't be necessary. I have come from a celebration that boasted a rather enormous food spread. I don't think I could force down another bite."

Although it was true the hotel's banquet had been filled with all manner of delectable treats, Laura had not partaken of much. Still, she didn't mention that her resistance was due to her emotional upheaval after the conversation with her father. Instead of betraying such things to this stranger, Laura moved to the vanity.

Mrs. Brady paused. "Would that be the reception at the Southern Hotel?"

"Yes, it would be." Laura turned back to the woman and peered closer. It wasn't possible that she had been there, returned, and changed into her more plain dress, was it?

"Casey Jones is married to my Janie." The woman beamed with pride.

"Indeed?" Laura smiled.

"Yes, do you know him?"

"Unfortunately, I cannot say that I do." Laura sighed and shifted toward the mirror, pulling pins from her hair. "My father was invited and opted to extend the welcome to me." She glanced at the woman's reflection to gauge her reaction.

"Oh, I see." The woman's warm grin fell slightly.

Laura quickly added, "But I would say it is to my own failing that I am not of Mr. Jones's acquaintance. He seems a rather fine train engineer...and a good man."

The woman's lips curled at the edges again. "That he is."

An awkward silence fell over the room. Should she be the one to break it? But her weariness overcame that desire.

"I will leave you to your ablutions, then, miss." The older woman dipped her head and made swift her exit.

Laura let out a breath. Maybe she should take an extra couple of days here. That may vex Father, but she needed some space. Her stomach twisted at the thought of another tense exchange with him, but she pushed it to the side and made short work of her evening routine. Before long, she settled into the bed, light extinguished, and closed her eyes.

Only, sleep did not come.

She tossed her body to the side and squeezed her eyes shut.

But images from the evening—of the heated interaction over the wine, her ire toward Mr. Patterson, and her difficult words with Father —all stymied her attempts to ease her mind into slumber.

What was she, then, to do? It rarely worked for her to force things from her mind. She pushed out a breath and set her gaze on the ceiling.

Heavenly Father, You tell us to cast our cares on You, that You give rest to the one whose mind is set on You. Give me peace. Help me let go of these things weighing on me.

And again her mind filled. She made the effort to turn her thoughts to focus on memorized Scriptures. She rehearsed every one of them and let her thoughts settle into the truth of them.

Her body relaxed, and the spaces between thought and the pull to unconsciousness lengthened.

And then her stomach growled.

The traitor.

Had she not partaken sufficiently at the party? But she knew...

between the heavy things of the evening and her ire at Mr. Patterson, she hadn't eaten much.

Perhaps she should have taken Mrs. Brady up on her offer of sustenance earlier. Maybe she could now?

She rose and pulled on a robe. Then opened the door to the hallway.

Foreboding silence met her in the dark thickness of the house.

She retreated back into her room and, closing the door, shifted her arms to pull off the dressing gown.

A painful churning in her stomach stopped her. She doubted sleep would come if she could not feed it. How did she find herself in these situations?

But she was not helpless. She didn't need assistance to find bread in the kitchen.

Pulling the robe back upon her shoulders and closing it with the cloth belt, she again crossed the room. Careful to step lightly, she moved into the darkened hallway. Where exactly was the kitchen? She looked about, remembering that a set of stairs brought her up. Her search needed to take her to the lower level.

Slipping down the steps, she scanned the area. The dining room sat to her right. Perhaps the kitchen would be just beyond. She padded in that direction. And was rewarded when she stepped through the door and found herself facing the oven. Now where would the bread be kept? She scoured the counter until she found a dark wooden breadbox, a small door concealing the contents.

The hinges squealed more than she liked. She halted her movements, but upon hearing no further sounds, she chose to be quick about it.

Removing a loaf half gone, she realized she'd have to find a knife. Thus she resumed her search of the room.

As she did so, she dropped the breadbox door. Another squeal and slam as the door banged shut, caused her to jump.

She held her breath.

Still nothing.

Letting out the pent-up air, she decided to tear off what she required to keep her stomach from its painful grumbling.

She pulled at the previously cut end of the bread.

A soft squeak startled her.

She halted, praying it was only something non-mousey in the kitchen.

But the sound became steadier. And seemed as if it came from the hall.

She swallowed. Had she wakened someone? How embarrassing it would be to get caught. Though it seemed unlikely she would not be.

Glancing about, she listened for the sound as it came ever closer—so slight, and her heart took to pounding.

"Ah, excuse me, I did not expect to find anyone about." The masculine voice sounded every bit as startled as she.

And familiar.

She turned to the door, swallowing against the rising trepidation in her throat.

There, in the doorway, illuminated by moonbeams coming in through the window, stood Mr. John Patterson.

JACK PEERED THROUGH THE DARK, WISHING HIS EYES WOULD adjust better so he could discern the features of the woman in the room. Likely, even if he could see, he wouldn't recognize her.

Her sharp intake of breath was louder than it should have been.

Did he know her? Did *she* know *him*? Or was her reaction borne of surprise at being caught?

"I didn't mean to startle you, miss." He stepped closer.

She moved back and hit the icebox. A hiss and grunt followed.

He halted, though he couldn't stop himself from reaching out a hand. Everything in him wanted to rush to her aid, but he held back from doing so. Perhaps because he had been reamed enough today for gentlemanly behavior.

"What are *you* doing here?" The accusing voice that cut through the darkness caused his heart to race, and he jerked his hand back. It couldn't be. "Miss Millington?"

She didn't move, nor did she acknowledge his statement.

His mouth suddenly went dry while his palms were anything but. He rubbed his hands down his pajama trousers. "Same as you, I suppose." The steadiness of his voice surprised him. "Looking for something to eat."

She remained quiet.

He squinted, an attempt to see her better. She was silhouetted against the moonlight coming in through the window behind her. Her features were denied him, but the gentle waves of her hair flowed freely. The urge to touch them overwhelmed him. Would they be as soft as they appeared? He scanned her form before he could stop himself. Her robe and nightshift prevented him from appreciating her figure, but the belted waist gave him some sense of her curves.

That did not help his unease. The perusal of her gave rise to a thickness in his throat. He attempted to swallow past it and failed. And he was given to a coughing fit.

He leaned over the counter and tried to catch hold of air again.

The patter of feet across the wooden floor whispered.

Then a hand rested on his shoulder. "Are you well?"

Was that concern in her voice? It only intensified his inability to steady his breathing.

The long fingers upon his shoulder gave way to a patting upon his upper back.

It did not help, but the fact that she attempted to aid, did.

When at last he was able to control his lungs again, he turned. She had come closer and that nearness unnerved him. But he couldn't make himself move away. Her features, in the light of the moon's beam, struck him. Her creamy skin fairly glowed.

"Are you well?" Her words were harsh.

Had he not answered her? No, he had become distracted and tongue-tied as a schoolboy. But he cleared his throat, hoping that would help. "I am."

She pulled back.

The loss of her touch bothered more than it should. That confused him.

Her head dipped away. Then drew up toward him again. "I...didn't find much. Just bread."

He looked at the loaf on the counter where she must have set it down.

She spun away. "Not that I pilfered. I just went straight for the breadbox." Her stomach growled. Loudly.

He nodded and fought the smile that pressed at his features. "Are you hungry?"

She jerked her head up and down once. He was fairly certain that if he could see better, he'd spy red upon her cheeks.

"Allow me." He moved past her, his arm grazing hers. Did she feel this heat between them? Dare he give it credence? Or dismiss it for simple attraction? For certainly that was all it could be. He'd become much more than a starry-eyed boy prone to flights of fancy. He was a man, and he had a real hot-blooded attraction for this woman. As any man would. She stole his breath.

He picked up the discarded half loaf and brought it back to where she stood, backed against the counter. Would she move away as he neared?

He broke off a piece of bread and held out a chunk to her.

She hesitated but for a moment before taking it. Still, she would not eat.

Perhaps it would be best if he made it easier. So, he pulled off another chunk for himself and bit into it. Sourdough. Firm on the outside, but soft in the middle.

She watched him.

"Please. I can hear your stomach. I know you're hungry."

Her long inhale was her only response.

"It's good. Sourdough."

She lifted the piece to her lips and bit into it.

Now he watched her. Until he realized he stared. And held his breath. Forcing out withheld air, he rested against the counter across the kitchen and continued to eat.

And so they sated their hunger in silence. But what might he say? Had he not apologized, only to have her strike out at him again? Did she have some sort of chip on her shoulder? As if she sought a reason to dislike him.

He shouldn't care. But he did. Swallowing the bite in his mouth, he spoke. "How long will you be in town?"

She paused chewing.

"Come now, we are in the same boarding house. It's not as if I won't know whether you are here or not."

Still, she remained silent. But her jaw moved as she commenced eating.

"I'm here for another week."

"Me too." Her voice sounded so timid that he almost missed her words.

Opting not to make much of it, he nodded. What more could he say? Did he want to prolong this interaction? Or make a way for other exchanges? His relaxed holiday had just become more complicated.

She popped the rest of her bread in her mouth.

"Do you need more?" He lifted what remained of the loaf, preparing to tear another bit off.

She held up a hand and shook her head. "That's not necessary. I think I will be fine until breakfast."

He set what was left of the sourdough in its wooden box. "Thank you."

"For what?" An edge laced her voice. As if she just then remembered that she had been angry.

He sighed. "For your assistance. Before."

She folded her arms across her chest. "Anyone would have done so. I wasn't about to watch you choke yourself."

He shifted his feet so he faced her. "Nevertheless, thank you."

A *hrumph* was the only response. So they were back to this?

It wouldn't do for them to interact this way. Not only was it unseemly behavior and wholly unnecessary, but it may also make unnecessary trouble for their hosts. "I truly am sorry."

Now that she faced the moonlight and he stood in the shadows, he noted her tightened mouth as she looked down.

"And I know I offended you."

She pressed out a laugh. Definitely not genuine. It really had bothered her.

"I assure you I only wished to determine if the woman was Mr. Jones's sister. I had heard talk of her and wanted to appease my curiosity. Still, it was ungentlemanly of me to do so whilst in your company."

Her face tilted up and her eyes widened.

He came across the space between them...uncertain that he should, uncertain of the wisdom of such an action. But his feet moved as if they had their own will. "Forgive me? Again?"

She watched him; the gentle beam of light coming in made it seem as if her eyes danced.

He waited several seconds, thick with this attraction between them and heavy with his regret before giving up. Shrugging, he moved toward the door. "I shall see you in the morning, Miss Millington."

"Wait," she called. Then pressed a hand to her mouth. Did she fear she had spoken too loudly?

He shifted to face her, intrigued.

"It is forgiven." Her words were terse, but he believed them genuine. "I have no desire to hold ill will."

He dipped his head briefly. "I thank you."

Several moments passed before she pushed off the counter and moved past him and through the door. But her hair, bouncing off her shoulders, left a whiff of lilac in her wake.

She did not pause again but disappeared around the corner. Then the low creak of the steps told him she took to the stairs.

As should he. But he waited until he heard the muffled sound of her door closing. Only then was it safe to let out the breath he held. This was trouble, and he knew it.

He must take better care to guard himself against such an entanglement. Not only would it end in naught but a wounded heart, it would likely not be tolerated by her father. Niceties at a banquet were a far cry from encouraging a match. Not with the vast difference in their stations. And that was a man he dared not anger.

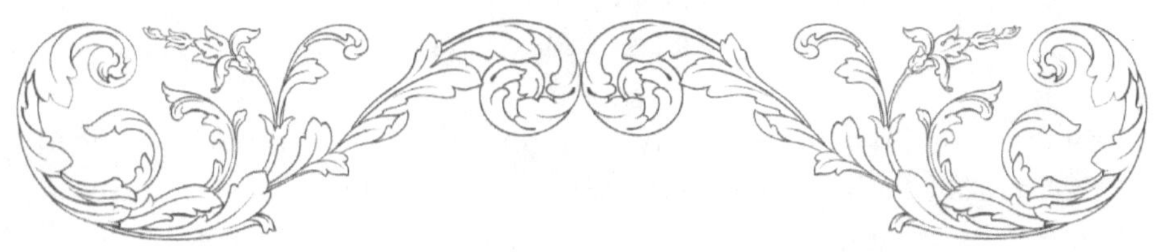

CHAPTER 4

Truce

J ack prepared himself for the day. With a bit of grogginess about himself. He had spent much of the night restlessly, thinking of his evening interaction with Miss Millington. What was wrong with him? Was he so taken with her that he would lose sleep? It defied reason. He'd spent time in the acquaintance of many a lovely lady before and not lost his wits. He would not lose them now. Hadn't Clarise been a rather becoming young woman?

That thought left bitterness in its wake. He had promised never to think of her again. And he wouldn't. Shoving an image of her face out of mind, he pressed on and descended the stairs.

He'd only come halfway when he heard the lilt of a woman's laugh. And he knew, somehow he just knew...Miss Millington. Who had made her so lighthearted? His heart thumped at the possibility of another man catching her fancy.

Straightening his jacket, he stilled his pulse. That should not concern him. It didn't. He had no designs on her. Nor the leeway to have designs.

Still, it irked him.

Stuff and nonsense! He picked up step once more, moving in the direction of the musical sound. Would he have followed it should the dining room, where her laughter originated, hadn't been his intended destination? Perhaps he would not have allowed himself to be drawn off course by curiosity over who pulled such levity from her hardened exterior?

He took a deep breath as he came off the last step and pushed into the nearby dining room. Though he told himself to not seek out her fine features, his gaze latched there first.

Her head tilted back, mouth parted and eyes closed, as she reveled in the moment. Could this be who she really was? Who she could be with him had he not offended her so?

Shaking his head to clear it, he ran a hand down the lapels of his jacket. When he looked up, everyone stared at him. Had his face reddened as much as he feared? The brief glimpse of her had seeped heat through every part of him. "I, ah, regret my late arrival."

Mrs. Brady waved him in. "Never mind that. Just sit yourself down and get some food. You must be starved."

He smiled. And again his gaze shot to Miss Millington. Would they exchange a knowing look—an acknowledgment of their shared late night snack?

But her regard had turned to her plate.

He nodded at Mrs. Brady and settled in a chair as far from Miss Millington as possible. Not as far as he'd have liked, but given the size of the table and room, it would do.

He scanned the room. An older couple sat near Miss Millington. They appeared to be dressed well enough, but not so fine as to be well off.

Mrs. Brady reached across him and scooped scrambled eggs onto his plate. She also plopped a biscuit and bacon alongside them. "A strong man like you needs good eating," she said as she loaded more bacon onto the pile.

He held up a hand. "I thank you, Mrs. Brady, that will be quite enough." Grabbing his napkin, he laid it on his lap. But he caught Miss Millington watching him out of the corner of his eye. It pulled his attention toward her.

She shifted her focus to the older, balding gentleman across the table. "And how long have you been acquainted with Casey Jones, Mr. Smith?"

"It's hard to say. I knew him back when he was a telegrapher...before he saw his dream of being on a locomotive come to pass."

"Oh, Harold, you are too modest," a plump woman beside the man piped up. "Don't be fooled," she said, looking to each person at the table, "My Harold talked him up. Perhaps even the reason he got on that first engine."

"You exaggerate," Mr. Smith muttered, pink about his cheeks. "He was a fine boy even then...though it's difficult to ever have called him a boy. That man has always been mighty tall...even as an adolescent."

"Shoo," Mrs. Smith said as she frowned.

"It's to his own credit he earned his place and reputation. I may have said the truth about his abilities to the boss, but I was one of many."

The Smiths' banter was endearing. While the chance to sneak another peek at Miss Millington tempted him, Jack focused on his food. He picked up the biscuit first. After the nicely flavored sourdough last evening, he expected magic. One bite into it, he realized his folly. The dry, hard puck instantly dried his mouth. But he chewed and swallowed all the same.

Mrs. Brady smiled and moved off into the kitchen.

"What brings you to Jackson?" Mr. Smith said.

Jack's head remined down, focus on his plate. He had no interest in butting into the conversation. Silence pervaded the table. Jack looked up and found all eyes on him. At least, he suspected as much. For he refused to look at Miss Millington.

Was Mr. Smith's question directed at him?

"Ah...I came for the celebration. And for a meeting with a certain gentleman." No need to disclose his business to these fine folks. Nor need he share of his intention to holiday beyond the opportunity to bend the ear of some important men.

"So, business and pleasure," Mr. Smith said before shoving a fork full of eggs into his mouth.

The whole room fell into silence.

Was Jack the cause? Or perhaps the awkwardness between him and

Miss Millington? The urge to look in her direction overcame him, but he resisted.

"I heard tell," Mr. Smith said, blotting his mouth.

Jack sighed, grateful for a refuge for his attention.

Mr. Smith set his napkin down and continued. "A wild tale really, of a heroic act by Mr. Casey Jones."

Miss Millington leaned in.

Jack pretended he hadn't just glanced at her.

"Do tell." Miss Millington's voice took on that light and airy quality again.

Why hadn't Jack brought out this more pleasant side? Was his mistake—or rather, *mistakes*—yesterday evening so egregious?

"There is a story—I wager it's true—about a time Casey's engine came through a small town. Not sure where exactly. Anyway, some children played about the tracks. When they saw the engine barreling down the rails, they rushed to get out of the way. All but one small girl. She'd been frozen to the spot."

Miss Millington paused her bite and lowered her fork. "Oh my."

Mr. Smith held up a hand. "Turns out, as the story goes, Casey was on the engine, oiling, and, as the engineer slowed the train, Casey maneuvered onto the cattleguard."

"No!" This from Miss Millington again.

Mrs. Smith had a grin the size of the Mississippi River, but she tried to hide it behind her napkin.

Mr. Smith paused his tale, as would any good storyteller. And his narrative capabilities shone.

Mrs. Brady came around the table, pouring more coffee for all prepared to receive.

Miss Millington leaned even closer. "And what happened?"

Obviously, Casey Jones had not been thrown from the train that day, but what chance of sparing the girl? If the story were even true.

Mr. Smith's voice picked up a lighter beat and he set a hand on the back of the chair next to him. "Casey reached out those long pole arms of his and scooped that child up. Safely."

Miss Millington's jaw dropped. "That can't be true."

Jack shook his head, so intent on Miss Millington's reaction, he'd almost missed the final note of the tale. "I'll say it can't be so."

Mr. Smith shrugged.

It must be a tall tale. The stuff legends are made of, to be certain, but not likely to be truthful.

Mrs. Brady stood upright. "As sure as I stand here today, it happened."

Jack watched the woman, her face solemn and sincere.

Miss Millington, hand to her chest, exhaled. "What a hero indeed!"

Once more Jack found himself jealous of Mr. Smith earning Miss Millington's regard. Shaking it off, he pushed back from the table. He needed space.

"Are you all right, Mr. Patterson?" Mrs. Brady stood at his side in the next moment.

"I assure you I am." He pressed a smile onto his features. "I just need some of this spring air."

"There are some fine gardens not far from here." Mrs. Brady took his plate, which had more food on it than he should feel good about wasting.

He nodded. "That sounds like a fine prospect." Standing, he then pushed his chair in. It took force of will to keep his gaze from wandering.

But the clatter of dishes and the scrape of chair legs made him more curious than he could deny.

Miss Millington had risen. "I would very much like to see those gardens." Her gaze caught his and held. Another challenge? If so, what could it mean?

"Well, I'm sure Mr. Patterson would escort you." Mrs. Brady stood near the kitchen, poised for some task.

After a moment's hesitation, Jack found his voice. "It would be my pleasure."

Miss Millington nodded and moved toward the stairs. "I will just need to grab my wrap."

Mrs. Brady watched her leave and moved about, clearing dishes.

Jack's skin prickled as if someone watched him. When he turned back to the table, Mr. Smith's knowing wink rewarded him. Though that did not make Jack feel more confident. Rather, he had never been so uncertain in his life.

LAURA STEPPED INTO HER RENTED ROOM. THE WARMTH OF the sun bore into the space, making her question if she needed the wrap. Still, she grabbed it from the nearby chair. Spring in Tennessee often meant a chilly breeze at the very least. So she pulled the shawl about her shoulders.

It became more difficult as her fingers trembled. Could she not calm her nerves? Why, then, had she pushed for an invitation? It seemed impulsive. Besides, what made her want to solicit an offer of escort from Mr. Patterson? She did not enjoy his company. There had been nothing but friction in every one of their interactions. What, then, caused her to reach out?

She shook her head and reached for a hat. This second guessing would amount to naught. For she got exactly what she wanted, didn't she? Mr. Patterson awaited her at the bottom of the stairs.

Glancing in the mirror, she set a hand to her quaking midsection. Every hair remained miraculously in place. She appeared a fine picture of a lady prepared for a stroll. What would her father think of her going about in the company of a tradesman? Likely such a prospect wouldn't be received well. It was one thing to share a dance at a social event. Quite another to make a regular practice of it.

Laura firmed her stance and dropped her hand, set in her choice. And that stilled her shaking. She would not avoid Mr. Patterson nor back down. No matter what her father might think. Perhaps even in spite of what he would say.

A nagging in the back of her mind bade her pay heed. She didn't want to examine any of it, but a thought crept into her awareness: Was this an excuse to anger her father?

She shook that off. It wasn't so. It couldn't be. She didn't care what her father thought. This was nothing more than an opportunity to let Mr. Patterson redeem himself.

With that, she marched out of the room and to the stairs.

Just as expected, Mr. Patterson stood at the base of the steps, hands behind his back, gaze trained out the front window.

She attempted to free herself from her earlier thoughts. Mr. Patterson was a kind man, even if those instincts had been misdirected. He *had* come to her aid last evening. What else should she expect from a gentleman? How could he know his lack of confidence in her ability to handle the oaf from the reception would chafe her?

Mr. Patterson looked up the stairway and caught her gaze.

She peered down at the stair before her and stepped down, ignoring the clarity of his blue eyes. And the intrigue within that pulled at her. Such was nothing to concern herself with. They would have this stroll and that would be that. Perhaps they might part on friendly terms. Yes, that was a fine goal. Her only goal.

Glancing at his face, she found him staring.

Must he? She felt almost caged by his scrutiny. But she offered him a smile. One that he returned as he shifted his focus downward. Though she spotted that his cheeks reddened. Was this some effect she had on him? That thought warmed her from within. Did it heat her cheeks as well?

Now taking the last of the stairs, she stood beside him.

He met her gaze once more. "Ready?" The word cracked his voice.

"Yes." She plastered on her best, most appealing grin. The one she practiced for social occasions, the one that always met with Father's expectations. Only this time it was more. Her heart beat behind it.

He shifted his feet and held an arm out toward the front door.

She moved past him, walking nearer than was necessary.

His breath hitched.

Yes, she did have some sort of effect on him. That excited her. Every nerve tingled, yet guilt tugged at her as well. She chose to ignore it.

He opened the front door and followed her outside.

She turned and threaded her arm around his.

He pulled back and her heart dropped, but he soon steadied himself and firmed his hold. Then he pressed onward, steering them toward the gardens.

Silence filled the space around them. Had she forgotten how to behave in such a setting? She didn't want to be a twit or mindless flirt. Did she even wish for his tender feelings? If not, why did she push boundaries by taking his arm? She had no answer. Not even for herself.

The perfume of roses and gardenias soon surrounded them. She paused and breathed in deeply.

Mr. Patterson halted as well.

She sensed his eyes on her once more. "Is it not absolutely delightful?"

He coughed. "It is." Again, his words broke as if he struggled.

And she knew...she had the power here. A still small voice whispered that toying with a man's affections would not be right. She pushed that down.

Stepping forward, she pulled him along as she feigned great interest in the beds of reds, oranges, purples, blues, and pinks around them. The flowers, most merely buds ready to bloom, made for a lovely distraction. But she sensed that *she* held Mr. Patterson's attention.

Laura reached out and, with gentle fingers, cupped a tiger lily blossom. "Is not God's creation wondrous?"

"Yes." That word came out more firmly than the others. It drew her gaze to his. Just as before, he stared for a few seconds and turned away.

Pity.

What? Why would she play the vixen? Not even the melody of birdsongs about them could drown out her self-accusation.

"Miss Millington." Mr. Patterson's voice sounded strained. "I beg you, tell me...are you still angry with me?"

She watched him for several breaths. "Did I not forgive all last evening?"

He coughed again. "You did. I but seek assurance it is so. I never intended to injure you in any way." His lips moved as if he wished to speak more on that, but then he seamed his lips.

She glanced at an arrangement of irises. "I suppose I know that." Then she looked at him more fully than she'd allowed herself thus far. "I should apologize as well. I...may have been quick to anger. Quicker than I should."

The words came from somewhere she couldn't explain. Was this how she truly felt—that she had erred in her ire?

He let out a breath, and tension fell away from his shoulders. "I thank you for your candor." He replanted his feet so they faced each other.

Uneasiness filled her middle. It seemed as if she'd lost her advantage. As she watched his azure gaze delve into hers, her knees weakened. How did he do that?

"I would like us to be friends." His words were soft.

She nodded. "I would like that very much as well."

A smile spread his features. And it warmed every part of her.

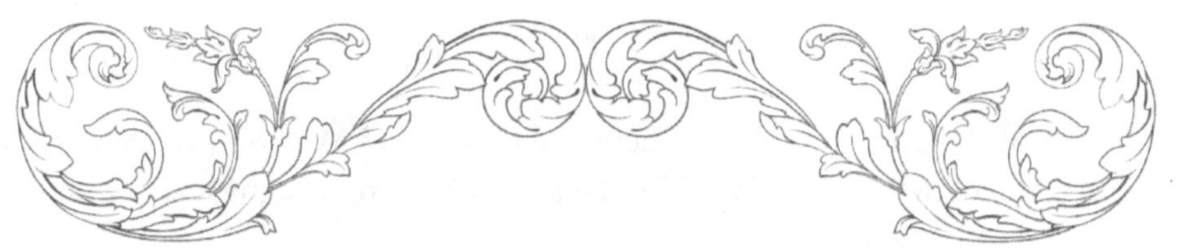

CHAPTER 5

Too Close

J ack walked up the slender path to the front door of the boarding house. His final meeting of the day had been good, but long. He needed a hot meal and the comfort of bed. The muscle behind his left shoulder burned. No surprise. He frequently carried his tension there. Plenty of that lately. Between these meetings and his interactions with Miss Millington, he stayed on edge. Though no longer due to ire between himself and the lovely lady. Quite the opposite. Their exchanges had been pleasant and downright enjoyable the last couple of days.

Still, tension had filled him during said exchanges. She brought something out in him. Something he wasn't ready to acknowledge. Although, his insistence on fighting it landed him with this aching muscle.

Ah, well. The soreness proved better than outright anger.

He stepped into the boarding house and his senses became filled to overloaded. First, the scent of stewing beef and tomatoes reached him. Dinner would be a welcomed comfort. Not all of the meals he had partaken in this house were. Secondly, music warmed the house. Someone created quite the skilled ambiance.

Jack glanced about. Other than the obvious clues, there were no signs of the other boarders. Where had they gone? Mr. and Mrs. Smith? Mr. Brady? Miss Millington? Perhaps one of them brought such a beautiful melody from the nearby piano.

He set his case by the door and wandered toward the parlor. The music, full and robust, held a hint of sadness about it. As he neared the front-facing room, the sound rose and quieted, rose and quieted. Whomever played had an impassioned touch. But he wondered...why the grave undertones?

Soon enough, he reached the doorway. Dare he disrupt the musician at work? He thought better of it. Perhaps it would be best to retire to his room until supper.

But the movement of the piece tugged at him. The emotion spilled upon the keys intrigued him. And he came closer and peered into the room.

The piano stood across the larger room positioning the pianist's back to him. Still, he discerned the identity of the artist whose shimmering brown waves fell down her back—Miss Millington.

Should he step within and call to her? Something stopped him. Was it the intensity of her movements? Or an unwillingness to bring an abrupt end to the music?

She leaned into the keys, her slender fingers flying across the intermix of black and white. She'd become lost in the piece.

He did not recognize the tune nor the identity of the composer, but the music mesmerized him.

The melody swelled and the rhythm slowed. And then suddenly it was over.

Miss Millington released a sound that felt raw and real as she hunched her shoulders and folded into herself. She pressed her hands to her mouth, but that did nothing to halt an overflow of emotion.

He could not stop his advance. In a moment, he was at her side. But what was he to do? Did she sense his nearness? He didn't wish to startle her or leave her embarrassed by such a display.

Still, he reached out and laid his larger, coarser hand on her delicate shoulder.

She jerked around. Her eyes were rimmed in red, her face a mask of pain.

He prayed she wouldn't send him away or rush off.

Words formed on his lips to entreat her, but he stopped them and sat upon the bench beside her. He faced opposite, his back to the piano, but turned toward her.

Their eyes locked, and he became overwhelmed with the sense of *her*.

"Miss Millington," he said, attempting to voice his thoughts again. But that wasn't right, not in this moment. "Laura." Her name slipped out on a breath.

Her eyes widened.

Would she chastise him for eschewing a more proper address and speaking so informally?

She looked down at the keys, likely still warm from her touch.

He swallowed. "Tell me."

She shook her head. It was but a slight movement, though done with finality all the same.

Jack drew in a ragged breath and pushed it out. He prepared himself. For certainly, she would run from him or ask him to permit her some privacy.

She leaned into him, her shoulder pressed against his chest. Then she laid her head there as well.

This position they had found themselves in would be considered highly inappropriate should anyone see them. But he was powerless to untangle himself. Instead, he wrapped his arms about her and pulled her closer. "I'm here, Laura."

She released a broken sob.

He held her as she fell apart. Biting back questions that might satisfy his curiosity, he remained steadfast. For such questions may well break the spell surrounding them. And he wouldn't risk that. If his presence could offer her any comfort, he would sit with her forever.

And that's when he knew...he was in trouble.

When did this happen? This turn of attraction to something deeper?

He should set her aright and leave her be. He should turn away and guard his heart better. This road was familiar—more than he wished. Hadn't he been to this precipice, this place of letting go and leaping?

Only, the door had been slammed in his face, with broken promises and betrayal all that remained.

He would *not* go there again. Forcing his arms back to his sides, he set firm hands to her shoulders and set her upright.

She sniffled but didn't question his actions.

Her pain mattered. Though it shouldn't, it did.

He'd best get out of this room before he lost all sense of the line between safety and giving over to deeper feelings. Of taking this road that led to naught but disaster.

With his drawing back, an awareness of what this intimate moment could mean for her reputation became heightened. He pulled from a place of sheer willpower and stood.

"I…" he started, but his throat and mouth were as cotton.

"I apologize." Her words came simply, yet they confused. "That was wrong of me."

He wanted to naysay her, to own his piece of it. But he bit his lip to keep silent in the face of her sweet vulnerability. The barrier between them must be re-established. For where they now approached—where *his* heart neared—was dangerous.

The awkward moment of silence between them stretched.

"I…" he said, then licked his lips in hopes of bringing some moisture back to them. "I should go."

She tilted her gaze up to him, eyes glistening.

Everything in him wanted her to bid him stay, though he knew he hadn't the power to deny her such a request.

And so, he turned on the balls of his feet and slipped from the room. As he moved to the stairs, his ears mutinied and strained to hear if her tears had resumed.

He could not discern any sound.

So he urged his feet to carry him up the stairway, to the safety and privacy of his room. Once there, he shut the door soundly behind himself. And found that while it may create a physical barrier, it did nothing to contain the bleeding of his heart.

LAURA DIDN'T KNOW WHAT TO THINK. SHE PRAYED THAT HER face no longer showed the ravages of her spent emotion. Even if it did, need she care? She was adrift on the sea, with no bearing and no place to make berth.

Jack had offered comfort in his arms, as if a lighthouse making a promise of safe harbor. But it was not to be. For he had obviously regretted his actions. He could not have removed himself with more haste.

And why shouldn't he? She had little to offer beyond a pretty face and a wealthy father. Neither of which did she wish to utilize in securing a man's devotion or affection. Were that the case, it would be nothing more than a vapor, a whisper of what could be.

The stairs creaked and Mr. and Mrs. Smith's gentle conversation echoed in the hall. Such a kind sort. Perhaps even a model of what she only hoped for. How could someone such as she, with a powerful father such as hers, dream that true love would ever be hers? No, she must marry for her father's advantage. She needed to accept that.

As the older couple stepped off the last step, Laura held her breath. Would they turn toward the dining room or veer into the parlor? Was she in any condition to entertain or be entertained? No, she needed a few more minutes to collect herself.

Thankfully, the Smiths seemed intent on their supper, for the altering of their voices indicated they had turned off into the dining room on the other side of the far wall.

She should join them. Perhaps she might make herself comfortable before she must face Mr. Patterson. That prospect soured her stomach. Could she have been more inappropriate with him? First, pushing him to invite her for a stroll the other day, and now spending her emotion on his jacket? She cringed at the reality of it.

Still, she had to face the other boarders. Was this not the very reason she practiced her brave face—the very one her mother had coached her on so many times? Those lessons instilled Laura with a practicality about her appearance and a warning to not let emotions get the better of her. While she could manage the former, the latter had already been lost in Mr. Patterson's regard.

Rising from the bench, she brushed her hands down her skirt. Was she still in order? Peering down, she noted a few wrinkles. These may well be excused by the creasing of the fabric upon sitting. Yes, that would have to be. With any luck, neither the Smiths nor the Bradys would suspect the disheveling of her dress due to her pressing into Mr. Patterson.

He had been a firm place to land, his strength offering her solace. For a moment, she'd been protected, safe. But that, too, was an illusion.

She gathered her skirts and forced herself to move into the dining space, putting on her best and most pleasant grin.

As she rounded the corner, she found the others already so engaged that she slipped in almost without notice.

Mrs. Brady moved to Laura's side as she sat and offered her something to drink.

Laura thanked her with a request for lemonade.

Then she scanned the room. A brief smile from Mrs. Smith and a nod from Mr. Brady even as he responded to something Mr. Smith said helped ease her. Maybe she wasn't so unpracticed with her mask.

However, inevitably, Mr. Patterson would join them. How was she to manage that?

The conversation flowed around her but did not induce her to join in. For she sought any hint, any indication that someone descended the stairs.

Mere moments later, his footfalls betrayed him. They were solid and sure like his broad frame. Her face heated. What were these thoughts? They were woefully out of place if she wished to present a nonchalance to the man as he entered.

Before she had fully prepared herself, Mr. Patterson appeared in the doorway.

She opened her mouth but forced it shut and feigned an interest in whatever Mrs. Smith had said, though Laura had little idea what that might be.

He came around the table to a seat as far from her as he could manage. Her heart fell. Yet she told herself it should not. She had better gain control of her thoughts.

Mrs. Brady brought Laura's glass to her place then clapped her hands. "Shall we begin?"

The conversations in the room quieted.

"We are having beef stew." The woman appeared well pleased with her pronouncement, though Laura wagered it smelled better than it tasted. Though cooked lumps of tomato and boiled meat had never been Laura's preference.

Mr. Brady returned thanks, crossed himself, and invited his wife to serve the meal.

Whatever the stew should have tasted like, Laura did not know. For nothing about the beef, vegetables, or broth could be sensed beyond the overwhelming amount of basil.

It mattered not. All of her effort was spent on avoiding Mr. Patterson while keeping a mind to what she might discern about his movements from her periphery.

He spent the meal quiet and reserved. More so than usual. Did the Bradys and Smiths have any idea? Or even take notice?

The meal had only started when Mr. Patterson rose.

"I beg your pardon," he said, dipping his head, "but I must excuse myself for a bit of a headache."

Mrs. Brady stood, on her feet in a moment. "Oh dear, shall I fetch the doctor?"

"No." Mr. Patterson waved her off. "It is nothing that a little rest won't relieve."

He nodded first to the kind hostess and then to the others. His gaze on Laura was brief, but her breath caught just the same.

"I bid you all good night," he said before turning.

"I fear we won't see you in the morning," Mr. Smith said. "We catch the train for Memphis first thing."

Something tugged at Laura's heart. She had become fond of the Smiths and regretted that her last evening around the table with them had been overshadowed with unsettled emotion.

Mr. Patterson halted. "I am even more sorry to take my leave, then.

It has been a pleasure to make your acquaintance." Then he shifted his focus without looking in her direction and retreated.

Laura could not bear it. She jerked to her own feet.

The two couples stared.

"I...must excuse myself as well." Her words were rushed. "I am rather tired."

A quick glance about told that none of those remaining in the room thought it coincidence. Did they think she and Mr. Patterson had an ill-planned rendezvous? That she would be so common?

She wished for something to say to contradict what they clearly thought, but she couldn't waste time. They would think what they wanted.

Stretching her legs the extent she could with her skirts, she fairly ran after Mr. Patterson. As she stepped into the hall, she spotted him halfway up the stairs.

Closing the distance as fast as possible, she reached for his arm and called out, "Mr. Patterson." Her heart pounded in her ears. Would she be able to hear anything else?

He continued upward, pulling free of her grip.

"Jack!"

He paused but didn't acknowledge her in any other way.

"Surely you can't be so cruel."

He turned slowly and gazed at her. What was that shifting in his eyes beyond the darkened blue?

"Miss Millington, I think it best for both our reputations if you return to the dining room."

Her vision blurred as her eyes watered. Not again. "I only...wanted to say..." What had she intended? An appeal? An attempt to make him rethink his behavior?

He arched a brow.

"I am...embarrassed by my earlier behavior and hope that you will not let it sully your opinion of me." There, that was well said. She prayed it would be well received. Did it even make sense to him?

He grimaced. "It has not."

Why then were his shoulders so stiff, his manner so cold?

"Will you not rejoin us for some coffee?" Even she heard the desperate plea in her voice.

He watched her, his eyes hardened as he seemed to look through her.

Thankfully, the house had darkened. Otherwise, he might be able to see into her...and find things she preferred to keep locked away.

Something shifted in his affect. Was that a softening about his eyes? "I will not."

An ache anchored in her stomach.

His gaze became icy. "I would entreat you to return to the dining room, lest there be cause for the others to think the worst."

She swallowed. He was right. Only a fool would refuse to acknowledge that. So she nodded and looked away. Could she bear to leave this tension between them even for the evening?

Letting out a breath, she relented. "Of course."

His shoulders relaxed a bit.

She tried in futility to move her feet and so appealed yet again. "But I want...that is, I..." Her words wouldn't cooperate. Perhaps this would all look better in the light of the morning. "I shall see you at breakfast... Mr. Patterson."

He jerked his head once and settled his gaze on her hand that remained but an inch from his arm.

She drew it back to her side.

"At breakfast," he concurred. And he remained as he was...waiting, watching.

Laura nodded and moved back down the stairs toward the dining room. But paused by the door and looked back.

He was gone. How he managed to continue with so little a sound, she didn't know.

She pressed on her trained smile as she came back into the room. "I...changed my mind. I could not pass up one of your mouth-watering pies, Mrs. Brady."

The others' faces betrayed a curiosity and doubtfulness, but they returned to their conversation as she reclaimed her seat.

As long as the evening at dinner was, the sleepless night was all the more so. Laura lay abed, restless and unsettled. Somehow, someway she had to make this right with Mr. Patterson. Finally, as dawn peeked over the horizon, she drifted into a fitful sleep.

When she awoke, the day had been fully realized. She dressed and came downstairs to find she was alone with the Bradys. Had Mr. Patterson gone to another meeting?

"Glad you are awake," Mrs. Brady said, "I was starting to worry. Let me get something for you to eat." The woman moved around Laura and set one of the horridly dry biscuits on a clean plate.

Then Laura noticed that only three plates lay upon the table—two that had yet to be cleared and one for her.

"Has..." Laura cleared her throat before continuing, "Has Mr. Patterson already eaten?"

Mrs. Brady exchanged a look with her husband, who lowered his newspaper.

"I'm afraid Mr. Patterson left this morning."

An early morning appointment as she had thought perhaps. Though something in Laura bade her tread carefully. "It's a bit early for one of his meetings. Did he say when he would be back?"

"No, miss." Mrs. Brady leaned over and grabbed the two used plates. "Mr. Patterson has left Jackson."

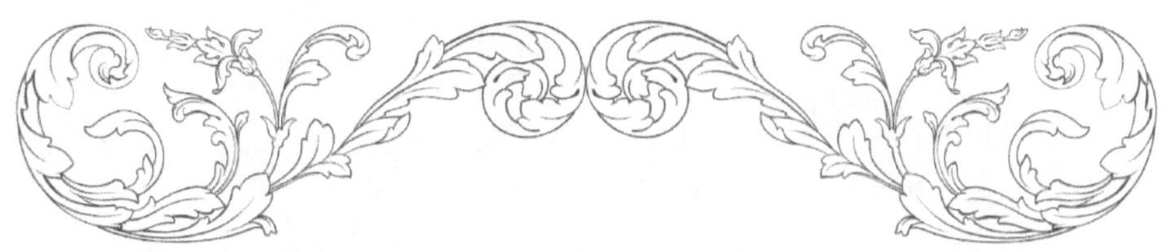

CHAPTER 6

Escape

Tennessee Midland Railroad Depot
Jackson, TN
March 6, 1899

Jack dropped onto the only remaining seat on the last bench. He had done it. He'd escaped the rush of emotions that bade him remain and give Laura a proper farewell. The tumultuous storm had been so thick in his gut he had scarcely managed to leave the boarding house. But it couldn't be helped. Every time he imagined seeing Laura again even to bid her farewell, his heart was left racing and his stomach turning. Even more so than it did now.

Letting out a breath, he scanned the small waiting area at the depot. It wasn't unsightly, though neither could it be described as comfortable. Certainly nothing that could calm his midsection from the torrent that now filled it. Because he would return home ahead of schedule? Or that he neglected his remaining business in Jackson? His superiors may not be pleased about that. Nor could he expect them to understand.

Who did he try to fool? He wasn't so completely out of touch with his own mind. Though he might attempt to lie to himself, he could not deny that the churning was due to what he had done to Laura. How had he even gotten here? The morning hours were a blur.

But two things he knew for certain: he had lied to Laura, and he felt every bit the oaf for doing so. Guilt gnawed at his gut, eating at him. He deserved it. She certainly hadn't earned his rebuff last eve. And he had delivered it so harshly.

The scent of tobacco overwhelmed his senses, returning his mind to the present. A pipe's warm aroma was not unpleasant, though perhaps unwelcome. Turning about, he spotted another waiting passenger across the room breathing out a stream of smoke. It reminded Jack of his father. It took little effort to fall into those memories for a handful of moments. In truth, he sought an escape from his present woes.

Soon enough, he would be home. Chicago always had been home for him. But it became a little less inviting after his father's passing. Though it had provided him a new home with the Pullman Company. One that he treasured.

Pulling out his father's pocket watch, he let memories of the man flow through his mind. His father had taken him to see the trains when he was but a boy. To say he had been fascinated would be putting it mildly. More aptly, he became obsessed. Even as his mother pushed him into the design portion of the industry as a railway engineer, he had longed for something very different—a life operating a train engine, driving the massive locomotives down the tracks leading to wide open spaces.

And what had he done with the opportunity his advancement afforded him? Disappointed his mother when his future with Clarise disappeared. What would he tell her now of his early return? Dare he mention Laura? Or how close he came to betraying his desire to better shield his heart?

How had Miss Millington gotten so close so quickly? Somehow... she had. And he could not risk that. Not again.

A discussion erupted behind him. An older man and woman with familiar voices. He turned to confirm what his ears had already told him: Harold and Eugenia Smith.

Had he not left early enough to avoid them? Could he escape notice now?

"I don't care," Mrs. Smith carried on. "This is a far too ungodly an hour to be at a train station."

"I assure you, my dear, I am not to blame. These were the tickets we could get." His kindly voice attempted to soothe her. Then he lowered his voice to a mild hiss. "Say, is that Mr. Patterson? Just over there?"

Caught.

Forcing a smile he didn't feel, Jack stood. "Mr. Smith, Mrs. Smith, what an unexpected pleasure." He shoved out a hand to meet Mr. Smith's.

The man shook it, but a curious peak of an eyebrow told that the older man was not as assured as to Jack's words. "I thought we had left you tucked in bed at the boarding house."

Jack shook his head. "My business in Jackson concluded, and I am needed in Chicago."

"I see," Mr. Smith said, though his tone betrayed him. There was little chance the man didn't suspect the real reason.

Was Jack so easy to read? Or worse...had he made overtures that were noticed by others? "I did not expect to see you two out and about quite so early."

"Yes," Mrs. Smith groused. "As I was just telling my husband. It was difficult to sleep with such an ill-timed venture looming over us. I'm not as spry as I used to be."

Jack's smile became genuine. He found the couple and their banter endearing. A whisper of a happy future he may never get. "Unfortunately, we do not dictate the train schedule, do we?"

Mr. Smith held out a hand in Jack's direction as if Jack had just supported his case.

Mrs. Smith narrowed her gaze and pouted. "Regardless, I need to get off my feet."

Jack scanned the area but didn't see any available seats. He gestured at his recently vacated spot on the bench.

"I couldn't," she sputtered, even as she stepped to the waiting space.

"Of course, you can. It wouldn't be gentlemanly of me to deny a lady some respite." Jack put on one of his most dashing grins. "Besides, I need to stretch my legs."

"What a fine young man," she cooed as she plopped down and set about fussing with her clothing as if preening. "I do hope you won't stay away long." She fluttered lashes at him.

Whatever could she mean?

Mr. Smith frowned and shook his head at her.

She all but ignored him. "I pray that Miss Millington doesn't get too bored in that house with naught but the Bradys for company."

Why must she bring up the beautiful brunette he had just shoved out of mind? It wasn't as if his conscience hadn't sufficiently speared his heart already.

"So lonely, she must be. She strikes me as a sad sort. Don't you think?" Mrs. Smith looked to her husband but made little effort to veil that she directed the question to Jack.

"I wouldn't know." Mr. Smith rolled his eyes.

"What do you think, Mr. Patterson?" Mrs. Smith's innocent gaze was laughable.

"I..." His words caught in his throat, thinking of Laura's disappointment when she woke to find he had left. He prayed she had rested better than he did with the prospect of today overshadowing his attempts at sleep.

Mrs. Smith batted her eyes and watched him.

"I imagine the lady has quite a number of acquaintances to occupy her time. Who knows, she may be headed home soon herself."

"I never did hear where exactly her home is. Did you, dearest?" Mrs. Smith continued to feign innocence as she turned her attention to her husband.

Jack realized that he did not know either. Of the time they had spent together, had his aversion to getting to know her on any level been so blatant? So egregious?

He was a cad.

At that moment, a whistle pierced the awakening sky and the heavy chug of an incoming train rendered any response moot.

Mrs. Smith grimaced and covered her ears. Soon enough, the locomotive pulled into the station and she declared, "Why must that infernal thing be so loud?"

Mr. Smith all but ignored her question. "Come now, it will be time to board soon. Won't be long until we're back in Memphis."

"It won't be soon enough." The woman scowled. "Jostled about as we'll be."

"Would you prefer a stagecoach?" Mr. Smith muttered.

Jack caught the man's eye. Would he pick at his wife so? But a half-cocked smile gave away that Mr. Smith only teased.

He helped his wife to her feet and gathered their suitcases before stepping toward the platform.

But Jack was stymied. Getting on that train would mean he shut the door on whatever he felt for Laura. And seal the misrepresentation he had made to her. The first weighed heavily. Perhaps he should return…if for no other reason than to explain himself. A far more appropriate response than running away. Was that what he was doing?

Mr. Smith turned. "You coming, Mr. Patterson?"

Jack opened his mouth and then closed it. Was he going to board the train and leave Laura assuredly in his past? He was more torn than he'd expected. Maybe she had pierced through his protected walls and touched his wounded heart.

It was decided, then.

He nodded at Mr. Smith. "I am coming."

A few short moments later, he settled in the passenger car and watched Jackson, Tennessee become a memory.

Brady Family Boarding House
Jackson, TN
March 7, 1899

LAURA'S EYES WERE SURELY GLAZED OVER. THERE COULD BE no two ways about it. The telegrapher had droned on for nearly thirty minutes. Laura had only wanted to check the post. Apparently, the man had a penchant for long stories. The one he told now was not only long winded, it had also lost her interest entirely. It took work to maintain some semblance of focus on him.

He had mentioned there was a post for her, but then he launched into his tale of woe. And so here she was, with her mind wandering to the prospect of the telegram. Was it from her parents? Maybe from Micah or one of her other brothers? Or, though it was highly unlikely, a part of her hoped it to be from Jack. She chided herself. There wasn't any sense in that. But still, she hoped.

For certain, she deserved an apology. Or an explanation. Preferably both.

The man's tone wound down and Laura jerked back to attention. What had she missed? Had it been noticeable? Would he be offended? Or worse—ask her a question as a follow up?

She put on her most charming smile as he concluded.

"And so, now my wife thinks we need that dumb dog. Guess it's ours. She won't stop feeding it."

Laura shrugged. "Dogs can be fine companions."

The man's brows quirked. Did she contradict something in his monologue?

She held her smile in place with much difficulty and shifted her weight to her other foot. The left one ached just slightly. How long had she been here? It didn't matter.

"I don't want to take up any more of your time, sir. Did you say there is a telegram for me?"

He shook off his confused expression and shuffled through his papers. "Ah, yes. Here it is." With a clearly forced smile, he extended the paper to her.

"I thank you." She plucked it from his fingertips. Though she didn't intend to read it in front of him, she couldn't help glancing at it for the sender's identity.

Father.

Would it be tempered by the social politeness of her mother? She prayed so. For Father would not spare her his ire or opinion.

Her face heated at the prospect. As well, she was keenly aware that the telegraph operator would know full well what it said.

She pressed her lips into another smile. He must think her inane the way she kept grinning. If nothing else, she could fall back on her social graces. Those were always a reasonable idea for interactions such as this, weren't they? "Have a good day."

He offered a quick nod but shifted his focus to the next person in line. Was he upset? Perhaps he was put out that she hadn't listened to him well enough. Somehow she had erred in her statement. Only, she wasn't certain how. Not that it mattered. But her lack of manners bothered.

She slipped out of the small office and down the boardwalk to find somewhere less...open...to read whatever her father had dealt out.

As she approached the mercantile, the smells from the bakery wafted to her—sweet rolls and fresh breads. How long had it been since she had enjoyed soft bread? Mrs. Brady proved a wonderful host, but whomever made the bread at the boarding house needed to recheck their proportions. How did it always come out so thick and hard? Inedible, Laura had long since decided.

Except that night...that first evening she stayed in the house. The night she and Jack caught each other in the kitchen. The sourdough they shared had been promising. In more ways than one. What had she been thinking? Such a passing attraction would never have led to anything.

Between the mercantile and bakery, she spotted a bench to the far side of the walkway. Not as private as she'd like, but the anticipation of what the message held became too much. Her heart raced. Must she fear her father's words so?

Steeling herself, she drew in a cleansing breath and pushed it out.

No more delays. The words wouldn't change just because she put them off.

Sending up a quick prayer, she gripped the paper and looked over the words.

As she suspected, Father demanded she return home. His reasoning? It was inappropriate for a young lady to be unaccompanied for so long. Reasonable as that may seem, that wasn't the whole of it. He wanted her where he and Mother could keep an eye on her. He believed she needed constant supervision.

She chafed under his constant scrutiny, but what could she do? It seemed unlikely she could convince him otherwise and even less likely she might outright defy him.

Blowing out her breath slowly, she hoped to calm her inner shakiness. Perhaps it was best Jack had abandoned her before anything further developed. Even should she have wanted it to. Did she?

That bothered her. He did not fit the image of a man that her father would approve of. Was that why she had been so forward with him? A way to poke at her father?

Such was not becoming of a lady...and certainly not acceptable. Why had she behaved that way? Guilt washed over her. God called her to something higher. Treating others in this manner did not line up with His teachings.

She dropped the telegram to her lap. Returning home was the last thing she wanted to do. Propping her elbows on her knees, she laid her head in her hands and fought the tears that threatened. This would not be her undoing. She was stronger than this. She had to be.

But what kind of life could it be, living under Father's thumb, at his whim, and with a future that would be decided by him alone? Could she tolerate it? Did she have a choice?

Maybe she had stayed away too long. Her mother relied on her to help keep the house running smoothly which permitted Mother time to participate in her clubs and socials—something that Laura knew little about and cared nothing for.

Collecting herself, she rose and tucked the telegram safely away. She would return to the boarding house and pack. Then apologize to Mr. and Mrs. Brady for her abrupt departure. That was how it had to be. For Mother's sake if nothing else. Laura had always held out hope that her diligence would somehow endear her to Mother.

But she knew that was just a well-worn excuse to cover the reality of what home was—a prison.

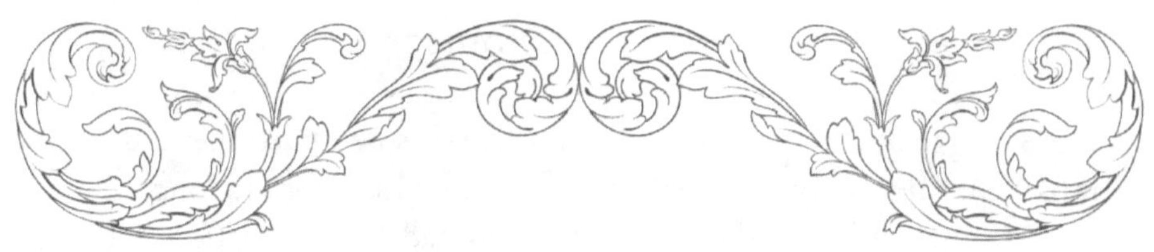

CHAPTER 7

Uninvited

Calhoun Street Station
Memphis, TN
April 29, 1900

Jack shifted on the bench. His job demanded that he ensure the comfort of passenger trains as well as their safety. The opportunity to experience them firsthand told that something in the design may be off. For he lacked an assurance of the former. Then again, how could a seat be anything less than restricting after so many hours? He stretched and glanced out the window. The two-story train station, though as luxurious as a station could be, suffered from the dirt and grime passing trains stirred up. Still, he could only somewhat determine such through the sheets of rain. That made everything worse.

He yawned. Did he hope they would depart soon? Or did he wish for a few more minutes of reprieve from the ricketing of the car on the tracks? Best to get to Canton and be done with it.

Passengers disembarking gave way to movement about him and offered some small measure of interest. Couples and families milled about and attempted to file out in a sort of orderly fashion. As more room came from their exit, he stood and allowed himself a much longer, more exaggerated stretch. His muscles ached as he pulled them, though it had been necessary. He'd been in the cramped seat for too long.

As much as he loved trains, and always had, the fascination of being aboard only lasted a few minutes before the downsides irked.

A conductor called for those waiting on the platform to board.

Jack best take his seat and permit those coming into the car some room to move about the aisle and find their perch for the next several hours.

That reminder made him groan. But he'd been on similar routes many times. He would manage.

As he sat, he looked at those waiting to gain their place. A lady, dressed in a red travel jacket, moving with a grace that defied the wet conditions, stepped carefully across the platform. She ducked her head, and her hat blocked his view of her features.

He averted his gaze. It had taken nearly a year to push down the memories of his last close call. The curves and lines of Laura Millington's face remained more easily recalled than he cared. She was fine of face, quite lovely. His heart ached at the mental image he conjured.

Closing his eyes, he breathed more evenly and purposefully. He must shift his thoughts to more productive things—such as the improvements he might recommend for these benches.

But the lady from before snagged his regard again. A gentleman clutched at her elbow, assisting her in the less than ideal conditions. Either way, Jack became more averse his notice of her even as he tracked her movements. Such nonsense. She traveled with a companion, likely her husband.

She neared the train and Jack's view then became obstructed due to the fact that his position sat higher than the platform. Just as well. He need not spend another second considering her. Leaning his head against the thin cushion of the seat back, he took another deep breath.

Though as she stepped into the car, he found himself peering in her direction once more. What was wrong with him?

She came off the final step and into the car. As she did so, she tilted her head up.

He gasped.

Laura Millington was in his life again.

By some miracle, she somehow didn't see him. Could he stay in the background enough that she wouldn't notice?

The man traveling with her came into the car. "Did I give you the tickets?"

She reached into a pocket in her jacket and produced the twin pieces of paper. "Yes."

Letting out a breath, the gentleman glanced about the car. Was he scouting for a pair of available seats? "Could we not secure a cabin?"

"This will be fine," Laura soothed, turning a loving gaze to the uppity fellow.

Jack's stomach twisted. And he wished it had not. Then he smirked. The man would have to sully himself and ride with the other passengers. For this car had not been equipped with private cabins. Jack enjoyed that realization more than he should. He realized quickly that if they were not headed for a private cabin, and considering his position in an aisle seat, the chance she would see him was great.

Could he not hide somewhere, somehow? He hunkered down as much as possible and wished he had a newspaper or something else to obscure his features. Taking out his pocket watch, he rubbed at the engraved design.

"Let's find a seat and get settled." Laura gripped the man's arm and tugged at him.

He nodded.

Jack noticed that the well-dressed, rather stocky man held himself as someone raised with money. That did not ease Jack's discomfort. Wasn't this privileged man the sort Laura deserved to be hitched to? Someone who could give her everything she wanted and needed. And whom her father would approve of.

Not like Jack—a simple tradesman.

There existed but one hope—that Laura's focus would be set on empty seats, not the passengers.

She moved down the aisle, scanning the car.

As she neared, he dipped his head even more, much like a turtle scurrying into its shell. What did he fear?

Jack's elbow bumped the man to his left, who had been dozing since the last stop.

"Ow!" The man rubbed at his side where Jack had made contact.

Heat rose in Jack's face. Turning to apologize, he realized too late what a mild spectacle he must have become thanks to the recently roused passenger.

"Are you all right?" A voice behind inquired...a voice he knew all too well, a voice that had haunted his dreams on many nights.

He wanted to disappear.

The offended man looked over Jack's shoulder. "Of course." He stood. "I only need to find a more accommodating seat." He jerked his head at Jack. "If you don't mind, sir, I would like to get by."

Jack swallowed. He would have to step into the aisle to allow the man space to do so. Nothing else could be done about it.

"You have cotton in your ears, young man?" The older man's voice rose.

Would this become a bigger scene?

Jack backed into the aisle, hoping he could keep his back to Laura.

A sharp intake of air and the rustle of clothing belied that he erred. Laura had stood much closer to him, and his movement pushed her back.

"What is this?" She gripped for the back of the bench.

Jack spun and grabbed for her lest she fall.

Too late, he realized. But her companion managed to keep her on her feet.

"What is the meaning of this?" Laura struggled to disentangle her limbs from the fine gentleman with her, her tone harsh. But as she looked up, she startled. He had been found out.

Her hard rebuke trailed, though her mouth still moved, and her eyes widened more than he'd thought possible.

He grimaced.

"Laura?" Her companion tried to move around her. "Are you well?"

She nodded and pulled her hands back. Then smoothed her skirt and tugged her jacket back into place. Licking her lips, she looked everywhere but at Jack. Even though he could not tear his eyes away from her.

"Laura?" the well-dressed man repeated.

"I'm all right." Her words were strained as her gaze met Jack's. The hurt within the amber was evident. Due to how he had left things in Jackson a year past? Or because she did not ever wish to see him again? Perhaps both.

"I apologize." He wanted again to just disappear. Still, he pulled out a handkerchief and offered it to her.

The man beside her stepped forward. "I think you've done enough."

Laura laid a hand to the man's upper arm. "It's all right. No harm done."

Was it Jack's imagination, or did she grow paler? It concerned him. Though it was not his place to worry after her.

"We are holding up the boarding." The stockier man's voice sounded gentle, but the look he shot Jack was certainly not. "We'd best find our seats."

She nodded, but she neither spoke nor averted her gaze. Nor did he.

If he thought his heart pained at seeing her with someone else— likely her husband—it was doubly afflicted by the anguish naked on her face.

She allowed her companion to tug her farther forward.

Jack watched as the man settled Laura into an empty row before putting their valises in their designated place.

The rich man shot Jack another accusing glare before taking the seat beside her.

Jack dropped onto the bench and laid his head in his hand, praying he might escape any further interaction with the couple. Forever.

LAURA RUMMAGED THROUGH HER BAG FOR THE SUGAR cookies she had packed. She needed something sweet and ill advised. After all, what were the odds? She could scarcely believe her bad luck running into Mr. John Patterson. Hopefully, he would not be on the train for long. But, then again, with her luck...

The iron hot heat in the pit of her stomach refused to quell. And if it so much as started to, an image of Jack floated through her mind, tossing the iron back into the fire. Why did he not explain himself? Why did he not apologize? Both of these things she was due. Yet he had not ventured near either.

Grabbing the wrapped cookies at last, she pulled them out and handed her bag to Micah, who put it back in its place. She bit into the white confection, taking in half of the first cookie at once. She peered up to find Micah staring at her. "Would you like one?"

He shook his head but did not look away.

"What is it?" She couldn't stand for him to eye her like that.

He leaned closer. "Are you certain you are well?"

She nodded and swallowed the barely chewed piece of cookie. Where could she begin explaining Jack? More...did she want to? What would be the benefit? The tall, well-chiseled man had been set firmly in her past. "I am perhaps a little shaken."

Sensing more than seeing Micah nod, she thought to lean into what comfort he could offer. But the thought of Jack watching her banished such ideas. Or...perhaps that was exactly what she should do. What would Jack think of that?

The train had jerked into action when leaving the station, and now it thundered steadily down the tracks. How fast were they going? And in this rain?

"Guess the engineer is trying to make up time." Micah did not seem to like the rumbling any more than she.

The older gentleman that had been sitting next to Jack looked at them from across the aisle. "Aye. Casey Jones is at the throttle. He doesn't tolerate being late."

Laura searched her memory for the visage of the man they had honored a year ago. The night she met Jack. She pressed those thoughts to the side. "Is he not? Never?"

"For certain, miss. He's had some trouble for traveling at speeds greater than warranted."

"Oh?" Should she be fearful? Looking to Micah, she hoped her anxiety wasn't too apparent.

"Not to worry yourself, he is a gifted throttleman."

How had the man read her mind? Perhaps her concern shown too readily.

The man continued, "And he has managed these speeds well."

"Does he not get penalized enough for such speeds?" Micah's words were rough.

The white-haired gentleman leaned closer. "To be sure. But the penalties for being late are far greater than the slap on the hand for driving the locomotive so fast."

That didn't seem right. She would have to ask Micah about it later. He knew far more about the operation of the engines than did she.

"Doesn't he make his daily run earlier?" Micah puzzled.

He would know—he had an uncanny ability to remember train schedules.

"I understand that the engineer assigned to this run called out. So, Casey and his fireman filled in."

Laura nodded and glanced out the window, noting that what she could make out went by rather quickly.

She shifted around to ask the man about his destination. Only to find that he had laid his head back and closed his eyes.

"Might I trouble you to switch seats?" Micah motioned toward the window.

Yes, he did prefer to watch the scenery pass. Not that he could see any more clearly than she had. Still, she cared less about her proximity to it. Especially when the world beyond lay so darkly covered. "Certainly."

They made short work of exchanging places. Now with Micah in his seat of choice, she settled her shoulder against his. "I am a bit tired."

"That is no wonder," Micah spit out on an odd sort of laugh. "Not only is this an ungodly hour, the day has been long."

She gave him that. And allowed her eyes to close.

He upset her position to put an arm around her. "Rest."

She offered what of a smile that she could muster and laid her head on his shoulder. She needn't give Jack another thought. Her awareness became dulled by closed eyes and ears that only perceived the clacking of the wheels on the track. Inasmuch, she gave herself over to what sleep could be had.

Still her thoughts raced, one tripping over the other in an effort to chase her consciousness.

Not again.

Sleep had been rather difficult the weeks following her encounter with Jack last spring. Their time spent together had been short, but the impact on her heart and mind defied the brevity of it.

Micah's breathing deepened. How could he find respite amidst the shaking? And in such a strange angle as his body found itself?

She sat upright, watching him. Had he slipped into unconsciousness so quickly?

He shifted further away and leaned the weight of his torso onto the window frame.

She frowned but couldn't be irritated. He had been a solace to her this past year—a needed distraction and necessary comfort.

Reaching out, she swiped fallen hair off his brow and smiled. He would be snoring soon enough.

Sitting straighter, she wished for some sort of light to enable reading or at least the ability to make out what passed outside. Rain and wind pelted the car and obscured any hint of the world about them. And was that fog? She squinted to enhance her vision. Yes, the thick tendrils blanketed the earth.

She prayed for their engineer, having to travel in such conditions, then attempted to turn her mind elsewhere—to ease her anxiety and push away her rogue thoughts.

How long she remained at war with herself, she did not know.

An intruding voice brought it to an abrupt end. "Laura."

She jerked away from the sound, bumping into Micah. Not that it disrupted his slumber. Glaring in the darkened car, she made out the lines of Jack's face. "You startled me."

He frowned. Or at least what seemed a frown. "I..."

Was he trying to say something? His words had trailed.

"You what?" Ire gave her words sharpness.

He dropped his regard to the floor. "This was a mistake." Turning, he gripped the back of the seat. Would he simply return to his bench?

She grabbed his forearm. "Just say what you came to say."

He halted and bent closer again. "I only wanted to apologize for any bad feelings between us."

She wanted to snort at that but couldn't. For the way his actions a year ago had cut her had been very real. And still wounded her heart.

"I never intended to cause pain." His words were solemn, sincere.

But she didn't want to believe them or forgive his previous disregard of her feelings. The lines of his features became more discernable in the dimness. He appeared stricken.

"It..." She swallowed against a thickness in her throat. "You need not worry yourself." Why did her tone still scold?

"Very well." His words held a finality, yet he didn't move. "I am sorry either way." He glanced at her companion and grimaced. "For all of it."

It almost seemed as if he cared more than she'd thought. As if his heart had been as engaged as hers. But that wasn't possible. She had rehearsed this line many times. Such a short acquaintance could not permit deeper feelings to take root.

Still, he didn't move, but hovered over her, his presence pulling at her. Why did she so want to reach up and touch his face?

"You're forgiven," she blurted. Then, with softer words and some amount of regret, she said, "Is that what you seek?"

"Partly." His voice deepened, sounding hoarse. Almost parched. "It is probably all I can hope for." He looked again to Micah's resting form.

What did he imagine? What did it matter? She'd best end this conversation and send him back to his seat.

All of a sudden, the speeding train screeched on the rails, pressing everything in the car forward.

Jack grabbed wildly for stability, but his body lurched.

"Jack!" She gripped the back of the seat in front of her to keep herself from being thrown as well.

Micah jerked awake, fingers clenching the bench, and her.

She watched as he, like her, struggled to remain seated.

Out of the window, she witnessed something fly from the train. What could that be? Had something damaged part of the train? Shook something free?

There was little time to think and less time to act as their rapid slowing came to a crashing halt. She pitched forward...and all was dark.

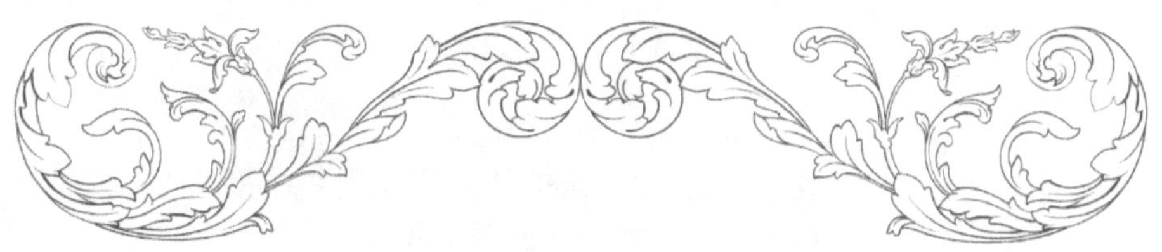

CHAPTER 8

Fallout

Train Depot
Vaughan, MS
April 30, 1900

Laura could not make sense of what had happened. Darkness engulfed her. Her senses had become muted. And while she discerned a chill, yet warmth surrounded her. She fought to find the surface of the thickness over her so that light may once again illuminate the world. She squirmed and reached out. Was it even real? Then a very real hand clamped over hers.

"Laura..." A voice called to her as if through deep water—muffled, insistent, and edged with worry.

She opened her eyes. All was dim, but shapes took form, though blurred. How long had she slept?

"Thank God! Laura!" The sound bade her draw nearer.

Was it Jack? Could it possibly be?

Awareness came rushing back—the jerking, the crash, and Jack being tossed. Was he all right? Bidding her vision clear, she blinked. Her eyes only somewhat obeyed. So she searched around herself with a hand.

The grip on her tightened. "You're safe."

Was she? What was this strangeness surrounding her? The bustle of people became more audible. As well, the shouts of men farther away. Had they crashed? Could they have survived that?

"Jack?" She tried to seek him out.

He leaned closer, his breathing falling as soft fluttering across her face. "I'm here."

Maneuvering her other hand, she sought his features. Why did everything ache?

He did nothing to stop her from setting her fingers to his strong jaw.

"Is it you?"

"Yes, darling." His larger hand closed around hers again. "I won't leave you."

She swallowed against a parched throat. "What h-happened?" Amidst the dim, cold world, she found comfort.

"There was an accident." His voice seemed calm despite what he said. "We're still trying to figure out what happened."

She searched her mind, replaying images from the moments she could recall. Had something come off the train? "I saw...something..."

His features became clear. "Don't worry yourself. I've got you."

That wasn't what she tried to say. Why couldn't he understand? Her hand slid from his face to the lapels of his jacket. She jerked him closer. "It's important."

"Not right now. I need to get you to a safer place."

Another man leaned over her. "Is she awake?"

Micah! He seemed well enough. Tears brimmed her vision.

But as she latched her gaze onto him, she noticed an uneasiness about him as he looked between her and Jack. She should have told him about Jack.

Micah dropped to a knee. "Thank the Lord. You had me worried." He motioned for Jack to move aside.

But Jack did not appear ready to acquiesce. He slid an arm under her back and helped her sit up.

"Say now," Micah said, his voice gruff, "I'm plenty capable to take charge here."

Would the two men do this right now?

Jack's grimace was the only indication that he had heard Micah. Instead of heeding Micah, Jack maneuvered Laura's body to lean against himself.

"I...think I can stand," she pressed out. Could she keep the tension between them from escalating?

"Are you certain?" Jack's voice was tight, but his gaze on her softened.

"I think she knows her mind," Micah objected. He set a hand to her upper arm in a protective way.

Not now. Her mind remained somewhat hazy. Despite Micah's grousing, she leaned into Jack.

"Let me help you." Jack's arm came around her and he lifted her as he stood.

She did not resist him, much to Micah's sputtering protest. If only she could find her tongue. The thoughts that formed sentences dispersed before she could make them words.

Jack's arm stayed around her, stabilizing her as she settled her weight onto her feet.

She pushed at him with a half-hearted determination to be upright on her own strength.

Micah appeared at her other side and grabbed for her arm once more. "Sir, I thank you for your assistance, but I can manage now."

How could she tell Jack she didn't want him to go? How could she explain that to Micah?

"I am well enough," she shot out even as she bit back the urge to groan at the pain spiking through her.

Micah jerked back.

Jack didn't move. Would he not even respond to her sharpness? He urged her forward. "Let's get you out of here."

Micah's breathing became heavier, a far cry from his more genial nature. Was he so perturbed?

She held out a hand, pressing against Jack once more. "I assure you, I am well enough to walk."

He frowned.

"Sir, I will tell you once more," Micah said, his words rather forceful. "Unhand my sister."

Jack halted, his whole body jerking in response, but a long exhale told that there was relief about it.

Relief? Had he thought Micah was her beau? Should his relief say something in that regard? Her whirling thoughts and feelings clashed, making it quite impossible to grab onto anyone.

"Micah," she managed, "This is not the time."

Her brother pulled back as if she'd stung him.

Jack's gaze tugged at her, but she wouldn't face him now either. There was too much she needed to know.

She stood straight and removed her limbs from Jack's hold.

"Laura, I don't think you understand." Jack came around to look at her. "There's been a crash. How we are all alive, I don't know. But we need to get you away from here."

She tossed Micah a look. Hoping it wasn't as pained as she felt. "I need to find out what happened."

"No," Jack's voice was firm, "you don't."

"This isn't the time." Micah came alongside her. "Not now. We need to get you to a safer location."

She held her ground, refusing the hands that closed over her forearms. "No. I saw something, and I have to know what it was."

Jack's eyebrows dipped in a quizzical way. "There will be time for your questions later."

She pulled back. "No. I need to know. I need answers."

"Not now." Jack's tone hardened once more.

"Why must you be so stubborn?" Micah groaned.

In the next second, arms came around her and her feet flipped up.

She tried to fight the chest she'd become pressed against, but it was useless. Looking up, she noted the stiff lines of Jack's face.

He carried her toward the exit of the passenger car.

"Put me down," she demanded. "You have no right."

Her struggles came to naught. Jack and Micah worked together to get her down the stairs and onto the grassy area beyond—damp and fog-covered. Even then, Jack didn't stop.

The fight went out of her at the sight that greeted her—the train's engine was crushed beyond recognition. And it had come off the track. As well, cars from a second train lay in a heap of twisted metal, demolished. In the darkened haze, she struggled to discern what was what. Something terrible had happened here. How had they all survived?

"Jack," she whispered, "please let me go." Her request came out softer than she'd intended, sounding more a plea than she'd like.

He held her firmly, but not in a possessive way. His strong, capable arms both eased and tugged her closer at the same time. "Soon."

They joined a collection of other passengers. Jack made good on his word and set her onto her feet.

She stepped in the direction of the wreckage.

His hand reached for hers, securing her position at his side.

Micah slid in front of her. "This is not the time for one of your investigations."

She frowned. He had been the only family member who never spoke ill of her drive to seek out truth and examine it through writing.

"But I can help." She glanced between Micah and Jack. How could she make them understand? "I saw something."

Micah let out an exasperated sigh. "There will be time aplenty to report it."

Still, she resisted their attempts to keep her away from the site of the crash.

Micah took hold of her shoulders, drawing her to look at him. "Laura, a man is dead."

That gave her pause. Such an accident was bound to have casualties. But he spoke of only one. How was that possible?

Micah's gaze landed on Jack. "Can you keep a rein on her?"

Jack did not respond at first. But, at length, he did nod.

Of all the... Why did these men feel the need to keep her in her place? To control her movements? Stop her ability to do what she did best? She would not have it. They would not hold her back.

Micah walked toward a cluster of men near the worst of the debris.

Everything in her wanted to follow. But she didn't. Had all of the fight left her?

Jack's hands pressed her shoulders. She moved to jerk away again only to discover that his movements were to set a coat around her.

She looked down. The navy pinstripe appeared to be *his* coat. When had he shed it? She gripped the warm cloth that smelled of bergamot and vanilla. Of him.

And she let her tears fall.

Was there no way to reach past her iron hard surface? Jack steadied a mug of fresh coffee as he approached the station manager's office where Laura had been settled.

How could she seem so frightened and yet so strong at the same time? What was the truth?

"Here," he said, keeping his tone gentle, "drink this." He eased the steaming cup toward her. "It's not much, but it's all the station had to offer."

She took the beverage, giving no indication that it was too hot for her fingers. Bringing it close to her chest, she breathed in the warmth.

What should he do? Sit beside her? Stay as he was? He wanted to offer comfort, or at least try to break through the shell she had erected around herself over the last hour.

Where had her brother gone? Micah had said he would be back soon but had yet to show his face. What could the son of a railroad tycoon glean from the situation? Perhaps more than Jack. Still, he itched to be in the thick of it. He'd heard only snatches of what happened, and none of it made sense.

He needed to do something to ease Laura's struggle—if not for her, then for himself. Watching her retreat into herself pained him deeper than he cared to admit. Did he truly care so for her?

His relief at discovering Micah was her brother and not her husband had been great. But what could he do? Was he prepared to make an overture?

Either way, he had to reach out, had to at least try and pull her back from whatever precipice she approached.

"Laura," he said, hoping his words soothed, "it will all be all right."

She brought the rim of the mug to her lips and sipped.

"I promise. All of your questions will be answered...in time." He leaned back in the chair.

Her lack of response left no opening to pursue her further. If he even should.

The silence between them stretched, punctuated by a sip here and a movement there.

"Where are we?"

He jerked forward, surprised at her words. "Vaughan, Mississippi."

She frowned. "Not a scheduled stop."

He nodded.

"The cannonball run should have been able to go right through the station."

Again, he sighed. "Yes, that's true."

The wheels in her head turned. He could almost hear them at work, attempting to unpuzzle this thing.

"It's nothing to be concerned about. The men in authority are gathering information now. I'm sure the investigation will unlock whatever happened."

"Our train's engineer is dead, isn't he?" Her words were flat, devoid of emotion. It was eerie.

"Yes. He is." Jack remembered the man—Casey Jones—from the reception at the New Southern Hotel. The man had been solid, admired, revered. It didn't seem right that such a giant of a man—physically and by reputation—could be gone in an instant.

"And...no others?" Her tone continued to disturb him. As well as the fact that she stared straight ahead.

"None that we know of."

She grimaced and took another sip. "So, he died at his post...saving us all."

Jack studied her. That was one way to look at it. He didn't want to tell her, but he'd overheard the railroad employees tell that flaggers had been at their posts. Casey must not have seen their signals, warning that a train blocked the way through the station.

"What are you not saying?"

He shifted his focus back to her.

She watched him, her eyes wide and pooling with unshed tears.

If only he could pull her into his arms again and assure her that all would be well, and that nothing happening here made a difference between them. But he couldn't.

"Jack?" Her eyes had a sheen to them, clear and serious. This mattered to her.

"It's nothing."

Her gaze hardened. Did she know he lied?

The desire to protect her from becoming emotionally entangled in this mess overwhelmed him. He couldn't fight it. So, he said nothing further.

"I..." she started, but that thought never came to fruition.

Just beyond the office where they rested, the station manager escorted another man.

Laura rose, immediately on alert. Would she move to intercept?

"Laura, no." He reached for her and just missed as she shuffled past. Why hadn't he shut that door? He followed her into the hall.

"Sir," she called after the man whose dark skin stood out in the lantern light.

The man turned. His eyes were wide and worn, and he looked as if he had been better. In fact, he appeared every bit as dismayed as anyone. His clothes were covered in soot. Had he been on the train? In the engine car? How had he survived?

"Yes, miss?" His voice came out thick and tired as if he had been weighed down in more than one way.

"You..." Her words were not accusing, but apologetic. "I saw you jump from the train."

The lanky manager urged the dark-skinned fellow along.

Yet he resisted. "Yes, miss. I'm the fireman...was the fireman."

Her eyes widened. "And you survived?"

"Casey..." The man paused and cleared his throat.

Was that an attempt to disguise his emotions? They were written on his face.

Then he continued, "Casey...told me to jump, to save myself. I didn't want to...honest. But I...did what he said." The man dipped his head. Sorrow fairly emanated from his pores.

"We've taken enough of Miss Millington's time," the manager said. "We need to get you bandaged."

Only then did Jack spot some abrasions about the man's face.

Laura opened her mouth, paused, then said, "I'm sorry for that."

He nodded but couldn't quite meet her gaze.

Jack wondered again what had him so bedraggled. Beyond his physical aches and pains, there was more. Something deeper. Something harder.

When the manager prodded the fireman forward again, he followed.

"What is your name?" Laura called after the man.

Jack drew closer to her.

The fireman turned, though several paces away. "Sim."

She offered a small smile, etched with sadness. How difficult was that for her to put on? "Thank you, Sim. And I will pray for your injuries."

Sim shook his head. "Don't need no prayers for me. Pray for Ms. Janie. And them precious babies."

Jack swallowed. There were others beyond the men and women here tonight, others whose lives would be forever impacted by these happenings.

Sim picked up step and followed the station manager once more.

"I will," Laura called in a voice so small Sim likely didn't hear.

Jack put an arm around her, steering her toward the office. "Let's get you off your feet."

She jerked away. "Do you not understand?" Her eyes were wide again, with a wildness about them. "I'm fine. But Sim...and Casey's family...they aren't. And they never will be again."

He grimaced. She wasn't wrong. But that wasn't his responsibility. Others would care for the family. And for Sim. Right now, she was the only one under his care.

She blew out a breath and spun away.

He feared she would bypass the manager's office and insert herself elsewhere, but she fled straight into the recesses of the small space and slammed the door, shutting him out.

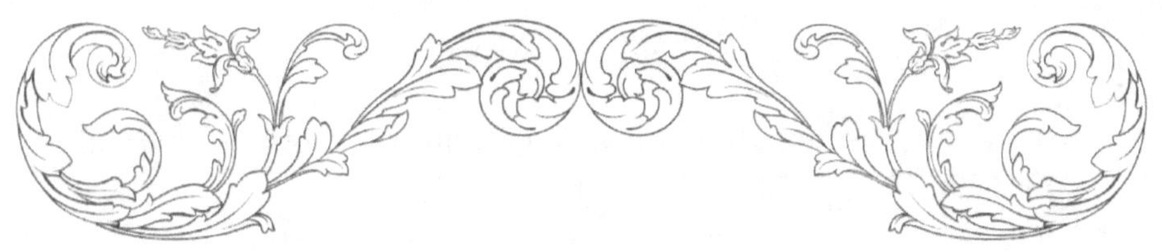

CHAPTER 9

Witness

Memphis Central Station
Memphis, TN
April 30, 1900

Home. They were home. The train had rolled into the station minutes ago. And Laura had never been more out of sorts.

Mentally, she remained in Vaughan, Mississippi, reeling from what had happened. Had she truly walked away from Jack and shut him out? Everything in her had wanted to plead with him to understand. And she selfishly had wanted to find comfort in his embrace.

She was hopeless. He just didn't understand. How could he? How could she make him? Casey Jones's death was monumental. At least to her.

Her fingers wished desperately for the ability to tell the story on paper, to help others understand and discover the truth of it.

"You coming?" Micah called over his shoulder. He shifted, preparing to descend from the passenger car and onto the platform.

"Coming!" Gripping her skirts, she moved after him.

In a few minutes, she stepped down onto the ground. That didn't mean she had caught up with Micah.

He made his way through the station as if he hadn't a care for her following. Did he not? True, he had been vexed at her behavior in the wee hours of the morning after the crash. Did that matter? Could she be anything less than the whole of who she was?

She dropped her chin. Who she was had never been quite acceptable in their home. She was too much...and yet somehow not enough. Could it be both? Either way, she felt them both...deeply.

Looking in the direction her younger brother had gone, she noticed his form in the distance, nearly out of visual range. "Micah, wait!"

He did not stop nor make any effort to slow his pace.

Which left her rushing to catch up.

And when she did, she asked through short breaths. "What is the matter?"

He didn't look at her, but his glower was evident.

"Don't be mad at me." Couldn't he sense her sincerity?

He did stop then and whirled to face her. "How can you say that to me?"

She tried to find words, but came up short, and instead fidgeted with the hem of her jacket.

"You made quite the spectacle of yourself. And created a mess for me to clean up."

An anchor weighed in her core. He was right. She had insisted on being heard, defiantly so.

Her desperation had grown all the more after hearing that Sim's testimony differed from all other reports at the scene. Of course, his word had been summarily dismissed. It did not surprise her. At least, it shouldn't. Sim's skin meant he had been viewed as less than. Laura fumed at the injustice of it all.

Her own eyewitness statement had been heard because of who her father was but not regarded seriously because she wore a skirt. The investigator coddled her and set her to the side. Yet somehow that had meant trouble for Micah.

She evened her breathing. Though she might be angry, he was right. He'd had to make excuses for her and made every effort to ensure that father did not catch wind of it. Micah may be irate...Father would be enraged.

Not that she doubted what she had seen...or Sim's word.

The men who swore they were at their post had everything to lose. Whereas Sim had nothing to gain by lying. Nor did she.

"Oh, come on," Micah muttered. "Why do I bother?"

She grabbed for his arm. "Please, Micah, don't hate me."

He released a long breath and watched her.

"I know I caused trouble for you...and I'm sorry for that." She glanced about and bit at her lip. "But you're the only one I can be honest with. Or trust. Don't make me hate myself for alienating you."

The area about his eyes softened. Yes, he cared about her. And he knew what she lived with, what she had to endure. Though she longed for an ease to his ire, she hated that pity drove him to relent time and time again.

She swallowed. "Can you forgive me?" The words were choked out. She couldn't disguise that.

He looked off in the distance for several moments.

Could he not find that pity for her today?

He shifted his focus back to her. "Of course, I will."

Air rushed out of her and her shoulders relaxed.

"But..." he said, holding up a hand, "You have to let me do the talking when it comes to Father. Don't go in half-cocked and make things worse."

She hated that she would not be able to defend herself. But the truth remained that Father would hold Micah responsible...at least in part. So for her brother's sake, she would be silent. "All right."

"If you aren't able to do that, Laura, I might as well—"

"No," she blurted. "I can."

He watched her, his eyes boring into hers.

"I will." She pressed on a small smile she didn't feel. "I promise."

It was his turn to release pent-up air. Everything about him eased. The forthcoming conversation with Father would not go well for him. But if she steered clear, it would go infinitely better.

He crooked his elbow toward her.

She set a hand on his forearm. "I see Father's carriage is waiting. How kind of him to send it."

"Let's not cause any further delay."

She understood his concern. Father would no doubt be eagerly awaiting them at home, intrigued to hear what they had seen and heard. Ever the businessman...he was only secondarily their Father. That's just how it was.

Laura let Micah help her up into the rather spacious carriage.

And she quickly discovered they were not alone.

Father sat within, a grimace set into his features. This would not go well for them.

Meriweather Home
Canton, MS
April 30, 1900

Jack dropped into a chair in the fine parlor. His friend paced to the open doorway and called for tea. Settling into the cushioned piece of furniture, Jack's heart warmed. Had it truly been but a few hours since he'd been thrown across that passenger car? And only mere hours ago that he had held Laura in his arms? That he had watched her shut him out?

None of it made sense—her resistance to his aid nor the depth to which he cared about it. That would not do. She was a stubborn woman...and that could only lead to trouble for him.

Or had it already?

He pushed that question to the side as Ernest rejoined him. "Are you comfortable?"

Jack hated that his friend bothered with such nonsense. "I am no longer standing in the rain, drenched and chilled. Of course I am."

Ernest shook his head. "I can't imagine how you pushed on to Canton. I would have demanded reprieve for the night in a hotel."

Jack shrugged, an attempt to shake off his friend's concern. "I had to come either way. It made sense to make the rest of the trip now. Who knows how I'll feel in the morning?" He chuckled.

His friend did not express such levity. "You could have been injured. Or worse. That whole thing could have had a much more devastating outcome."

Jack nodded. It wasn't as if he didn't know that. But he couldn't extend his time in Vaughn. Not with Laura there. Not with the thoughts that invaded his mind whenever she was near. Could he have managed himself should he have had another run in with her?

"I made some inquiries as you were en route. It seems the investigators' early determination is that the engineer did not take heed of the flagmen. So sad. So pointless."

Jack frowned. He'd heard that same conclusion thrown around at the station. Except...the words of the fireman who had been in the engine with Casey. He'd been rather adamant that it was not so. The muscles in Jack's chest tightened. This was not his job nor his concern. He pushed out a breath and hoped the tension would ease.

"It's not as if engineers have the best track record with safety. Such dangerous business," Ernest said low.

Jack's thoughts fell to his own father's career as an engineer. Ernest spoke truthfully about the dangers. But not necessarily all engineers' lack of concern about safety.

A maid came into the room with a tea tray and promptly served the men.

Jack accepted his cup, grateful for something to take his mind off the accident and the events surrounding it.

"Makes one glad we are not that brand of engineer." A smile played at Ernest's lips.

Jack lifted his cup and sipped the hot liquid. But it only reminded him of Laura, taking some measure of comfort from the mug of coffee. He remembered the way she had gripped it and held it close.

He shook his head and directed his attention back to Ernest. His friend dismissed the maidservant. Taking a sip from his own teacup, he glanced at Jack. "Are you certain you are well?"

Jack balked at that, bristling under his friend's constant inquiry of his wellbeing. But hadn't Jack asked that same thing of Laura? More than once.

He refocused on Ernest. "I am. Perhaps I am a bit tired."

"I have no doubt of that."

Setting his cup on its saucer, fatigued weighed on Jack. It seemed a struggle to keep his eyes open. How had he not noticed before? "I should make my way to the hotel."

"Nonsense," Ernest declared. "I implore you, stay here. There is plenty of room, and Franny won't mind a house guest in the slightest."

There were reasons he had declined Ernest's offer before, but they no longer held up under his hazy thoughts now. It seemed a rather fine arrangement in this moment.

Ernest's cup clattered. "I won't take no for an answer."

Jack looked at him.

The man had set his tea down rather forcefully on the tray.

"I..." Jack tried to remember why this hadn't been ideal but came up at a loss. "I accept."

Ernest's face brightened. "That is the most sensible thing you have said since arriving."

Jack's weariness settled more heavily on his shoulders.

"In fact, I insist you take your leave at once. I'll have your bags sent up to the second floor. There is plenty of time to rest before the dinner hour."

Again, Jack had not the wherewithal to argue with his friend and simply nodded.

Ernest rose. "Shall we then?"

Jack stood, every ache in his body screaming. Perhaps the impact of the trains had done more than jostle him.

Ernest stepped to the door and into the hall.

Jack, for his part, did his best to keep up. He followed as Ernest climbed the stairs. "I heard that two of Richard Millington's family members were aboard the train."

Jack wished that had not come up. "Yes, his daughter and a son."

"That will not be good for any at fault." Ernest gave Jack a sideways glance. "Did you have an opportunity to speak with either?"

"I did. Briefly." Would Jack's lie be obvious? The last thing he wanted was talk of Laura. How could he forget her if their interactions were constantly thrown in his face?

But he knew...that wasn't Ernest's intention. His friend had no clue how the mention of her name pained Jack.

Ernest continued upward and down a hall. And soon stopped outside a fine room.

Was this ill-advised? Should he impose? Surely Ernest would have said as much if it was an imposition. In their friendship, honesty was acceptable—and encouraged—at all times.

Maybe, then, he could be more forthright about Laura. If they did, indeed, have that manner of friendship. Ernest was his oldest and closest friend. They had worked together for many years, side by side, until Ernest married and transferred to Canton.

Jack opened his mouth to speak further, but Ernest cut him off. "If you need anything—anything at all—don't hesitate to call for someone." Ernest waved an arm toward the room. "I am glad you are in one piece." Ernest's words were heartfelt.

"As am I." Jack stepped into the room. The bed and the promise of sleep called to him.

"Rest well." Ernest reached for the door latch. "I shall see you at supper."

Jack offered a quick nod before turning toward the bed.

The door clicked shut and he was alone. Truly alone. As he had not been since many hours before the horrid crash. And now he was.

Jack removed his jacket, thankful to put it and the lingering scent of lilac—a reminder of Laura—to the side. Such was an unavoidable result of having offered her his jacket. Should he freshen up before lying down? The weight of his fatigue drove him to the bed.

As he lay down and closed his eyes, he struggled to find rest. A mental image of Laura's face visited him when he shut his eyes. So he opened them.

This would not do.

He refused to be plagued by her visage. Would he have no peace? Setting his mind on the door she had shut between them, he forced his eyelids to fall once more.

And her soulfully sad eyes stared back at him.

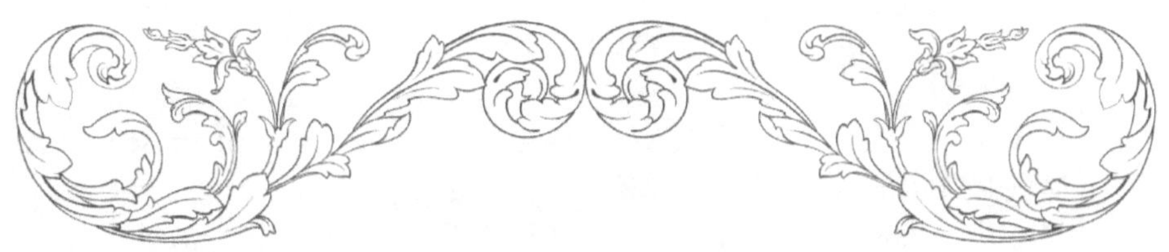

CHAPTER 10

Captive

Memphis Central Station
Memphis, TN
April 30, 1900

Laura shrank back. Father's ire was evident in the redness of his features and the way his nostrils flared. This was not going to be pleasant.

She shot a look at Micah, who at least tried to disguise any hint of upset he may feel.

Forcing herself to breathe, she lifted her chin. Maybe she would appear braver than she was. Would that help? Or make things worse?

"Father," Micah said, "how good of you to come see us home."

Raising a hand, Father grunted. "I know all about what happened."

Micah stilled and swallowed. Why must he bear such a burden on her behalf? He had always protected her. But this was her mess. It was time for her to make a stand.

"It was quite an ordeal," she pressed out.

Micah gripped her hand.

She didn't dare look at him. She didn't have to. He would most likely give her a silent warning. Should she heed it? Leave him to the wolf that was their father? Never. She set aside the hasty promise made to Micah. The time had come for her to take responsibility.

Father's stare intensified, and she shifted under his glower. But courage was about being brave when things were hard, right?

Laura pushed on. "I'm not certain that all is as the station manager said. It bears further investigation, does it not?"

Father scoffed. "By whom? You? Would you like to write one of your little stories about this incident?"

What was the right answer here? The truth? Or a lie to spare her discomfort? "I just want to find the truth."

"The truth," Father spat out his words. "As if that matters. As if it will change anything."

How could he say such a thing? Did he honestly believe that?

"But Mr. Sim Webb's testimony—"

"Is inconsequential," Father said. What efforts would he go to in order to silence her on the matter?

"You can't mean that. I myself saw—"

"I don't say things I don't mean, Laura." How did Father make her name sound as if it were a curse?

She dragged in a breath. This was not going well. Fear weighed her down.

"I, for one, am glad it is in the past," Micah said. So brave in trying to divert Father's attention.

Father shot him a hard look. "Fortunately for you, it is." He turned toward the window. Was it difficult to be so cold?

"Father," Laura started again, "I saw something just before the crash that I think is—"

"No. You saw nothing."

"If you mean that I didn't see the flagmen, I would—"

"Don't." The word was spoken with force. "You will not say it now, and you will never say it again."

His treatment pained her, but could she sacrifice Sim's name and his word so her father wouldn't be so hard on her?

"Surely, you can't turn a blind eye." Her voice sounded smaller than she wished.

Father's anger heated his glare. "And what do you know about it?

You flit about here and there, telling stories and stirring up trouble. Trouble that your brother," he said, pointing at Micah, "Or I have to cover up."

She bit her lip until she tasted blood. Was there too much truth there? Did Micah find himself covering for her often?

"Do not forget...we have an arrangement."

Yes, they did. She forced air to continue moving. How long had she been made to live under their 'arrangement'?

Micah sighed loudly. "I think the scene was relatively orderly."

"Be quiet," Father said, the words demanding. "I shall tend to your conduct in a minute." He jerked his regard back to Laura.

Could she not disappear into the bench? Fade into the soft red velvet cushion? Fair enough that she would be upon this pillowed surface when she walked on pins and needles in this exchange.

"Let me remind you...lest you have reason to forget." Father's frown deepened. Could she withstand his harsh words any longer? But she must.

She reached for Micah's hand, but he tugged it away. Would even he back down?

"Your little articles have done enough damage to our family, to *my* reputation. And I will not allow that to happen again. Especially when it involves *my* railroad."

Her hands trembled, and she ached for Micah's strength. But it was not to be had. The articles she'd written about the Women's Suffrage had been innocent enough. She only reported the facts. And she had disguised her identity with a pseudonym. But Father had discovered them. Somehow. And declared that everyone could trace it back to him.

Thankfully, she had been spared his anger that day. For she had moved on to her next stunt reporter assignment—the asylum. And that's where he found her. And that's where he threatened to leave her if she ever penned another article.

But this was different. She only sought the truth...as much for him and his precious railroad as anything. The truth would not be hidden forever. Couldn't he see that? Wouldn't it be best to be on the side of right?

"That's better." Father leaned back. "You keep your mouth closed and your pen and paper sealed away. Forever."

She wanted to glance in Micah's direction, but his breathing was uneven and his body stiff. There would be no help there this time.

"And you," Father turned to her brother, "had best learn to stay in your own corner. No more rushing to her aid."

The quick nod from Micah devastated her. Was she now to fight her battles alone? Micah had been her last vestige of help. She had nothing left to cling to and sank into desperation.

"What will you do?" The words came out shakier than she'd have cared. But a life imprisoned in the asylum did elicit fear. And darkness. Would he commit her?

"I will marry you off to the first good offer I can cobble together."

Marry her off? Which life sentence would be better? To be joined to someone she didn't love? Someone who would keep a firm hand about her the same as her father? Or to be rendered to the insane ward?

Neither appealed. And both made her spine shiver.

But she did not doubt her father for one second. He was capable. Beyond that, he was serious. All would be done as he said. She had only to pick her prison.

Patterson Home
Chicago, IL
May 8, 1900

Jack stepped into the modest townhome his parents had always kept. It was far from grand. And even more limited than the townhouse he kept. But, then again, a railway engineer's salary bested that of the highest paid engine worker by far.

In this he was thankful. But why? Had he let the size of his childhood home make him feel claustrophobic? It did now.

But it had always been home in one respect...and always would be.

His sister stepped into the small entry. "Jack, you're home!"

He forced himself not to balk at the reference but knew he failed. Annie knew him well...perhaps too well. Opening his arms, he embraced her more petite form. Blonde hair only partially pinned up filled his vision.

Allowing himself to hold to her a little more firmly, he took comfort from her genuine affection for him.

She started to pull back but halted when he did not release her. Her small voice whispered, "Are you all right?"

He gripped her a little tighter but let up quickly for fear he might steal her breath. "I am. Just tired."

She leaned back, still gripping his upper arms, and examined his features. Would she see beyond the surface? She always did. Her brow furrowed. "What is it?"

Was he ready to share? He wasn't certain he should.

"I am glad you're back in Chicago," an older voice interjected.

He glanced around his sister to see his mother standing in the parlor doorway, leaning heavily on her cane. A pang shot through him for the weakness he discerned easily in her affect. The once strong woman had been through much these last five years. And it showed.

"Mother," he said, turning his sister loose and shifting to greet the elder Patterson woman properly. Though he did not hug her nearly as fully as he did his sister.

He told himself it was because she was more fragile. But he wondered, as he always did, if there may be more to it.

"Can I get you anything?" Annie placed a hand on his arm. Her gaze promised that their conversation was not over.

Shaking his head, he shrugged out of his jacket that was more needed in Chicago than it had been in Mississippi.

Annie reached for it just as he pulled free of the sleeves.

He nodded to her and she hung it on the coat tree.

"Please have a seat, Mother." Jack hoped his voice didn't betray how little he regarded her ability to remain on her feet.

She shot him a look that was hard but soon softened. As if she were resigned to her situation. Setting her free hand on his forearm, she leaned on him.

"To the parlor then?" He offered her what he hoped was a smile. He had wanted nothing more than to lie down after his travel. For his fatigue went beyond the train ride home. Indeed, he'd not had one solid night of sleep since the incident in Vaughan.

He led his mother into the tiny parlor, his sister trailing but then parting for the kitchen. He didn't have to ask. She would gather some manner of refreshment for him.

Would it be coffee? He hoped for anything to help him stay awake—but guessed it would be tea.

Mother tugged him toward her favorite chair and let him settle her there.

Then he sat on the adjacent settee.

"How was your trip?" Even Mother's voice seemed weaker.

He shook that thought—and its implications—off. "Fine. It was good to see Ernest and his family."

"Ah. How is the little one?"

"Perfect." Jack grinned as memories of the scampering toddler filled his mind. "And energetic as anything."

"That must be wonderful."

She didn't say anything further on the matter, but he caught the implication. It wasn't her forte to be subtle. Her desire for grandchildren to fill her home weighed in the air. And she assigned that task to him. Annie had only now reached a respectable age to be matched, a thought that didn't appeal to him.

His mind drifted to images of a small girl with ringlets of chestnut like Laura's. Shutting his eyes, he forced it away. Would he ever banish these thoughts of that infuriating woman?

"Something troubles you." His mother's words were a statement. Yes, she knew him well also. Better than he'd like.

He grabbed for the same explanation he'd given Annie. "I am only tired from the trip."

Mother's narrowed gaze did not engender confidence. He'd been pinged. "Would you prefer to lay down?"

Nothing would please him more. But he sensed that Mother would like his company. Perhaps he could sit with her for tea and then excuse himself. The question then would be if he should rest here in his old room that he stayed in much too often of late? Or go to his own bed in his townhouse?

"I am able enough to stay awake and take tea."

Her small smile spoke volumes. Did she know he but appeased her?

There was little time to consider that as Annie returned with a tray bearing tea cups and a teapot. Did she expect them to linger over a second or third cup?

He wasn't certain he could manage that. His shoulders lost their stiffness as he considered having to keep them entertained for so long. They had little else to engage them except each other most days. Perhaps he should be more cognizant of that and placate their desire for varied conversation more often.

"Thank you." He stood and helped Annie set the tray on a nearby table.

He picked up two cups, but Annie beat him to Mother with the third cup. So he smiled at her and offered her the second one he had carried over.

She took a seat beside him on the small couch.

They all fell into silence, each sipping their tea. What should he say? His brain was so fogged he doubted he could broach a conversation coherently.

"How is Ernest?" Annie asked, setting her cup in its saucer.

He looked at her. Hadn't he spoken to that already? Some seconds later, he realized it had been Mother who asked earlier. Goodness, his brain had become addled.

"Did I say something wrong?" Annie glanced between him and Mother.

"No," he said more forcefully than intended. "I just..." How was he to finish that sentence?

Annie quirked an eyebrow. Yes, he would likely not find rest until they conversed privately. Something he did not look forward to.

"He is well enough...as well as Franny and the little one." Time to change the subject. "I had several meetings about changes coming for our passenger cars."

Annie dropped her gaze to her tea. Yes, talk of work did not really interest her. Why?

"There was an incident on the way to Canton, though," he offered. Maybe that would be more interesting.

"An incident?" Mother said on a sharp intake of breath.

Why had he brought it up with her in the room? She did so worry. Especially since Father's death.

"It was nothing." He shrugged as he took another sip.

"Nothing?" Annie pried.

Dare he lie? It would assuredly be in the papers soon, if not already. "There was an accident."

Mother gasped and put a hand to her chest.

Annie set a hand to Jack's arm and squeezed.

He sighed and continued, "Not to worry, I am fine enough...as you see."

Mother looked more closely at him...closely enough, it seemed, to see through him. "Were there...casualties?"

He could kick himself for mentioning it. "Only one—the engineer."

Mother's eyes widened and glazed over.

Annie was on her feet in a second. "Mother, it is all right." She put a hand to her mother's shoulder. "Jack is all right, as he said. These things happen." Her words were choked out. The injury to their hearts was too fresh.

To his heart as well. Father had been a good man. He didn't deserve to die at the throttle any more than Casey Jones did.

He drew in a breath. "I can see that I have upset you, Mother. I am sorry, that was not my intention."

Annie offered a small smile and a gentled gaze.

Mother appeared less ready to calm.

"Maybe you should lie down," he suggested. Yes, it would be better for her to struggle with those thoughts in the privacy of her room. That was, after all, as she had always preferred it.

"I *am* weary." She relented and reached for Annie's arm.

Jack stood and grabbed her teacup and saucer.

He watched as Annie helped Mother rise and move out of the room. And he wanted to kick himself. Of all the dull-witted things to say, why had he chosen that one?

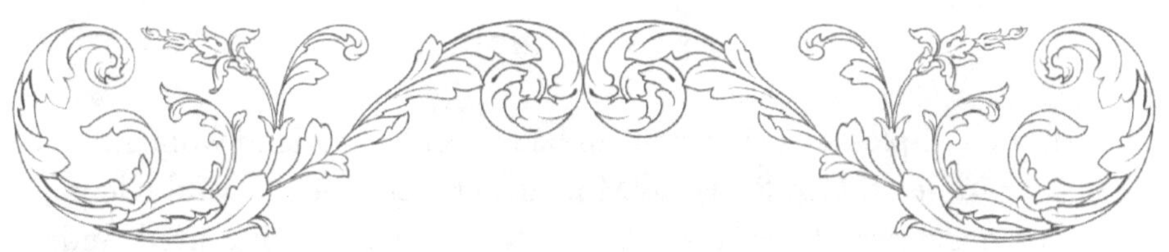

CHAPTER 11

Plans

Millington Home
Memphis, TN
May 8, 1900

Laura settled into her chair at the finely dressed dinner table. The China fairly shined and the wine glasses sparkled. Everything was the epitome of elegance. Her three brothers took their seats as well, but the chair at the head of the table remained empty.

Was she surprised that Father would continue to avoid her? Or just thankful? Not that the dinner would be pleasant either way.

Thomas and Samuel all but ignored her presence. Micah met her eyes but then looked away. Could he not do more than that? Had her sin been so great to now alienate him too?

She dropped her gaze to her plate. How would she bear another dinner like this? Never mind the countless others that would come.

Mother took her place near Laura. The soft scrape of the chair and movement of skirts were all Laura needed to confirm that. She still could not face the matriarch of their family. Not with all that had happened. And the pitiable state of Laura's being.

What sin had Laura committed that would make Mother look at her with such displeasure? The woman had never been a kind woman. Not to Laura at least. Had life jaded Mother so much that she would despise her own daughter? Or was she, too, a product of a life lived under Father's thumb?

Servants moved to the table—one filling goblets with wine and the others bringing food around. As a man servant approached Laura's glass, she shook her head and put out a hand to stop him from filling it. She didn't need anything impairing her judgment or loosening her tongue. No matter how the prospect of easing her mind with alcohol appealed.

Her mother's piercing gaze drew her attention in that direction. Though her mother's features were always difficult to read, a slightly elevated eyebrow told much. Mother questioned Laura's decision—even this small one. Not that it was different from any other dinner. Laura never could seem to please the woman, no matter what she did.

Laura leaned back and squared her shoulders despite her lack of confidence. Better to show some amount of strength than become easy prey.

"Where is Father?" The words were out of Laura's mouth before she could stop them. She wanted to sink into the floor. Why open herself up like that?

Mother's gaze hardened. "He has work that he cannot step away from. Not everyone has that privilege."

Laura swallowed and tried to keep her face a neutral mask.

"Tell me, Laura, why you are concerned about your father if all you care to do is bring ill upon him?"

Ouch.

She had walked into that. Freely. And the comment found its target quite well. Heat crept up Laura's neck and into her face...such that she was powerless to stop it. "I didn't intend to—"

"It doesn't matter what you *intended*," Thomas snapped. "The fact is you repeatedly create challenges for him. For all of us." Thomas waved a hand about the table.

God, help me.

She cleared her throat. "I don't do it on purpose."

"What did you do this time?" Samuel broke in. "Write more of your little stories?"

She was certain she shrank in size from their ridicule. If only she might be as strong as the front she put on.

"This roast is delicious," Micah said, somewhat timidly. Ever her rescuer. Even after what her actions had cost him.

Mother turned a venomous gaze on Micah.

"Is it not enough that she insists on pulling you into her messes?" Thomas challenged. "Why do you still feel the need to come to her aid?"

Micah bit at his lip and looked at his plate of food, then shoved a bite into his mouth.

The smell of the pot roast turned her stomach. Would she even be able to swallow one bite?

"You'd best eat," Mother said. "You will have quite the morning ahead of you tomorrow."

Would there be more to her day than sitting about at Mother's behest? Dare she ask?

"Yes, Mother." She speared a carrot with her fork and stuck it in her mouth. It was more metallic than savory. More due to the fear, she could almost taste bile than the quality of their cook.

Laura gripped the lace-trimmed napkin in her lap. The edging created a rougher texture for her to work with her fingers.

"Are you not curious?" Mother lifted a fine eyebrow again. Then she exchanged a rather wicked smile with Thomas and Samuel.

Micah reached for his wine and took a long gulp.

Whatever it was, Laura had no doubt it would be meant to punish her. Was she curious enough to play this game? For certain not. She had become resigned to her fate. But would her mother leave her be if she didn't further engage this point?

Laura let out an extended exhale. "What does the morning hold for me?"

Mother's lips twitched as if she fought a smile. "Your Father has arranged a suitor to visit."

Thomas sputtered behind his napkin. Must he enjoy her misery so much? What had she ever done to him?

Just as well, she would act her part in this charade. "And who might the suitor be?"

"Mr. Higgins." Mother made no effort to disguise her glee.

The heat that had flushed earlier now abandoned her, likely leaving a pallor in its wake. "Mr. Higgins?" She couldn't hide her chagrin.

Mr. Higgins was older than Father. Even more, his quiet, timid wife had passed last year under rather mysterious circumstances. Everyone had assumed the difficult man would not seek to remarry at his age. An assumption that was apparently untrue.

Her stomach lurched, and she pressed her napkin to her mouth lest she lose her few bites in an unladylike way.

The intense gaze of her mother and brothers pierced as she sucked in a breath. Even Micah watched her, albeit with pity behind his green eyes.

Between the rising fear and the churning of her stomach, Laura fought a losing battle. She jumped up, still holding her napkin to her mouth, and pushed out a muffled, "Excuse me." Then bolted from the room.

Laughter chased her from the dining space. It was cruel and unholy. But it was her due.

She raced to the water closet before the contents of her stomach upset their position. Then she sank to the floor, hot tears pouring down her face. Truly, she was hopeless.

Patterson Home
Chicago, IL
May 8, 1900

JACK HAD NO IDEA WHY HE STAYED. BUT HE DID. AND NOW he moved up the stairs and toward the room that had always been his. Stepping within, the things from his boyhood that remained haunted him, taunting of the things he needed yet to attain. He wanted to earn more, climb higher, and be as self-sufficient as possible. His journey was off to a good start, but he could not afford any distractions...be they an ailing mother or a pesky brunette.

The bed called to him, and he settled on the edge, running a hand over the quilt his mother had made many years ago. Her diminished eyesight did not permit her to continue doing such, but he had always loved the pattern she had made for him. There weren't many things that he received in his life that were so meaningful as his quilt. The fabric had softened over time and no longer had any stiffness about it.

He considered what he might do to better prepare himself for rest. But the haze about his thoughts bade him to simply retire. He reached for the pillows then fluffed them. It would be so nice to lie down.

A knock on his door unsettled that notion. He would be daft to pretend he didn't know who it was.

"Come in," he called. Just as there was no sense in acting surprised by her intrusion, it was likewise useless to deny her entry.

The door cracked and opened slightly. Annie peered in. "Can we talk?"

He let out a breath. His hopes that it would allow him to release tension was for naught. The tightness in his chest remained.

Without further invitation, Annie stepped within. "I am worried about you."

He jerked his head. "It's Mother you should worry about."

A sharp look met his gaze. "Don't do that."

He shook his head.

"Don't deflect my concern." She leaned against the wall just inside the room. "I have every reason to worry after you." Pushing out an exasperated sigh, she then continued, "You go here and there and everywhere, landing in this house when you are in Chicago. And now you appear again, only more fatigued than I've ever seen you."

His head ached...as did his heart. He hadn't meant to elicit such concern from her. As he crossed his arms, he considered her words. "I have work..." The words were weak, and he knew it. One glance at Annie told him she did as well. So, he let his comment die.

"Why do you even keep your own house? You sleep here almost every night...and have since Father's passing." Her tone was even.

He shrugged as he rose. "I suppose I thought you and Mother needed me."

"We do." Her words were emphatic. "You know we do. These last couple of years, it has been a gift to have you here so much."

He settled into his stance. It was good she understood.

"But what about your own life? Your future?"

He grimaced and stepped to the window. The world beyond was busy—people bustled about without much thought to the way the world spun within these walls.

"What distracts you so?" She moved across the room, now standing an arm's length from him.

He jerked his regard to her. "Nothing." An easy lie. "I'm just tired from my trip."

She scoffed. "That might work on Mother, but not me. Something more is weighing on you. What is it?"

Crossing his arms again, he watched the clouds move across the sky, subject to the direction of the wind. Was he like that? Did his heart direct which way he would go? Did it dictate what he would do? He sighed. That would never again be the case. Not after what he had been through.

"Please, tell me it's not Clarise."

He shut his eyes. Why must Annie bring up that woman's name? It wasn't as if he had forgotten. Or that the memory of her still held power over him...not anymore surely.

"You have to put that in your past. She didn't deserve you."

Of course, Annie would say that. She saw him in a light that no one else did...or could.

"Is it...someone else?" There was a glint of hope in the way Annie's voice lilted up.

He shot her a look.

"It is!" Where did the enthusiasm come from? This thing with Laura was nothing more than a disaster. "Tell me about her."

Jack scrubbed a hand down his face. "It's not like that. This woman has been nothing but a thorn in my side."

Her brow scrunched. "Is that so?"

He scanned the horizon again—a refuge from Annie's disappointment. And her hope. "Laura is...spirited and stubborn."

"Is she beautiful?"

"Yes." Jack conjured an image of the tycoon's daughter. The gentle waves of her hair curving about fine features. And those amber eyes...breathtaking. "Very much." He drew in air and turned to face his sister. "But don't go getting any ideas. She shut me down...she is not interested in allowing me to pursue her. Even if I were thusly tempted."

Annie watched him as he struggled for words.

He pushed a hand through his hair. "Not that it keeps her from my thoughts, day and night."

Annie's mouth shifted into a quirked smile. "I see."

He glared at her. "A minor inconvenience."

"Oh?" Her tone held a hint of teasing.

He would not have it. "Yes."

"Jack," she said, her words soft, "I may not understand fully how you feel, but I would hate to see you give up hope for future happiness because of what Clarise dealt you."

He shook his head. Annie was right about one thing—she couldn't know what it had been like. The mental image of Laura shimmered, replaced with one more well-worn—Clarise having snuck out into the night with another man...the eve before she and Jack were to wed. The image of him standing at the altar, awaiting a bride that was not to come...it still pained him.

As if that betrayal wasn't enough, he had let his heart become overly involved. Yes, that had been the worst of it. He had given his emotions full rein, believing his affection safe with Clarise, never knowing how dangerous it would be to put his heart in such a precarious position.

That part of him was buried. And he would not resurrect it for a woman such as Laura Millington. She was every bit as risky as his one-time fiancée. Not that Laura had given him any real encouragement. All the more reason not to let his wayward thoughts pursue it any farther. But how to shut them down? They were his constant companion.

"Jack," Annie's voice had become quieter, and deeper.

He had forgotten she was there, lost, once again, in memories.

"You have to tell this woman how you feel."

He shot her a narrowed gaze. That would certainly leave his heart teetering on the edge. "No."

Her eyes shone with moisture. "You must."

There was little chance of that, no matter what Annie insisted. Laura would remain as much in his past as Clarise. What he needed to do was banish all thoughts of her to the abyss. And focus on the things he could manage.

But what if...

What if he could pursue Laura and keep his heart safe? Was it too good to be true? Maybe if he made an arrangement with her father, it could be more of a business proposition. And that, he could handle.

"What is in your head?" Annie, yet again, knew his thoughts before he voiced them.

"I think I may take your advice. Talk to her."

Annie seemed uneasy with that. "Truly?"

He walked to her and took her hands. "It may be the only way to maintain my sanity."

Her eyebrows met and her lips turned downward. "I'm not sure you understood what I—"

Jack leaned in to kiss Annie's cheek. Yes, this might work.

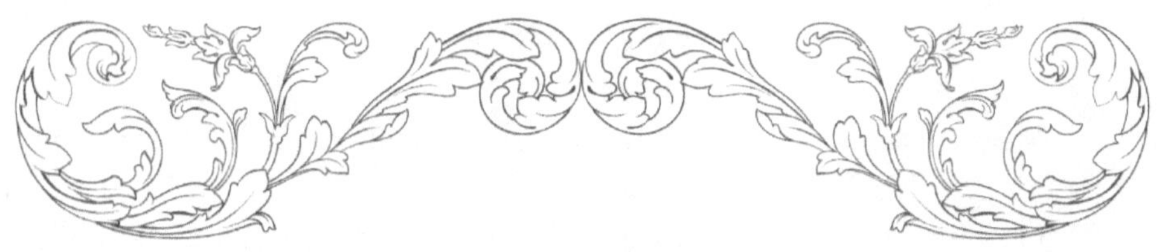

CHAPTER 12

Shaken

Millington Home
Memphis, TN
May 10, 1900

Laura awakened to another dreary day. The sky beyond her room was clouded and gray. Fitting. Her heart was the same. As she sat for the maid to fix her hair, she stared out the window. Was there any hope for her to cling to? Father was determined to have her married off...to someone like Mr. Higgins. It couldn't be. Surely her mother merely threatened, only wanted to see her reaction. That man could not be a serious consideration, could he?

She wouldn't put anything past Father. He clearly wanted her to suffer. At the very least, she was merely a commodity—a pawn to be used in whatever way Father chose. There was little she could do about it.

The bedroom door jerked open, slamming into the wall behind it the force was so great.

Laura spun as her heart fluttered as if prepared to take flight from her chest.

Mother stood in the opening...and she was not pleased. "What is the meaning of this?"

Looking to the maid, who had paled, Laura shrugged. "I don't understand. I'm finishing my ablutions."

Mother's stern expression burrowed a hole through Laura. "Mr. Higgins is in the parlor. And has been for nearly an hour."

Laura gulped. Why had no one told her? Another opportunity to watch her squirm? "I did not know."

Mother scoffed. "I informed you at dinner that he was coming. He will not be pleased at having to wait all this time."

Laura rose. "I can go straight away." The thought of facing Mr. Higgins shot cold fear through her core, but she would do it.

"Not as you are." Mother's words were ice. "Let Hattie finish your hair. And quickly."

Face heating, Laura sat once more, praying she wouldn't say or do anything to earn further ridicule. Perhaps, if she behaved well enough, her parents would reconsider this matchmaking.

The maid's fingers flew about Laura's hair, tucking and pinning.

But Mother's huffing could be heard from across the room. Why did she not go to Mr. Higgins? Attempt to ease his ire? Yet she remained, rooted to the spot, glaring and fuming.

Hattie stepped back only a few moments later.

"Finally!" Mother's anger indeed boiled hot. Was that for Hattie? Or more for Laura? It wasn't difficult to determine...not the way Mother's gaze landed on Laura.

Standing, Laura took care to school her features as she crossed the room. It would not behoove her to have Mother upset more than she already was.

"Come on," Mother groused, "I won't have you delay me one more second."

Laura picked up step behind her mother, rushing to keep pace with the taller woman. She fairly puffed as they reached the bottom of the stairs.

She tried to even her breathing as she followed her mother to the sitting room but found only modest success. The emotions coursing through her made it nearly impossible.

Soon enough, they stood at the door to the parlor. Mother halted and jerked around, her eyes narrowed, and her voice lowered, heat seeping through it. "Do *not* embarrass me or your father. And you will *not* disappoint us. Is that clear?"

Laura didn't trust her voice with her breathing so out of kilter. So, she simply nodded.

"I hope you find your words in the next minute or it will not go well for you."

Again, Laura nodded. "Yes, Mother," she eked out.

"Lord, help us." Mother spoke the words as if they were a curse. "Do better than that."

Laura swallowed, unsure how to proceed.

Mother blew out a breath and turned back to the door. After a brief moment to straighten her shoulders, Mother pushed the door in and entered. "Mr. Higgins, we do apologize for your wait. I hope you will indulge me a little longer and allow me to present my daughter, Miss Laura Millington."

Laura followed her mother into the room but froze at the man's intense glare. His features were lined and hard. Her delay in preparing herself did not appear to be well received at all.

Beady eyes took her in, up and down. It could not be described as anything but a leer. For once, she was grateful for her mother's presence.

Mr. Higgins stood and muttered a response that Laura did not catch. Because he kept his voice low? Or because her heartbeat thundered in her ears?

Mother waved Laura into the room and urged her to a chair across from his.

She hoped mother would sit beside her and offer somewhat of a buffer.

"I will leave you two to get acquainted." Mother smiled.

Laura's thoughts swirled. Mother couldn't mean that. Such would be highly irregular...and rather inappropriate. She shouldn't spend time with him alone...especially if he had expressed an interest in her on a deeper level. Which he clearly had. Wouldn't her reputation be left in tatters?

She fought a chill that threaded down her spine. It became quite difficult to hold herself firmly and not shiver. "Mother, I would prefer you—"

Her look speared Laura. Mother shot out, "I have things to attend to. Surely you can entertain Mr. Higgins."

The man's smirk was not comforting.

"Yes, Mother."

Then the door shut, sealing Laura inside with Mr. Higgins.

"Please, sit." Mr. Higgins gestured toward the chair beside her as he lowered into the one he had just vacated.

At least he wasn't going to request she sit beside him. She would be thankful for these small mercies as they came.

"I said 'sit,'" he barked. Any pretense of kindness quickly evaporated.

She all but fell into her chair, catching herself at the last moment so she wouldn't knock the winged back chair off balance.

He settled onto the settee, leaning back and watching her.

Was she to carry the conversation? What was she to say? What *could* she say? It was difficult to pull her thoughts together with him staring at her so intensely.

"Do you have a voice?" he bit out.

She blinked. How was she to respond?

"Of course, you do, I heard you speak to your mother. I would have you use it now." His gaze became stony.

"Yes, sir," she managed. Could she be anywhere else? At any other time? Her mind transported her to the last piece of comfort she had known—Jack's arms. That surprised, but she gave herself to the memory of his arms holding her up, carrying her from danger. If only he were here now. For her position had become rather precarious indeed.

"It might not be a terrible thing to have a quiet wife," Mr. Higgins said, his voice cutting through the pleasantness of her memory. "As long as you know your place."

She focused on him and swallowed against the bile rising in her throat.

He stood and walked about the room. "Your father has grand ideas about a marriage between us. It could be very...advantageous, you see."

She closed her eyes, wanting to escape into Jack's blue gaze—a warm ocean to bathe in.

A finger trailed down the side of her face and she opened her eyes. The lecher stood over her, his small eyes gleaming.

She jerked back.

He frowned. "That will not be tolerated." He reached for her again.

She jumped up, nearly toppling the chair as she pulled away. "You are old enough to be my father...or grandfather! You cannot be serious."

His eyes flashed. "You will not speak that way to me. Ever."

She shook her head. This was a nightmare.

He took a step toward her. "I may be older than you, but you will belong to me. And I will not have you disrespect me."

She backed up again, and his eyes widened.

Before she could react, his hand snapped forward and he grabbed her arm. His fingers dug into the flesh of her upper arm, his hold stronger than she'd have believed possible.

She tried to twist free, but that only caused him to grip her tighter—a feat she did not think possible. Then he dragged her to his chest, his scowl causing her stomach to flip. "You're hurting me."

His stare sliced through her. "You will learn your place." His words were tight and forceful.

She tried to shake him off. "Let me go or I'll scream."

He laughed. The sound was menacing. One minute he held her tight enough to make bruises, the next, he shoved her away.

She reeled, catching herself on a sideboard as her hip slammed into it.

He scooped up his hat and cane.

For a moment, she feared he would turn that on her, but he simply set the hat on his head and strolled to the door. Looking back for a moment, he chuckled. "You'll do."

Then he was gone.

She sank to the floor. Her mother would be quite irate to find her in a puddle of skirts, but she didn't care. Nothing mattered. Nothing.

Patterson Home
Chicago, IL
May 10, 1900

JACK EAGERLY AWAITED HIS TURN AT THE TELEGRAPH office. Many people milled about...too many. Would he wait to read the post until he had privacy? Could he wait that long? He hoped that Mr. Millington had responded...which wasn't a sure thing. The man could have very well ignored Jack's request for an hour of his time.

The couple in front of him finally stepped to the counter and asked after their mail. He was next. He buzzed with anticipation, his body vibrating to the shuffle of his feet and tapping of his toes. There was much invested in this venture.

He pulled out his father's pocket watch and checked it. More out of habit than need.

Had he risked his chances by sending a veiled request? Perhaps he should have been more forthright. But when he had come to send the wire, he'd been caught up in fear for his heart. What did he risk by seeking Laura Millington's hand? Could he keep his heart guarded and secure? He had reason to doubt.

He paused. What was he doing? It was certain his heart would be at risk. Could he recover if it were to be rent in two yet again? How?

"Sir?" the telegrapher called, an edge to his voice.

How long had Jack been standing at the front of the line, leaving the man waiting?

There was no way to know, and it didn't matter. Stepping forward, he said, "John Patterson."

"Ah, yes, I have something." The man's tone remained even. Was there any chance it would alleviate? Or had Jack managed to completely irritate the man?

Either way, he reached for a stack near the counter and, after ruffling through the papers for a long moment, pulled one free. "Here you are."

Jack took the paper, feeling every bit of its coarseness between his fingers. Dare he read it now?

"Do you have a reply?"

Had he been staring through the words enough that the angered telegrapher believed he read them?

"I will let you know." He stepped to the side and then toward the exit.

"Next," the man called a little louder than necessary.

Jack walked onto the sidewalk beyond the office, seeking a place he might read the words he had put so much stock in. He strolled in the direction of his mother's townhouse with the sound of passersby chatting, yet none of it penetrated the haze around him.

If he waited to read it until he got to the townhouse, he would have Annie and Mother to contend with. That would not do.

He spotted an unoccupied space by some nearby buildings that promised some level of privacy. Only then did he pull the telegram out of his pocket and pour over the few words.

It was, as he had hoped, an invitation to Memphis to speak with Mr. Richard Millington. The man also extended an invitation to stay with the Millington family.

Jack shoved the telegram into his pocket and let his fingers graze the pocket watch. He tried to let the words settle into his mind. He had little choice now but to go. Mr. Millington was a powerful man who would not take a change of heart too kindly.

The only way out would mean conjuring some reason—other than Laura—as to why he sought such an invitation. But did he want to? Could he bear it at this point if he were to back away from his desire for her hand?

Even more, what if all of it came to nothing? If Laura were already promised to someone else? Or if he were viewed to be a substandard choice?

She came from much. And he did not.

He squared his shoulders. While that may be the case, he had made much with the small start he'd be given. His ambition had served him well. If he could make a solid offer, it was possible he could secure the marriage.

And if not, what then?

A train whistle blared nearby at the station. Would he be back here in the following days to board one himself?

Regardless of what might be, he had to try.

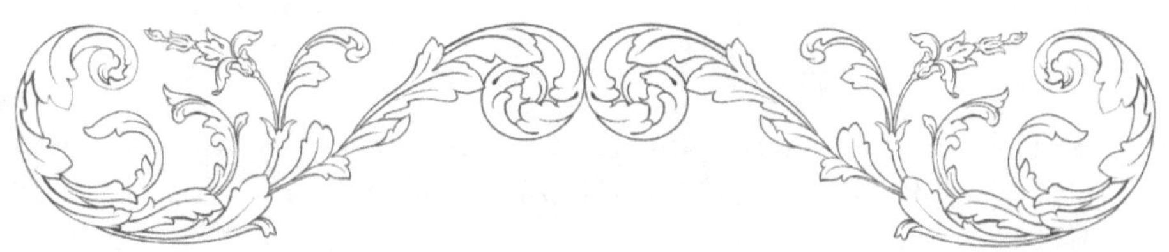

CHAPTER 13

Eager

Memphis Central Station
Memphis, TN
May 12, 1900

Jack had never experienced such a train ride. It wasn't horrid in any sense. Rather, it was as smooth as possible. But *he* had been jostled within himself the whole trip with uneven emotions. Should he follow his plan to secure Laura's hand? It would be an advantageous match for Jack. And it would solidify his future in the industry.

Though he could not deny that his feelings were involved. And *that* was not something he wanted to risk. Therein, lay the question: Did he seek her hand for his career and what he might gain or because of Annie's urging regarding his deeper desires?

The former would serve him well. The latter may lead to his ruin.

How was he to know? His heart thudded in his chest, belying his feigned ignorance.

Pushing those thoughts to the side, he settled within the fine carriage that had been sent for him. What would it have been like to have always lived in such finery? To never know want. To never know need. What had Laura's life been like? How had it shaped her?

The fact that he was so intrigued gave him pause. He would not let this care for her sway him. This was for his career, for his stability. That was all.

As the horses slowed and shifted their direction, Jack turned his attention out the window. And there, in the not so far distance, sat an opulent house—the largest he had ever seen. The fine entrance mesmerized him. Would he ever have this manner of home? He could dream.

The building became even more foreboding as the carriage brought him closer. He looked up in an attempt to take in the totality of the structure. It was more than he could have ever imagined. A part of him, perhaps layered far beneath the surface, whispered in his father's voice. *What would a man need with such a place? To what end? Meaning is not found in the size of a man's estate, but in the number of people who value him.*

While he loved and revered his father, he wasn't certain that life could be summed up so simply. Didn't Jack want to provide for a family? His ambition had placed him well enough for now, but the future...

The door to the carriage opened, and a footman announced that they had arrived.

Jack was tempted to apologize for his distraction but opted not to. How would that look, him explaining himself to a servant? So, he simply nodded and grabbed for his hat as he stepped down.

He had donned his finest suit for this first experience at the Millington mansion. And what would be another meeting with Mr. Richard Millington himself.

As he alighted from the carriage, he again tried to take it in with a thought to not appear a country bumpkin who hadn't the manners nor the acumen to navigate such a situation.

The footman made quick work of unstrapping his luggage as another man came to assist.

There was little left for Jack other than breaching the entry. Walking toward the large door, he climbed the few stairs and, steeling himself as he straightened his coat and tie, he knocked.

The door creaked open to reveal a nicely dressed man who was likely the butler.

"John Patterson. Here to see Mr. Millington."

"Ah yes, Mr. Millington has been expecting you." The servant ushered him within. "Shall I take your over things?"

Jack nodded numbly, removing his hat, and passing it to the man. But he'd best keep his jacket. His shirt and vest had probably wrinkled beyond any reparations he could make before seeing Laura's father.

The man handed off the hat to another manservant who appeared from nowhere and, stepping aside, allowed Jack to move into the center of the entryway. It was more spacious than the whole lower floor in his townhome. Beyond that, the grandeur surrounding him was unparalleled.

Did he truly think he could tempt Mr. Millington to give his daughter's hand to someone without family or position? Swallowing, he decided to shove that thought to the side. There was nothing he could do but present his best case.

"Shall I escort you to your rooms?" the butler asked without emotion.

"I should like to speak with Mr. Millington directly."

If the man was surprised, it barely registered on his features. "I shall have to ensure Mr. Millington is able to receive at this time."

Jack's bravado wavered. Then he reminded himself that he must press on. He stiffened his spine and said, "Then make haste."

"Wait here." The butler afforded him a long, meaningful glare as he moved past Jack and down the hall.

There was nothing to do but wait. Where had the other man taken his hat? He scanned the area, but there was no indication that the man or Jack's hat had ever existed. The whole of it became more than a little disconcerting...especially given his mission here today.

The passing moments gave allowance for Jack to become increasingly uncomfortable with his plan. What was he thinking? Did he actually believe this would amount to anything?

Should Mr. Millington inquire as to Laura's preference, surely she would turn Jack down. But a mental image of Laura visited him, and his anxious heart quieted. And beat harder for an entirely different reason. He remembered the feel of holding her, of having her in his arms. There was nothing for it...but to move forward with this ill-thought-out plan.

The butler appeared again. "Mr. Millington will see you now. This way, sir." Then the man strode off down a hallway.

Jack picked up his pace in order to not be left behind amidst the maze of rooms. He maintained only a short distance from the butler. At last, they arrived at yet another ornate door that had been left ajar.

"He is expecting you, sir." The butler moved out of the way.

There was nothing left for him but to enter the room. He would have supposed Mr. Millington would receive him in the parlor, but this room lay much farther in the home.

Jack took in a deep breath and pressed into the darkened room.

Dim light only partly illuminated the massive office designed as well, it seemed, to function as a study. The dark reds and browns only deepened the foreboding nature of the space.

Mr. Millington rose from behind his desk as Jack entered. The older man extended his arm as he came around the desk.

Jack shook the proffered hand.

The tycoon's grip was firmer than Jack expected.

Mr. Millington indicated for Jack to sit in a nearby chair and dismissed the butler with a wave almost in the same movement. He seemed perfectly genial and even offered a small smile. "What can I do for you, Mr. Patterson?"

Did he remember Jack from the celebratory gathering for the ill-fated engineer last spring? Did it matter?

"I—ah—was hoping to have a few minutes of your time, sir."

Millington nodded. "As you see, you have it." A slight chuckle threw Jack nearly into a nervous fit.

Jack grimaced. What an idiotic thing to say. "I hoped, er, that is I *wanted* to seek your opinion on a matter." Then Jack paused.

Mr. Millington stared at him for several seconds. "I don't wish to sound ungrateful for your time in coming to Memphis, Mr. Patterson, but I am a rather busy man."

"I do thank you for the invitation. As well as for your hospitality."

Millington waved dismissively just as he had for his butler. Was that the level he put Jack on? "Think nothing of it." He returned to his chair behind the desk. "But I am rather curious what a railway engineer could wish to speak with me about. Unless..." Millington smiled enough to show teeth.

"Unless what, sir?" Jack leaned forward, praying the man would somehow just guess what he wanted.

"Unless you are seeking to jump ship with Pullman and find a place in my railroad operation. I could use a man of your skill and knowhow."

Jack straightened, hoping his momentary confusion had not been evident. Was that so? He had never considered looking elsewhere. Not only was he content with his job at the moment, he planned to better his position within the Pullman company. What kind of proposition could a railroad owner have for him? What need could he have for a designer on his payroll? Wait...did Millington have some knowledge of his experience and abilities? How?

"Don't be so surprised." The man's smile broadened. "I have followed your career closely. You are a star on the rise. Reminds me of myself at your age."

"You, sir?"

"Yes." There was that chuckle again. "I haven't always had all of this. I worked my way up."

Jack wanted to hide his surprise, but he wasn't sure he was at all successful. His face always told what he thought and felt. Without a doubt.

"But I'm getting ahead of myself. Tell me, what did you want to talk about?"

"I..." *Why* was he here again? Oh, yes...Laura. The gleam of opportunity with Mr. Millington's company, as well as his praise, had proven quite the distraction. "I wanted to speak to you about your daughter."

The man's eyebrows came together. "Is that so?"

Jack nodded. "I have had the opportunity to make her acquaintance."

"Yes, I remember. The banquet at the New Southern Hotel last March. If I remember correctly, she wasn't too keen on becoming more...acquainted with you."

Jack swallowed. "That is true. Still, I would appreciate if you would hear me out."

Millington nodded slowly. "I should tell you, she has other interested suitors."

Jack's eyes widened. "Oh?"

"Yes. Well, she is a very attractive young woman. And I have to consider any offer for her hand very carefully. I would...perhaps feel more inclined to hear from a man who would align himself with my company. I have a duty, you understand, to look out for her and keep her in the lifestyle she is accustomed to."

"Of course, sir." Was he saying what Jack thought he was? That Jack would have a horse in the running if he would give up his job with the Pullman Company? The company that had given Jack an opportunity when no one else saw his potential? Didn't Jack owe Pullman more than to jump ship right now?

Millington's brows arched. "It really is up to you. As I said, I have to know that my daughter will be cared for. As well, that any interest she might have in my railroad would stay in the family and in my company."

There, then, was the rub. Was it that clear cut?

Mr. Millington stood. "I don't want to belabor the point, but I am going to need to know what to tell others that come knocking. And what to tell Laura."

Jack wanted more time to think, time when he wasn't under Mr. Millington's watchful glare. "I...don't know that I can make a decision in this moment. That is...a bit to think about."

"I understand," Mr. Millington said as he set a hand to Jack's shoulder. "And I can be patient. To a point."

There was a clear message. Jack didn't have long to consider it, but he was being gifted some time. How long? That was less clear.

Mr. Millington walked back to his desk, all but dismissing Jack. "You must be tired from your trip. Take some time this afternoon to get settled. We can speak again tomorrow."

And that was, Jack supposed, his deadline.

Millington Home
Memphis, TN
May 12, 1900

LAURA DIDN'T KNOW WHY SHE TRIED ANYMORE. WHAT WAS the point? She stood at the top of the stairs, stymied by the prospect of another dinner and a table with her family about it. Looking over the portraits around her did not soothe. Even though her mother had specifically chosen these paintings for this hallway to do just that. The figures stared at her. Even her ancestors judged her.

Micah had always been her saving grace during the periods her parents found reason to be ill with her. But even that was not the case anymore. He'd become increasingly quiet and subdued of late. Was he giving way under the pressure to disregard her?

Had she not given up enough? Sacrificed her dream for the benefit of her father's gain?

A door shut behind her. Had she been standing here long? Turning, she spotted Micah strolling down the long corridor as he fastened the buttons of his jacket.

She ached to call out to him. What would that gain her but further rejection? Perhaps...but maybe he would show her some kindness in the absence of their parents and other brothers.

So, she waited for him.

He looked up across the space between them and startled, halting in his tracks.

"What is it?" she asked. She wanted to take the words back immediately. There were few things he might say to make this any better...and many things he would likely say that would sting.

Still, she waited.

"I didn't expect to come across you." His frame stiffened.

That was curious. Their bedrooms were not far from each other. It had aided their developing closeness in years past. Was it now a challenge for him?

"I..." What to say? How might she express the fears lying under the surface? "I only paused for a moment."

One of his eyebrows lifted, and they stood in silence for several moments.

She wanted to reach out again, but her trepidation got the better of her and she remained silent.

"We'd best get on," he said, his words flat as he moved closer. Then walked past her and began his descent down the stairs.

She stared after him.

He stopped and turned, taking a deep breath, and letting it out. "Come on, then. No need to make things worse by delaying the whole dinner."

His eyes caught hers and, for a moment, she believed him truly concerned. Of course, he was. He cared for his sister. No matter what.

Guilt swirled about her. How could she doubt that?

She nodded, not trusting her voice. Stepping down, she was thankful he would escort her to the dining hall.

But he picked up his pace before she reached him, hurrying down the remaining steps, and turning right at the base and through the open arch. And then he was gone.

Her steps slowed but continued. Yet another meal where she would have to endure ridicule and harsh words from her mother. And Father, if he were present.

She caught her breath, pulling in air as deeply as she could. Then forced herself to let it out slowly. Only then did she proceed toward the dining room with eyes downcast. Because she felt such despair or because she did not want to face her family? Perhaps it would communicate her submission.

As she neared the dining hall, she prayed for strength, for guidance, for purpose... That caught her off-guard. Purpose? Had she not given that up? Indeed, she had. What more could there be for her in life? She would be forced to marry the horrid Mr. Higgins and simply endure what years remained before her.

She stepped into the room lit with candles lying about the table. Her brothers, including Micah, stood off to the side conversing with a fourth man she couldn't quite see. Samuel's stockier frame blocked her view. Did it matter who came to join them? Perhaps Mr. Higgins? Her heart dropped. How could she sit through a meal with that man?

She paused, deep in thought, as her father came from the direction of his study a few paces away and moved toward the dining room. Only, he would have to pass her. She swallowed. Having an interaction with Father did not appeal. But to avoid it, she would have to move farther into the room and make her presence known—a likewise unappealing prospect.

"Don't just stand about." Father's gruff voice filled the hallway. "Are you ill?"

She froze.

He came alongside her and set a hand to her arm. "Come, we have company."

She nodded weakly and allowed him to press her into the room.

Samuel, Thomas, and Micah turned. And the fourth man became visible.

Jack.

Her heart stopped. It couldn't be. How was he here? Why was he here?

The memory of his rebuff at the boarding house returned, and she frowned. There would be nothing but hardship here.

Father continued on toward Jack, leaving her in his wake.

She was buffeted by waves of apprehension. Her heartbeat returned, albeit faster than normal. It made her light-headed. She backed up a step.

"Laura." Father's tone was one of warning.

"I..." She set fingertips to her forehead, tugging her gaze from Jack's piercing one. "I must excuse myself. I seem to have developed a slight headache."

Father scowled.

But she spun before he could say anything further. Ducking, she pushed her legs onward, needing desperately to quit the room. Now.

She only managed a few paces before a claw like grip clamped on her upper arm.

Jerking her regard in the direction of the offender, she found her mother's matching scowl.

Hoping her eyes adequately communicated a plea to let her keep going, she gazed at her mother's frank expression.

"I think you should sit with us for a while."

It was not a request.

Laura glanced over her shoulder to where Jack watched across the room. Was God even listening? Did He care? She wasn't sure about anything anymore...not in this house.

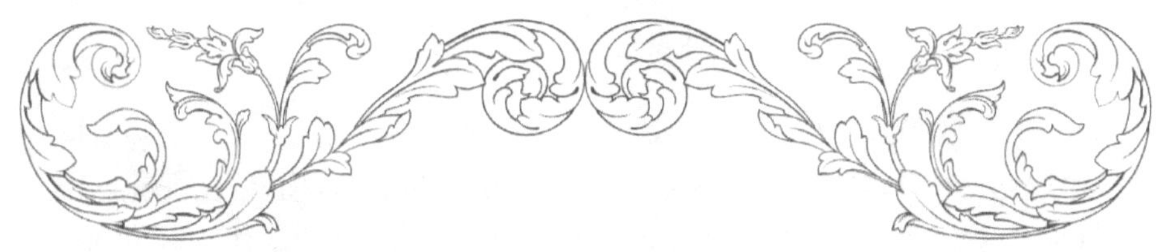

CHAPTER 14

Linger

The dinner conversation had been far from flowing. Jack tolerated it as Laura's parents and brothers made polite chitchat and had plenty of questions about his work. But Laura sat with her head dipped. Was it possible she did indeed have a headache? It had seemed a ploy to escape the forthcoming interaction.

A glare bored into Jack from the right. He didn't have to look to determine it was Micah. The man had not given him a moment's peace—watching him intently. Jack shifted under his scrutiny.

Perhaps Jack deserved it. He had left Laura in the worst of situations in Vaughan.

Why he had done so was still a mystery. Though now that he had some distance and space, he was certain his heart had become better protected.

"Shall we retire to the drawing room?" Mr. Millington glanced about at the men around the table as he set his napkin beside his plate.

Samuel and Thomas rose. Micah a moment behind them.

"I would like that," Jack said, then cleared his throat. "Might I excuse myself long enough to see Miss Millington to her room?"

Laura's head jerked up, and her gaze collided with his.

Mr. Millington shot a curious look at Jack, but it wasn't quite what he expected. There was no accusation in his eyes, no visible concern that Jack might intend to take advantage of his daughter. It was more... amused. As if he were intrigued by his daughter's discomfort.

Laura's words were sharp. "I thank you, Mr. Patterson, but I am quite capable of—"

"That would be kind of you." Mr. Millington's voice drowned out Laura's retort.

Then something happened that Jack did not expect—Laura gave way to her father.

She shrank back at his tone. It was pitiable.

Jack's chest tightened as he wondered what she feared of her father. And just how the man might have instilled that fear.

"Thank you," Mrs. Millington added, her voice dripped with a honeycomb sweetness. "She can be rather sickly."

That astounded as well. Laura had only ever seemed a strong and independent woman. This was, for certain, a different side to the fair lady.

Nodding, Jack came around the table and offered Laura his arm. "Shall we?" His eyes were on hers alone.

She peered at him for a second, the swollen redness of her lips belied that she had been gnawing at them.

Then he realized he stared at her mouth. Heat flushed through him.

At length, she set a hand upon his arm and stood.

Without anything further, he led her from the room. Though he did spot her father and brothers moving off in the direction of Mr. Millington's study.

Jack kept his steps even and his pace slow. He had to know, had to assure himself that all was as it should be.

"Are you well?" he whispered as they strolled toward the stairs.

She bit at her lip. Why must she draw his gaze there once more?

"Only a bit of a headache," she repeated the words she had used earlier.

He grimaced. Something wasn't right. He had asked an improbable and highly inappropriate thing in requesting to escort Laura to her bedchambers. And he had fully expected one of the men to protest. Were her father and brothers not concerned about her virtue?

He did not doubt her innocence, but he questioned the behavior of her family members. It seemed backward. It felt wrong.

"I...confess I wished to speak with you again. After the way things happened in Vaughan, after—"

"After you all but dismissed my accounting of what I saw? As if the word of a woman could not hold up to the report of a man."

Jack swallowed. She spoke the truth. He had done that. Not intentionally, but he'd done so all the same. "That's not exactly what I wanted to say."

She looked down and muttered, "I'm sure not."

He wanted to respond, the urge to combat her words gnawed at him. But he held back, and for several paces neither spoke. Then he tried a different approach.

Turning toward her, he tried to catch her gaze. "I meant to...apologize for my behavior. For leaving without another word."

She did not shift her focus from whatever she spied in the distance. "I should say that your leaving was one of the better things of that evening."

That stung. Her verbal dagger hit its mark. What did he need of this? Why would he continue to allow her to berate his efforts?

She drew in a long breath, then pressed it out. "Forgive me."

He halted, dragging her to a stop as well.

Sliding her gaze toward him, she met his eyes. "I am...tired."

The last word was fairly breathed out, and there was more behind it than simple fatigue. But what? What did she hide? And why did the forlorn look about her pain him so?

She dropped her gaze to the floor. "Would it be all right if I continued on my own?"

He examined what of her features he could see. "I should not think to leave you to find your way alone with a headache plaguing you."

A simple, brief nod was her only response.

After a moment of attempting to gauge her thoughts by what little he could discern of her face, he picked up step once again.

They reached the top of the stairs, and she indicated a room to the left. "Here we are."

He paused once more, this time just short of the door to her bedchambers. "Are you certain you will be all right?" His intent had been to assure her rest, but just as her words seemed to be a front for a deeper meaning, so were his.

She looked at him and a slight smile graced perfect lips before it disappeared. "I will manage." Her words were hoarse.

He could not shake free of the thought that something ill befell her. But what? And what might he do about it?

She tugged her hand from his grip and reached for the doorknob.

"Laura..." he said before thinking better of it.

She turned and her gaze caught his. Did he but imagine the pleading depth to her amber eyes?

He took in a breath. "Miss Millington," he corrected himself.

One of her eyebrows lifted. She waited for him to continue.

"I shall see you tomorrow." Then he bent forward and grabbed for her hand. With tentative movements, he brought it to his lips, pressing a kiss to the perfectly gloved and delicate limb. There was no chance he touched her skin through the satin, but a fire ignited in that space all the same.

Unable to linger in the moment, yet dreading its passing, he released her and forced himself to keep his attention on where he was going and not on the lady who had stirred him so deeply.

The encounter should leave him prepared to run for sake of his heart. Still, a protective desire he couldn't explain flared in him. Beyond that, he was uncertain if he should risk his rather secure future with the Pullman Company for a risky venture with her father.

All things considered; he knew what he would say to her father once they had a private moment. There could only be one answer.

LAURA COULD NOT IGNORE THAT SOMETHING WAS AFOOT. Something with Jack. Why was he here? Did he have business with her father? If so, what? Did he know more than he let on about her situation?

She stared out the parlor window, all but forgetting the book in her hands. The trees beyond had blossomed in the last few weeks, the world becoming bright and alive. Even as she died a bit more each day within these walls.

The question should be why did it matter? Had she not decided weeks ago to forget the tender moments shared between them? She should. For there could be no future there. Those weeks ago, he had spoken to her as if she were a wayward child...just as her father and older brothers did. Even if there could be more to their acquaintance, she would not stand for it. What manner of friend treated another in such a way? And last night, even upon his apology, he had not denied it.

As soon as he concluded whatever brought him to Memphis, he would leave. Just like he did before.

Good riddance. Indeed.

She took her fill of the vibrant world beyond the windowpanes. If only she could soak it in and let something akin to hope spring in her. But it would be for naught...for what hope remained?

The book poised in her grasp had become a bother. She wasn't reading it anyway, so she set it on the side table.

The door to the parlor swung open, and she released the book just inches shy of being on the table. And the bound pages fell to the floor.

She swooped toward it, her thoughts whirling. Who would invade her private moment? Had Mr. Higgins come to renew his malicious intentions? Could she stand another such episode?

But as she gripped the binding with a trembling hand, fingers grazed hers. She lifted her gaze to find Jack crouched in front of her.

"Let me help you with that." He lifted it from her hands and assisted her to a standing position with one hand on her elbow.

Her face heated as his nearness overwhelmed her senses. And she hated her rebellious body. Had she not just decided to be done with him?

"Are you quite well?" His words were soft yet had an edge to them.

"I...am fine." She would not show weakness.

"And your headache? Improved?"

She touched her forehead. Had she completely forgotten her excuse from the evening before? "I...yes." Why did her tongue fumble now?

He held out a hand toward the settee she had been perched upon. "Please, rest yourself. You do look a bit flushed."

She touched the side of her face. Must her whole body betray her? This would not do. Instead of abating, the heat within her intensified.

Jack set the book soundly upon the side table as she had failed to do before.

He backed away and watched her rather curiously.

"Did you need to speak with my father? I can fetch him for you." She rose.

But Jack set a hand to her forearm. "No. I...came to speak with you."

With her? Had they not said their piece last eve? What more could he want to say? Did he intend to belittle her further?

She tried to catch his gaze. Perhaps she might read something in his expression.

Though he had begun to pace again. Had something agitated him?

"You seem ill at ease, Mr. Patterson. Please, sit, let me call for some refreshment."

He was in front of her again, preventing her from standing. "I am well enough. But I would speak with you, Miss Millington."

Helpless to offer anything more, she watched as he fidgeted with his sleeves.

"I'm not doing this right," he mumbled.

She worried at what may come next. Was there horrid news to deliver? What could be worse than the prospects she had already faced?

Jack halted and, drawing in a breath, faced her. Yet his focus seemed to be on the floor between them. "Miss Millington, our acquaintance has been a bit...uneven."

Quite the understatement.

"And I have not always represented myself as well as I should."

That was also true.

"But I find myself caught...in a place that I wished not to be."

That piqued her interest. What exactly was he trying to say?

"I have spoken with your father."

He appeared to be sweating. His words were coming more frantically.

At last, he looked at her. "And I fear the only remedy is to ask for your hand."

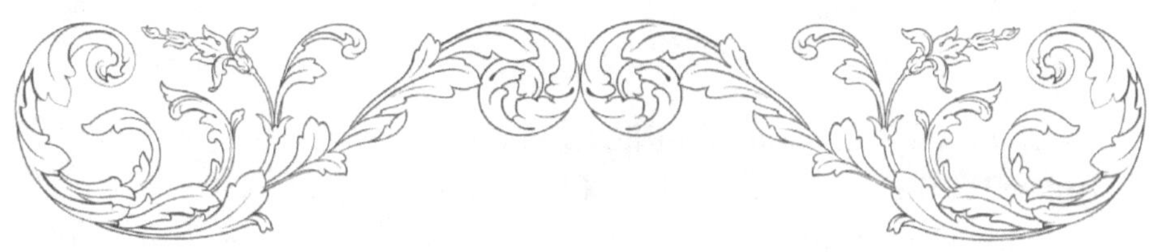

CHAPTER 15

Closer

J ack held his breath. The moments passed unimaginably slow. And, as he watched her features fall, his heart did as well. She would say no.

After all he had promised Mr. Millington. After all that was at stake—his career, his good relationship with the Pullman Company, his integrity—she would deny him.

Should he reach for her? Perhaps it would have been better had he taken her hand. Glancing at her fingers, gripping the fabric of her skirt so tightly they paled, he doubted such a move would be prudent now.

He had strived to keep his heart protected, but it became more apparent as the seconds ticked by that he had failed. Should he, then, tie himself to this woman? Give her the opportunity to hurt and betray him? Or might he retract the offer before she had the chance to reject it?

Her lips twisted and her eyebrows puckered. Was she so deep in thought? Struggling with an answer?

He looked down, perhaps it would be best to pull back from the exchange. He took a step away from her. The urge to take another over-whelmed him. But he refused to let her know how she affected him.

Look at her, he admonished himself. *Be strong and show no fear.*

Blast it all! It wasn't as if he faced down a wild animal. He almost laughed at the precarious position his heart found itself in.

This was a business arrangement. Her father had made that quite clear. And though the conversation with her father had been tense, Jack had made promises that he must keep no matter how difficult. He would be a man of his word. Regardless of the thinly veiled threats her father had made. Jack wasn't daft. It was clear that if he didn't follow through, his future in the industry would be in peril.

His gaze collided with hers, and she looked away.

She pulled her bottom lip between her teeth. Was her answer so difficult in coming? Perhaps she only wanted to ease her refusal.

He swallowed, the movement painful in his throat. "I...ah...might have overstepped."

What was he saying? He had done everything correctly—he had asked Mr. Millington for her hand, he had treated Laura with kindness, and he had put his future in jeopardy...for her.

Her amber eyes fell on him again and there was moisture in them.

That tugged at his heart all the more. Blast it all, indeed.

He cleared his throat. "Miss Millington..." Why did it feel wrong to address her so formally? Had their circumstances not permitted him to speak her Christian name?

Releasing her lower lip, now swollen from her teeth, she tightened the muscles around her mouth.

And he regretted that his gaze was drawn there at once. He couldn't do this. There was too much at risk—both for his heart and his career. He'd best find a way out. "Miss Millington, I have been too zealous, I fear. It is obvious that you—"

"Yes." The word came out forcefully. And she reached for his arm, grabbing at his sleeve.

Nothing prepared him for that. All at once, his heart swelled and beat harder. This would not do.

He straightened his tie, not trusting his voice just yet. But as he glanced back at her face, her eyes pled with him. To do what, exactly? Did she agree out of fear? Perhaps she didn't wish to marry him at all. Had he not put his very livelihood on the line—both his career and his future?

Stepping closer, he lowered his voice and forced himself to retain his hold on her gaze. "Laura, I do wish to marry you. But not out of some sense of obligation."

She dipped her head. There it was—her reluctance. This would not do.

"I see."

Lifting her gaze, she moved her grip to the lapels of his jacket. Holding firm to him as if his strength was desperately needed.

"It's not that at all." She paused, licking her lips.

Why was his attention so drawn there? Did he want to seal their arrangement with a kiss? His breaths came heavier. But he could not lose himself in this moment. Too much was at stake.

"What is it then?" His words were huskier than he'd expected. As if he were some love-sick school boy.

Her gaze held his. The intensity there bade him rise to the occasion, to protect her from harm, from herself.

That was craziness.

Wasn't it?

"I..." Why did she have such difficulty speaking? Was it evidence of her reluctance? "I...would be pleased to become your wife."

This was not the Laura Millington he knew—the impulsive, spirited lady that had flared at him on more than one occasion. Right now, she fairly cowered. Her vulnerability unnerved him.

His fingers moved up her arms as if of their own accord. Gently. Seeking to soothe.

She trembled. Because his hands were on her? Or from some unseen fear?

Still, his hands moved, seeking out the silken skin of her face. His left hand retreated to cover her hands on his chest while the other cupped her face.

"Truly?" The word was tortured. Did he need reassurance from her? Or did he seek some response other than fear?

Something shifted in her eyes. What exactly was difficult to discern. But her gaze upon him was different. Hungry, somehow.

She leaned into him. The warmth of her searing his skin through the layers of fabric.

Her eyelids lowered and her face rose toward his.

Would she kiss him? The pounding of his pulse in his ears was maddening. And the pull of this woman was beyond what he could stand. He closed the distance between their lips and claimed her mouth.

She softened under his movements but tensed at the same time. Did she think he would behave abhorrently?

As the seconds passed and his mouth explored her sweet lips, she moved in his arms and her lips parted.

It was more than any man could resist. And what had started as a simple, tentative touch deepened. How could any man—much less one with such consuming affection coursing through his veins—pull back from that?

He wanted more. And so, his mouth explored hers, tasting and taking...and promising.

Her body shifted at some point—straightening and pushing against him.

As he returned to himself, he released her and stepped back.

She stumbled as he did so.

His hands reached for her again and she leaned away, intensifying her balance issues. Though she did, at length, find her footing. Her fingers grazed her lips and she glared at him.

Yes, he felt it too. Something powerful had passed between them—a fire he could not tame, a desire he could not deny.

"Forgive me," he said, his voice hoarse. "I did not intend to..."

She shook her head and held up a hand. "Don't." The word was harsh and clipped.

Did she think he prepared to make light of it? The happenings of the last few moments rocked him to his core. "I only wish to—"

Pressing her hand out again, she said, "Please. Don't."

Then, without lowering her arm, she walked across the room and out through the door.

Uncertainty and shock held him in place. What was that? What was this...this thing between them? And would he become hopelessly lost to it? More...had the chance to preserve his heart at all costs failed?

LAURA RACED FROM THE PARLOR. THESE LAST FEW MOMENTS had consumed all of her. And she had lost herself...for a time. That scared her more than anything else.

She'd had a glimpse of what it might be like to belong to him, to be loved by him.

Then he tried to take it back.

That had crushed her.

She'd rushed from the interaction as if her life depended on it. Indeed, her heart surely did. And the fact remained...she would not be subject to another man's whims.

As if she had a choice.

She leaned against the wall in the hallway, her shallow breaths rushing in and out. That kiss should not have happened.

When he had spoken of marrying her, a thrill that surprised had taken hold...only to come crashing down. He didn't care for her...not as she had thought. Only for what marrying her might do for his career.

At least, that's what it had seemed before the kiss.

Even should she wish to turn him down, her options were few and horrid. She could do much worse than a man who infuriated her at every turn—she might be married to the overbearing Mr. Higgins or find herself in the asylum for good.

What made her think Jack would be any different once they were wed?

The delivery of his proposal told of how he did not really want this. He was clear about how he fought against it.

"But I find myself caught...in a place that I wished not to be."

So, Jack and her father had plotted. And *this* was her only other choice.

Movement on the stairs stilled her heart. Who would come and find her thusly in the hall? She pulled herself off the wall and straightened her dress as best she could. She recalled how Jack had held her, crushing the fabric between them. It had seemed real—his passion and his regard for her. But it couldn't be. She would be a fool to trust it...to trust him.

"Laura?"

She looked up and found Micah standing just a few steps up. What would he have to say? She drew in a deep breath.

He came down the final stairs and stepped closer. "Are you well?" Though the hall was dimly lit, she discerned a light of concern in his eyes.

She looked to the side. Could she bear his kindness? And after the last few days when he seemed more worried about himself than her?

"Laura?" His words became demanding. "Has someone hurt you?"

Her regard jerked toward him. What did he mean?

Then she glanced down at her still wrinkled and somewhat disheveled clothing.

His hands cupped her shoulders. "Tell me. Was it that man? Jack Patterson?"

She slid a hand to his forearm. "No. It was nothing...untoward."

He released her and stepped back. "I see."

"No," she protested anew. "Nothing like that happened."

He glanced up and down the length of her, doubt clouding his features.

She wanted for more time to compose herself, to muddle through her wayward emotions before being called to speak to what had happened.

The parlor door opened, and Jack emerged.

"What have you done to my sister?" Micah demanded, stalking toward Jack.

"No!" Laura grabbed at Micah's arm. Could she stop him from attacking Jack?

Jack recoiled. He looked at Laura and then back at Micah. "I will be square with you. I secured permission to wed your sister."

Micah's eyes widened and his jaw slackened. "Wed her?" He glanced at Laura. "Is this true?"

She nodded weakly.

Micah glared at Jack. "I will speak with my father about this. You can't just—"

"It was your father's idea." Jack's words slammed into Laura.

Was it true? It hadn't been Jack's hope to marry her to further his career, then, but he was cajoled by her father? To what end?

Jack's gaze on her softened. "That's not quite what I meant."

She pulled away from Micah and ran for the stairs. She could shut herself in her room. But would she truly be safe anywhere?

Jack rushed to intercept her. "Laura, listen to me. I—" His words were cut off.

Laura glanced over her shoulder to see that Micah had intercepted him. She didn't care. She had to find space to breathe, to sort out what swirled within her. How could this be so? Only now, she had lost control of her feelings for Jack. And he knew it.

She reached the top of the stairs and then tripped over her hem as she rushed for her room. Once inside, she slammed the door and set a hand over her mouth to muffle her sobs. Then she sank into a nearby chair and gave herself over to the torrent.

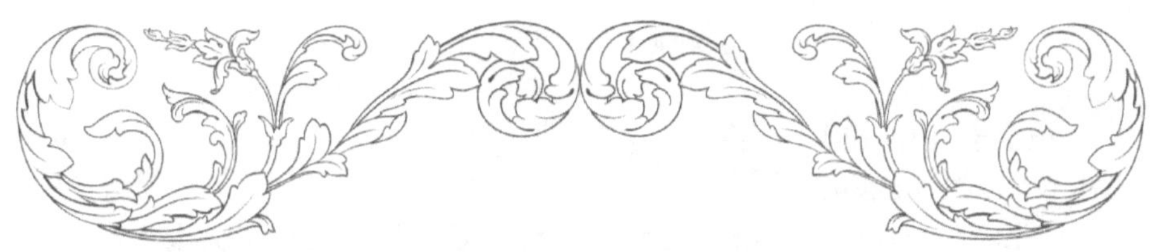

CHAPTER 16

Reassurance

Jack prepared for the day, sliding his arms into shirt sleeves. He pondered the trees just beyond the window, unsure of what the day held...or the future for that matter. After Laura's reaction to their kiss, he wasn't certain her word to marry him would hold.

She had warred enough within herself before answering. Such that her refusal to keep her word seemed unlikely as well. Would her reason for agreeing outweigh her resistance after their shared intimacy?

And what an intimate moment it had been. His nerves still vibrated at the memory of their kiss.

Though, as much as it thrilled him, that must not happen again. He would not permit her reputation to become tarnished. Even if they were engaged.

At least Micah would appreciate some reasonable distance between Jack and Laura. Would the man ever be well with Jack's presence in his sister's life or in the Millington home? That was doubtful. One more mountain to climb. But first, he had to discern what Laura thought... and felt.

Jack shrugged on his jacket and slipped from the bedroom afforded him for his stay. Now in the hall, he closed his door, but another sounded as he did so. Turning, he found Laura exiting her room just down the corridor.

She looked in his direction and startled. Then pulled back into her bedroom as if to retreat.

"Laura," he called before thinking better of it as he rushed toward her. "Wait."

Whether from his entreaty or surprise, she paused.

He would not waste his chance. "Please..." He slowed as he neared. "Let me speak."

She stood with one foot in her bedchamber, one on the threshold, her hand still gripping the knob. With wide eyes, she jerked her head once in assent.

He licked his lips. He had to get this right. There was little room for error. "I wanted to apologize for my...forwardness last evening."

Glancing up and down the wide hallway, he ensured that no one else lingered about. He couldn't quite look her in the eye, so great was his shame.

He dipped his head. "I should not have presumed such an inappropriate gesture."

Peering at her, he noted reddened rims about her eyes and a glistening that belied tears were soon to fall. Was she hurt by his words? They had been meant to soothe.

She drew in a ragged breath.

It pained him that he had clearly wounded her. But in what way? Because of the kiss? Or something else he made a mess of yesterday? Maybe it was what he had said just now? That didn't seem right.

He watched her as her slow breaths dragged in and out. And was no closer to discerning the source of her injury. Why would she not say anything?

"I beg you, Miss Mill—" He closed his eyes and sucked in a breath. If he wished to forge a connection here, using her formal address for his own comfort was not the way to do it. "Laura..."

Her eyes sparkled. Was that a glimmer of hope? Or evidence of tears all the more ready to fall?

He reached for her hand, grazing the curve of her fingers with his.

She jerked her hand to her chest as if burned.

"I know I have no right to ask anything of you, but I must." He pushed out a breath and, squaring his shoulders, he firmed his jaw and lifted his chin. He would brave her reaction and whatever may come of this interaction if it meant he had a chance for her hand. "Will you keep your word? And say you will still marry me?"

Her mouth became a thin line, and she rubbed her lips together. Did she consider him? At length, her gaze dropped, eyelashes falling over the amber orbs. Would the tears now fall?

She clasped her hands at her waist and steadied her own stance before looking at him again. "I will."

The urge to pull her into his arms and kiss her again overwhelmed him. But he held back. Such a gesture would be unwelcomed most certainly, and even more so, it would be unseemly.

But what to say now? Should he excuse himself and settle his dealings with her father? That was another conversation he did not look forward to. Less so, his forthcoming exchange with his overseers at the Pullman Company.

It would be worth it to have Laura as his own. For certain, her father's company would be a secure place for him, a son-in-law to be.

Then he realized he and Laura still faced off.

"I don't know if you have plans this evening, but I noticed yesterday that the circus has come to Memphis. I would very much enjoy taking you to see it."

Her eyes widened. Surprise? Or fear of an evening alone with him?

He opened his mouth to speak further but resisted. It was best he give her space.

She cleared her throat. "I would be well with that."

What a perfectly amiable response, one given appropriately and with careful thought. Not what he had hoped for. Or wanted.

He forced a smile onto his features. "I look forward to it."

She remained as she was, an arm's length away, neither moving nor speaking.

"I was just on my way to breakfast." His words sounded more dejected than he'd like. He must do better at disguising his feelings. If this was to work without him losing himself. "It would be my pleasure to escort you to the dining hall."

She took in a slow breath. Then nodded.

His heart beat a bit faster, thudding out a betrayal of his determination to be at odds with it.

Jerking his jacket into place, he put out an arm.

She turned and closed her door, a movement that, with her skirts, forced him to take a step back to give her space.

He kept his proffered arm at the ready.

But when she had secured her room, she simply moved off to the stairs.

So, she may still be well enough with marrying him, but the general mood about it was one of last resort only. He didn't know how to connect her tear-stained eyes and emotional outburst to this, in which she seemed to not care in the least, and the fervor of her kiss the night before. Something he could not have imagined. But, it had been real enough—perhaps a heated moment of lost control. For all evidence now was to the contrary.

Was he but a means to an end? The lesser of the evils presented her? That couldn't be so. A woman of her status and beauty must have had many offers. Why, then, would she accept him? That remained a mystery. But was it one he needed to untangle?

LAURA WATCHED IN THE MIRROR AS HATTIE PUT FINAL touches on her hair's pinned up style. This evening would be difficult to say the least—an evening with Jack, after their kiss. One that he clearly regretted.

True, she was intrigued by his behavior of late. And more than a little interested at the prospect of the circus. Her parents had always said the spectacle was not worth their time or effort.

Laura would be lying if she thought herself less interested because of that. The posters, the whispers that were surely exaggerated about animals and performers, and the sense of energy that filled the city whenever the big tent came...all of it shouted at her curious nature. She had to know what it was like. But had never, even on her own, afforded herself the opportunity.

And more, what would an evening on Jack's arm be like? They had spent time in each other's company. Surely, with pending nuptials, this would be the first of many outings they took together. Her pulse quickened at that thought.

She enjoyed being with him. And something about it brought an anticipation, a thrill from somewhere in her core...like flames licking upward. Could she maintain her indifference? For surely once they were wed, he would treat her as her father had. She was little more than a trophy, something to be toted about and made a spectacle of. Not something to love and cherish.

Had she hoped for more with Jack? At one time, yes. She had thought it was possible, had thought he had a genuine care for her. And she had allowed herself to dream as she dared not before. Though it was over-reaching...she knew that now.

"There," Hattie said, stepping back. "Perfect."

Laura looked at her own reflection. Indeed, every hair was in place. Only her downcast expression spoke to anything less than perfect repose. She doubted that would change. Still, she attempted to lift the corners of her lips for the sake of her servant. "You have performed a miracle."

The young woman waved a hand in her direction and then moved to the bed and gathered the clothes discarded for the burgundy dress she now wore. Much more fitting for an evening out on the arm of the man she would marry. Not that she cared.

Even she knew that was a lie. She did. And that was the problem.

Regardless, it was time. Jack must be waiting downstairs...perhaps had been for some time.

She stood and maneuvered around the bustling servant intent on putting the room to rights. If only her life and her heart could be so easily sorted.

Laura paused at the door. Setting a hand to her midsection, she took several breaths. She could do this. She would.

"Everything all right, Miss Millington?" Hattie called from across the room.

Laura looked over her shoulder.

The girl appeared rather concerned. What did she know of the situation? Did she understand what all of this meant for Laura?

"I am well."

"Is your corset too tight?" Hattie moved toward Laura, the day's dress on her arm.

"No," Laura assured her. "I tell you, all is well." She forced another smile onto her features.

The girl did not seem appeased, but she halted. "Have a good evening, miss."

Laura nodded and, pushing open the door, moved into the hall. No longer in the safer confines of her room, she felt exposed. That didn't make sense. She was fully covered. And safe.

Then why did she feel so vulnerable?

Forcing one foot in front of the other, she made it to the stairs. Only to find Micah staring at her.

Not now...

He had stopped his upward progress to take her in. Did he discern that she was out of sorts? He knew her better than anyone.

"Good evening," she pressed out as she started down.

But as she passed Micah, his hand set to hers and bade her pause. She should push on, but she stopped.

"Are you certain about this?" His voice held a good dose of worry.

She wanted to feign ignorance and say something about the draw of the circus. But he spoke of much more than that.

Fighting fresh tears, she put herself in order and looked at him. "What choice do I have?"

His Adam's apple bobbed. He was worried for her; it was apparent in his affect. Something else was apparent—his inability to contradict her.

She tugged her arm free of his grasp. "We all do as we must."

His frown deepened. "If I could..." The sentence hung between them. He straightened. "You know I would do whatever it took."

She nodded, fighting a swell of emotion. Micah did care for her happiness. But he, likewise, was powerless. In fact, he walked a tightrope himself.

The door to the parlor below opened, drawing her attention downward.

Jack emerged. And he jolted as his gaze collided with hers.

Micah's eyebrows dipped and met. Would he ever be well with Jack? The man wasn't all bad. Even if he was under the power of her father. And likely more similar to the tyrant than she cared for. Either way, Jack was her future.

Resuming her descent, she shook off Micah's gentle hold. Would he stop her? Try to rescue her somehow?

But he remained silent. Though she sensed that he stayed and watched.

Soon enough, she reached the last stair and found a small smile for Jack.

"Laura," Micah called to her.

She turned but slightly.

He fumbled with his words, but at last said, "Have a pleasant evening."

Her smile widened. And she fought to keep her tears from spilling. Micah was on her side. Always had been. And, despite the last few days of distance, he always would be.

She shifted her focus to Jack.

He extended a hand.

Laura set her fingers in his palm, thankful for the glove that kept their skin from direct contact. Though when they touched, it was as if the thin cloth did not exist. She could not let her heart win here. There was too much at stake.

Jack took her in, letting his gaze wander briefly to her dress, but then holding on her eyes. "You are lovely this evening."

"I thank you, Mr. Patterson."

He grimaced at her formal address but didn't say anything about it. Instead, he waved a hand toward the front door.

A servant appeared to open it.

"Your father has graced us with the use of his best carriage."

Her father. Again. Why must everything come back to him and his allowances?

"I wondered..." Would Jack see right through her façade? "Perhaps you would be well with a walk?"

The lines of his features deepened, and his mouth turned downward. "It is a few miles from here."

"But the weather is so nice." Why did her voice become pleading?

"I would prefer not to walk back in the dark of the later evening."

And that was that. Just like her father, Jack made the decision despite her thoughts on the matter. More and more, Jack proved to be patterned after the man she most feared. Was this truly her best option?

No. It was her only real option.

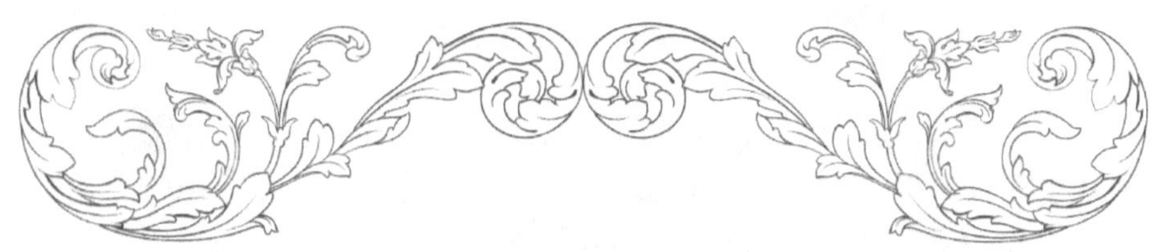

CHAPTER 17

Vulnerable

Jack could not determine how their easy interactions just months ago had turned into these awkward silences that seemed largely impenetrable. How was he to close that gap? More, dare he shed light on his feelings? Would that make him weak? For certain, he would become vulnerable. And that, he had promised never to be again.

Yet...when he considered what he knew of his parents' marriage, it gave him pause. They had always been open and honest with each other in a loving way. That had led to a security for him and Annie that went beyond their meager circumstances. Didn't he want that for himself and Laura? For the children that would come from their union? Was that worth the risk to his heart?

He had wanted that with Clarise. And had been burned.

Glancing across the carriage at Laura, he wanted for words. She had been quiet, eerily so. While he hated that she agreed to his proposal because he was her father's preference, he ached for her pain. He did want to see her happy. Could that ever be with him?

She seemed lonely. And stuck. Was that so? Maybe...just maybe...she was as stuck as he.

Dare he reach out and risk rejection? What did he desire more—to hold his ground or soften for the chance for a better relationship?

Drawing his shoulders back, he hoped that would create some ability to withstand any barbs sent his way. He cleared his throat.

"Laura?" He kept the word gentle, seeking.

She shifted toward him, a haunted look about her eyes. That pained him.

"I...do want good things for you. For us." There. It was out. And there was little place to hide.

She sucked in a breath and watched him, almost as if she weighed the veracity of his statement.

Leaning forward, he held out his hand, praying she would respond in kind. He determined that he would not take her hand but wait for her to come half way.

She looked at his extended hand and then back up to his face.

The dimness of the day and within the carriage made it difficult to discern her features.

He held his breath. Waiting.

Her features smoothed and she set tentative fingers in his palm.

He wanted to close his eyes and praise the Lord for small victories. Instead, he held her gaze and offered a smile.

She broke the thick silence. "Maybe this could be the beginning then."

He nodded. "I would like that."

The carriage halted. Had they arrived?

He released her hand with some reluctance and looked out the window. Indeed, the circus tent was visible just beyond the steady stream of people, its canvas reaching high into the darkened sky.

His father had taken him and Annie to many circuses—something he'd always enjoyed and remembered fondly. But had it been the clowns, or the animals...or perhaps the precious time spent with the man he missed so much.

Turning to Laura, Jack was riveted at her awed expression as she, too, looked beyond the window. Had she never been to the circus? It seemed as if she saw for the first time. Her parents were of plenty means to have thusly indulged her and her brothers.

He bit back a smile at her innocent delight. "Ready?"

She looked at him, her expression altering to his dismay. Though her features did not scrunch in a hard way, a gentle smile had appeared. Did she, too, want for good things between them?

The door swung open.

"Shall we?" He detected a hint of levity in his own voice and prayed she would not be offended. For he truly was enthralled with her child-like expectancy. He craved even more as he would show her the wonders that could be found within the circus tents.

He stepped out of the carriage and reached in to help her down.

She gripped his hand as she exited, her gaze latched on the big tent and the people milling about. Once on the ground, she marveled, "It's all so...big."

He grinned. Memphis was a far cry from the bustling city of Chicago. Had she truly never had the opportunity to see such grand things?

The coachman watched them, and Jack became a little uneasy about the way the man stared. But Laura's father was a powerful man, who likely monitored the comings and goings by way of his staff.

Jack released his hold on Laura's hand, even though such an interaction was not inappropriate.

But she maintained her grip, as if he were the only thing anchoring her.

Pushing thoughts of her father to the side, he firmed his hold on her.

He leaned toward her and murmured, "There is more to see. Much, much more."

And he would revel in sharing it all with her.

LAURA COULD NOT HIDE HER FASCINATION, NOR DID SHE really care to. How must she appear to Jack? A simpleton for sure. But every act that stepped to the center of the big tent amazed. The clowns were a lighthearted act, the lions were frightening, and the ring master was capable.

Even now, the boisterous man introduced the next performers. His pomp and booming voice were unmatched. He called the trapeze artists to the center. A man and woman, scantily clad...shockingly so, came to the middle of the ring. They waved their arms and bowed, hands linked.

What would it be like to reach for Jack's hand? Hold onto him during these various happenings? Would it bring her comfort and stability? Or be frighteningly vulnerable?

The acrobats climbed to the top of the tent on separate ladders across the ring from each other.

Laura couldn't help but gasp as they went higher and higher. How could they do that? Were they not fearful?

Now up on the high stands, facing off but apart from each other, the two made eye contact across the space. What was communicated there? Did they reassure each other? Speak something undiscernible? More, were they an involved couple—married or engaged?

The male acrobat took his place on the swinging bar. He pushed it to go higher and faster, each swing causing Laura to catch her breath.

Then he clamped his legs on the bar and securing wires and turned his body upside down.

The lady across the top of the tent swung in opposition. When had she taken to flight?

But now she, too, drove the momentum of her swing, drawing even closer to the man. At some point, she released her secure hold and, flipping through the air, reached for her partner.

There was a moment when everything was precarious. Would she make it? Would he catch her? Or would she fall to the net below? But just as she reached for him, he did so for her. And their hands secured a hold that kept her safe.

Laura unclenched her jaw once the woman reached safety, and loosened her grip—a grip that had, at some point, taken Jack's hand. His warm fingers surrounded hers, offering her the same security as the trapeze artist offered his partner. But could she trust Jack? Would he, too, keep her from falling if she were to let go?

Though the real question was deeper than that. Could she trust God? So much about her situation was unpredictable and out of her control. But not out of His. He was more than capable of catching her, but not if she wouldn't let go and trust Him. As long as she held tightly to the bar, she would never know what it was to fly. Or how much she could indeed rely on His faithfulness.

She had always trusted Micah. He had been good to her, over and over, protecting her, covering her...to his own detriment. But even he was human and subject to their father's whims. Likewise, Jack may not always have been steady and sure. That did not mean she floated on a churning ocean without respite. For God was with her and always would be.

In that moment, she realized Jack still held her hand. Even more, his thumb caressed the back of her hand, making small circles. She tore her gaze from the couple turning even more flips in midair to look at the man beside her.

He watched her with a softened gaze that spoke of a tenderness beneath the surface. Could it be? Did he care for her more deeply than he betrayed? More, would she trust God and let go of her illusion of control? Trust the story He was telling and the path He had laid before her?

For there was truly no more secure place to be.

Her father may have a distorted view of loving her—if one could call it that—but God's love was sure and complete, untarnished by the sinful nature of the flesh. That, she could depend on. Whether she understood the path or not. What would it look like to extend love and forgiveness to Father?

She balked at that thought. For certain, God could not ask that of her. The Bible taught of forgiveness. Christ forgave even those who nailed Him to the cross. But did she have that in her? The ability to extend forgiveness to her father?

Clasping Jack's hand even more tightly, she settled in her heart that he was God's plan for her. And she would trust in Him. And hope that He wouldn't ask the impossible of her.

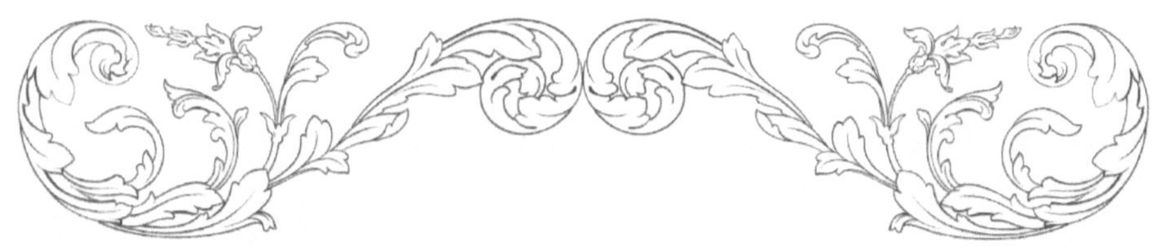

CHAPTER 18

Caught Up

Laura's heart beat in rhythm with her steps. There was so much to take in. The performances had been fantastical, but she now found herself surrounded by even more wonders as she clung to Jack's arm, walking around the circus tents. How could so many curiosities exist in one place? There were tattooed men and barely clad women in sequined fitted dresses that gleamed in the firelight. Even more, an elephant, led by its trainer, paraded about. And they offered anyone who would pay a chance to get closer.

How could one person take all of it in? She certainly could not. And she was thankful for Jack's steadying presence as she tried to absorb it all. Although, his closeness did strange things to her heartbeat—it quickened as she awakened to a better awareness of him amidst the oddities.

He did not seem to mind her holding to him so tightly. And, if she did not conjure up such notions, he drew her all the more closely to his side.

She must be imagining things. For his interests were in what he could gain from her father. But as she peered at him, he grinned. And it warmed her from her head to her toes. Was this just a reaction? Surely

149

she but daydreamed there was more to it. She turned away, focusing instead on a man who twirled a flaming baton.

Laying a hand over hers, he leaned closer. "I need to get you home."

Her heart sank. Whether from their time together drawing to a close or her having to leave such a place, she did not know.

She nodded but could not look at him. She dared not tempt fate in guessing what his expression might mean should she gaze upon it.

"I will call for the carriage to be brought around." With some amount of hesitation, he loosened his hold on her.

She didn't want to release him, though there was little option left as he pulled away.

He sighed and leaned close again. "I don't want to end our evening so soon, but your father would prefer it."

Her father... That brought a mixture of repulsion and guilt—both slamming into her at once. She should not think so ill at the very mention of the man, but it was a reality. She didn't wish Jack to see, though, so she maintained her attention on the man at play with the fire.

"Perhaps," Jack's words were hesitant, "I can let you watch a little longer as I send for the carriage."

She didn't want for him to leave her, but she didn't want to admit it either.

"Laura?" His voice deepened. If only he spoke in such a way out of a depth in his heart.

She gave him her regard despite her reluctance. "Yes?"

"Will you stay here while I do that? I shan't be long."

She looked down as she nodded. "I will." Did her voice betray how much she wanted him to remain?

Regardless, he pulled back and walked off.

Then she was left to gaze at the muscled man, muscles she could clearly see because his shirt sleeves had been removed. The play of the fire light against the contours of his arms added a bit of intrigue. She wondered if Jack's arms were muscled as well. She imagined they must be for him to have carried her after the train accident, for him to be able to hold onto her so capably.

She shook her head. Such thoughts were dangerous. Her heart may become too involved. It may be already.

"Miss Millington," a chilled voice spoke nearby. The voice was familiar...uncomfortably so.

She spun to find Mr. Higgins standing closer than necessary. Her body jerked away, but his hand shot out and grabbed for her.

His fingers landed on her forearm and gripped her painfully tight, preventing her from stepping back.

"How odd to find you here...unescorted." He sneered. The strength of the thin boney grasp defied his lanky appearance. "I should think one would take better care of such an asset."

"Release me," she said through clenched teeth. Her heart beat faster. Would he drag her off somewhere? "I am not alone. My...escort has gone to call for the carriage."

His features twisted into something far more sinister. "I see. And did he not think twice about leaving you vulnerable?"

The way he spoke that last word—drawn out and layered with his hot breath—unnerved her.

She attempted to jerk her arm free again. And again was surprised at her inability to do so. Mr. Higgins appeared docile enough—almost as if she might be able to push him over—but the iron of his grip now spoke to his ability to do as he pleased.

"Don't you remember?" His words ground out as he narrowed his eyes. "You belong to me."

What game did he play at? Her father could not promise her to two men. Just who had her father's blessing?

"Excuse me." Jack's warm baritone cut through the cloud of fear surrounding her. "I will thank you to release Miss Millington."

Her heart leapt at the sight of him, striding straight for her.

He slid his body in the very small space between her and Mr. Higgins.

The older man, for his part, frowned and gripped her even tighter.

She seethed but bit back a cry.

Jack leaned into Mr. Higgins's face. "I will ask you once more to let her go. Or I will be forced to remove your hand myself."

She secretly hoped that would be the case, that Jack would not back down, that he would stand her side and rescue her from this horrible situation.

"I don't think you understand." Mr. Higgins stood taller, though he still fell a couple inches shy of Jack's firm build. "I have an understanding with the lady's father."

Jack stiffened, but his voice did not alter. "I don't know what that could be." He leaned closer to Mr. Higgins's face. "But no understanding gives you the right to accost a lady in such a way."

Mr. Higgins glared at Laura, then his gaze swept the area. Indeed, several onlookers had shifted their attention to the three of them. He swallowed and shoved Laura away.

She stumbled, but Jack's arms steadied her precarious movements.

"We'll see who is misunderstanding what." Mr. Higgins straightened his jacket and hat. "But be assured," he said as he peered at Laura, "there will be a price to pay."

Laura shivered and leaned all the more into Jack as Mr. Higgins sauntered off.

No longer fueled by her desperate attempt to not show weakness, her knees became unable to keep her upright.

Jack's hold tightened. "Are you quite well?"

She expected his words to be hard, for him to hate her for causing such a display. But his voice was gentle, concerned, as if her wellbeing was the only thing he cared about. She blinked away moisture as she looked up at him. "I...think so."

His mouth became a firm line. He was not pleased. But something whispered that perhaps...just perhaps his anger was not for her. "Let me get you home."

She nodded and allowed him to lead her away from the prying gazes and murmurs. There was little else she could do but lean into him.

He accepted her weight easily.

Beyond that, she craved the warmth he offered...whether or not he realized it. He was a rock in the swirling current she had been caught up in. Could she trust it? Trust *him*?

Dare she dream that this was God's answer?

JACK MAINTAINED A HOLD ON LAURA, MORE SECURELY THAN he probably needed to. But he could hardly see straight he was so overcome. What gave that man the audacity, the notion that he had a right to touch Laura? When Jack had seen the man gripping Laura's arm... and more, saw the fear in her tight features, it was all Jack could do not to rage at the man. Still, he held his ire at bay. That itself was a miracle.

Even then, with such fury rushing through him, he had to make a conscious effort to keep his hold gentle. That would be the worst thing —to injure Laura after she had just weathered such a storm.

Shifting his mental energy from his thoughts to her condition cooled his anger somewhat. What must she be feeling? Thinking? Though his hold had eased, her trembling remained. But instead of fueling greater ire, it pulled at his heart. She had been through something difficult. This wasn't about him; it was about her.

They neared the carriage and her grip on him tightened. Did she think he would release his hold? Not as long as he could help it. He maintained that connection as he assisted her into the interior, and then he slipped in behind her.

It would not do to take the opposite bench this time. And he would not have it. He slid onto the bench beside her. He wanted desperately to pull her into an embrace but held back. Would that be more for him than for her?

The choice was not his, however. As he settled to the bench, she leaned into him, clinging to his jacket. She seemed so frail, so vulnerable. Would he be taking advantage of this moment if he pulled her closer?

Her tremors intensified and he lost the ability to fight with his better judgment. He wrapped his arms around her, wanting to crush her to his chest the intensity of his concern was so great. Again, somehow, he held back. But his embrace was secure and sure. There was little doubt she could feel the pounding of his heart.

"Are you truly all right?" he breathed into her hair.

She nodded against him.

He rubbed a hand down her back.

"No," she said, the word surprising him. "I'm not."

He needed to seek her gaze, the desire to do so nearly overwhelmed his good sense. Could he maintain his vow to not kiss her again until they wed if she did look up at him? If those eyes pled with him for that manner of comfort?

"I'm here. And I've got you." The words felt right. And true. More so than he'd have thought from their tumultuous relationship. But the depth of his care for her was undeniable.

Her hands fisted, no longer clinging to him, but pressing to her mouth.

"Everything will be all right." He didn't know if he could make such a promise, but he did. And he would do everything...*everything* in his power to see it through.

"Will it?" Then she leaned back. Her eyes were reddened by her tears. It shot a dagger through his chest. "How can you say that?"

Did she want him to let her go? He prayed not. For as vulnerable as she was in that moment, he doubted he could.

He searched her features, looking for some indication that she did want for space between them. What he saw in her widened eyes was fear and uncertainty...and pain.

"I promise you, Laura. I won't let him touch you again."

The corners of her mouth tensed. What did he hope for? Some declaration from her?

A tear trailed down the side of her face. "You can't promise that."

He wiped at the trail with his thumb. "But I am. Whatever it takes."

She sniffled. "I wish that were enough."

His heart broke for her struggle. "Tell me what I can do, what I can say...to make you believe that I won't leave you."

"It's not that. My father...he is the one who holds my future."

He let out a breath. It was clear she and her father had an unbalanced—and unsteady—relationship. But Mr. Millington had agreed to Jack's offer for her hand. And Jack would pay dearly for it.

Not that he regretted it. She was worth every sacrifice.

"But he has given me his word. We are to be wed."

She stared at him. Had she heard him?

"Laura, we *are* to be wed." Did he speak so forcefully to convince her? Or himself?

That was nonsense. The deal had been struck.

"I know our interactions...our paths have not been without trouble...and I own my part in that. But I promise you," he said, taking her hands in his, "No one will separate us now."

Her eyes moistened anew. The tears were more than he could bear, more than his heart could stand. Were they shed due to happiness at his declaration?

"You don't know my father." Her hoarse whisper cut through him. "He..." She bit at her lip, stilling her trembling lower lip.

"What is it?" He ran his hands up her arms, offering comfort in every way he could. "You can tell me." The words seemed right, but he realized as they were out that there was little basis for trust. Not after all he had done to push her away.

She sucked in a breath and let out a ragged exhale.

His thoughts raced with all manner of things her father might have done. It almost stole his breath. "What did he do?"

Her clouded gaze cleared and settled on him. "If I defy him, he will have me committed."

"Committed?" Surely, she didn't mean that. Perhaps her father had threatened such a dastardly thing, but he wouldn't act on it. That was ludicrous.

"I spent time as a reporter."

There wasn't much she could have said that would have shocked him more. At the same time, it fit her passion and desire to unearth the truth at all costs.

"I used a pen name. I was certain I wouldn't be discovered. But he..."

Jack almost spoke into the silence but stopped himself. This was her chance to share what she would, that she needed to. No matter how much he doubted he could bear the whole of it.

"I was in an asylum, doing a report on the conditions and treatment of the inmates."

He couldn't help as his eyes widened. She was serious. This was no passing hobby. She had risked her dignity...and much more.

"He found out. He came to the asylum...and threatened to leave me there should I ever fall out of step again."

"You don't think he would..."

The gaze she pinned him with was hard. "He put his mistress there. And I watched her be tortured with shock therapy and..." Laura paused as if gathering the strength to continue. "...a lobotomy. Until there was nothing left of who she had been."

Heat rose in Jack. Did the man see everyone as a tool—a pawn for his use? Jack wanted to ask more but sensed she had reached the extent of her ability to delve into the matter.

He lifted a hand to cup her face. "I don't care who he is. I don't care what he said, I will protect you in every way I can."

The corners of her mouth twitched in an almost smile.

"I know you will." She looked at her hand that had flattened against his chest. Almost as if she hadn't realized she still leaned into him. "At least..." Her face darkened. It was more than the dimness of the evening. "I know you will try."

Her very real fear shot through him. He had never experienced such sheer helplessness.

Without another thought, he pulled her close again. But she was wrong. He *would* protect her. No matter what. He looked heavenward. *God, help me.*

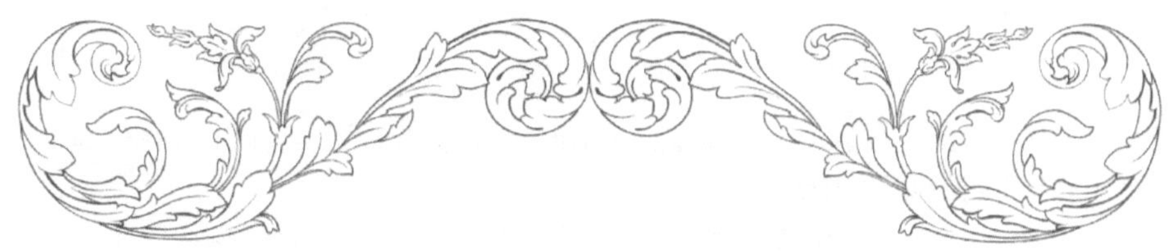

CHAPTER 19

Close

Laura's heart dropped as they drew closer to the house. Not only would she have to face that hostile environment again, but she would also have to relinquish her hold on Jack. And more, let him release his hold on her. That, she was certain she would loathe. For she had found his embrace to be life-giving in so many ways.

But she struggled with the reality that his closeness had given her reason to dream again—of love, of happiness, of all the good things life could offer. That would be dangerous indeed. For nothing pained like dreams ripped away.

The canter of the horses altered as they turned in the direction of the Millington home. It would not be long.

Yet Jack did not loosen his hold. Did he regret that it would have to happen soon? Could he possibly want this moment to last the way she did? Was there hope here after all?

It was too wonderful to fully trust in.

"Laura," his deep voice grazed her temple.

She could guess his intent. As thrilling as his warm breath's caress had been, it could not last. So, she tugged away.

He hesitated in releasing her but did so before the carriage had come to a halt. But he maintained a grip on her hand, squeezing it as the footsteps of a servant neared.

The door opened. And the spell that had been cast in these last moments was broken.

He moved past her to exit and extended a hand back into the carriage for her.

She took it, soaking in his touch for a little longer.

As she stepped to the ground, she felt a glare upon her. Looking to the side, she found the disapproving scowl of the driver. What had he heard? What did he think he knew? And what would he report to Father?

She offered a small smile, but it did nothing to alter his grimace. At length, he shifted his focus to the horses. With a slap of the reins, the carriage moved on to the carriage house.

Jack pulled free of her touch.

It bothered, but she knew it was necessary. They had to be thoughtful now that many eyes and ears surrounded them.

Jack set a hand to her elbow and assisted as she climbed the few stairs into the massive foyer.

Never had the place felt so stark. A simple light illuminated the space, but it was as cold as it was foreboding.

She caught Jack's gaze, or tried to. He seemed intent on avoiding her eyes. Her heart ached for it, though she told herself he but played his part well.

"I thank you..." she blurted before thinking. "For the fine evening."

His eyes met hers, and he nodded. "It was my pleasure, Miss Millington."

"Forgive me," she managed to press out, "I must excuse myself. I am rather tired."

Again, he nodded. His manner belied the moment they had shared. But his eyes held a warmth that reinforced it.

"Ah, Mr. Patterson, Laura," a voice called from the other side of the foyer.

Turning in that direction, she let her eyes confirm what she knew—Father.

He settled his gaze on Jack. "Mr. Patterson, I would invite you to join me in my study. There are things to discuss."

Laura spotted movement within the darkened room and her breath caught, but she soon discerned that it was only Thomas and Samuel. Was Micah there as well? She doubted that. He had become nearly as ostracized as she.

Jack offered Father a nod. "It would be my pleasure." And he moved off in that direction without so much as a parting look.

Again, she told herself it was part of the front he had to put on, and she consoled herself with the reality of the position he was in.

Still, she watched him join Father and follow into the study. Then the door closed. But not before Father's glare found her. Was that a warning? It seemed so.

Not that she had any inclination to disturb the men or violate Jack's line in the sand.

Father didn't know about the words she and Jack had shared. He couldn't. Even if the driver had overheard something, he had not the opportunity as of yet to let Father know. Jack would be fine.

The butler watched Laura but made no move to intervene. Or direct her.

She smiled with all the politeness she could muster. It wasn't his fault he was beholden to her father. He had always been kind, if not more often aloof...such she might say of the entire staff.

Did they see? Did they feel for her? Or did they worry more about their own good standing in the house?

It didn't matter. And it wasn't something she needed to concern herself with.

She moved to the grand staircase, taking the steps slowly. Did she want to listen in on Father's conversation with Jack and her brothers? It would be impossible from this distance...and useless.

Yet as she neared the top of the stairs, she was given to wonder...and worry. What did they converse about? Might Father ferret out Jack's care for her? What would happen if he did? Father had made a promise to Jack. One that was not easily dismissed. Not that her father didn't have ways to bring an end to an agreement while maintaining his status as a gentleman of his word.

Laura slipped into her room, but thoughts of what occurred below plagued her. Even as Hattie came to take down her hair and prepare her for bed, Laura worried herself with it.

"Are you all right, miss?" The woman barely spoke two words to Laura on any given day. What brought about her concern?

Laura looked at her, but Hattie's gaze was on Laura's arm, just now exposed as the maid removed her waistcoat.

Following the woman's gaze, she found that her arm had reddened and started to bruise where Mr. Higgins had gripped her.

That exchange seemed a lifetime ago.

"It is nothing. I...tripped."

Hattie sucked in a breath but said nothing further.

What did Laura care? It wasn't as if she had any delusions about the woman's loyalty. Nor did she fault this simple servant. The woman's livelihood—and perhaps that of her family—depended on Father's good graces.

So, Laura simply bore the unspoken scrutiny of the maidservant as she helped her mistress prepare for bed. It wasn't soon enough before Laura was left to herself. She stretched out in the bed, trying to get comfortable enough to drift off. But her thoughts swirled with memories of the evening. As well, she wondered what might be passing between her father and Jack.

She could sneak down the stairs and listen for herself.

That would be unseemly—her prancing about the house in naught but her dressing gown. The thought brought back images of her and Jack in the boarding house kitchen. Yes, even then, she had felt more for him than she probably should have.

Rolling to her side, she forced her eyes closed and searched inside herself for a sense of calm and respite.

But her wonderings were louder than her attempts.

She jerked upright in the bed. Dare she slip downstairs?

That was nonsensical. Did she not trust Jack to do the right thing? For her and for him?

Though her curiosity—typically her downfall—got the better of her. Soon after, her feet hit the floor and she grabbed for her robe. Then she was out the door and down the stairs, thankful that the gentle padding of her bare feet was silent.

Carefully scanning the lower level, she moved to the wall outside Father's study. She could hear the rumble of conversation but wasn't altogether certain she could distinguish the voices or the words.

She tiptoed closer to the door and pressed her ear near the crack.

"I don't envy you, sir, trying to keep that one reined in."

That sounded like Thomas. She frowned. Were they talking about her? Though it should not surprise that her brother thought so little of her.

"She has a propensity for trouble."

Samuel, that. His speech was slightly slurred. Had he imbibed too much?

"I have little doubt that Mr. Patterson has her already firm in hand."

Laura held her breath. How would Jack respond? A very real part of her wished he would speak in her defense. Yet, she knew he must stay quiet lest his support give her father reason to rethink his choice of Jack.

"How difficult can it be?" Jack said, his voice calm and confident.

Her eyes widened. It was difficult to hear that. Did he but assuage her father? Or did he toy with her heart? She pulled back, her stomach turning. This had been a bad idea. Ill-formed intentions.

She stepped to the stairs, her movements slowed and pained. What if Jack did think these things about her? Could she trust him? Trust the things he had said? Had promised? Or was this all a part of her father's game?

After what she had shared with Jack, and the things she had given into feeling for him...there was no way she would come out of this unscathed. It was too late for her. And for her heart.

JACK COULD NOT HAVE FATHOMED THE THINGS LAURA'S father and brothers said of her in the last hour. It had been an all-out, no-holds-barred complaint session. Blaming really. But he wondered...

did her brothers lean into this pointing of fingers in hopes their own faults wouldn't become an issue? Or the subject of this manner of conversation? Perhaps they merely created a common enemy.

The Laura he knew was strong-willed and independent, yes, and no crime there. But that didn't mean it must reflect on her family. Must they find her actions to be a personal affront?

Jack, for one, had decided that this aspect of Laura was refreshing. She knew her mind. More, she sought justice and truth above her own self. The world could use more of that.

"The hour grows late," Jack interjected into the tirade. "And I am long since wanting for my rest."

The brothers exchanged a look between themselves and then with their father.

Mr. Millington cleared his throat. "We shall see you in the morning, then, Mr. Patterson."

Jack was less certain about the request weighing on his shoulders. The one he had to find a way to make. Might he put it off? Address it tomorrow? Decided, he moved in the direction of the room's exit. Then paused. He had to push on. For Laura.

"I wondered if I might impose on you, sir, to allow Miss Millington to accompany me to Chicago."

Mr. Millington's eyebrows shot upward, but only for a quick moment. Then his features fell back into place with no more hint of surprise. "And why would that be necessary?"

Jack, in turn, tried to school his features to keep them from giving anything away. "I would like very much to introduce her to my ailing mother, who is unable to travel."

Mr. Millington dipped his head and looked at his steepled fingers. A few uncomfortable breaths passed before he looked up again.

But it was Thomas who cut in. "Would that be wise? For us to risk our sister's reputation for such a venture?"

"Perhaps her lady's maid might accompany her. For propriety's sake, of course. And she would be able to stay in my mother's home. I have my own townhouse." Jack spoke to Thomas, but his gaze was on Mr. Millington.

It didn't matter what the elder brothers thought or wanted. The answer would come from their father.

"It is not that I wish to deprive you of your daughter, sir. But I need to make the trip myself to speak to my superiors at the Pullman Company per your request."

Mr. Millington nodded slowly. "I think we can trust you, Mr. Patterson, to take care. And exercise all prudence."

"If it would ease your concern, perhaps Micah could be called upon to make the trip."

"No," Mr. Millington was quick to say. "Micah is needed here."

Jack watched Laura's father. How much of that was true? Or did he now find the need to keep Micah under strict watch?

"I understand, sir. And, if I do have your permission, I would like to leave as soon as Miss Millington can ready herself."

"That will not be a problem. She can be prepared to leave on the noon train."

Now that was quite the volunteered statement on behalf of his daughter. But this provided Jack what he needed—a way to get Laura away from here. There may be the potential to keep her away from here for good, but he would take it one step at a time.

Jack nodded and bowed his head ever so slightly. "Then I will take my leave." He half turned; half backed his way to the door. In the next moment, he slipped out.

Catching himself with a hand on the stair railing, he forced his breaths to come and go slowly, steadily. He had survived the tense exchange. And withstood the many statements hurled against Laura's fine character. It had truly pained him to do so, but it had been necessary.

Jack took the stairs carefully, his gaze on the limited view of the floor above as if he might see into Laura's room. Was she at peace? Would she be well with his plan to take her away? Would she trust him?

Stepping up onto the second-floor landing, he found himself plunged into darkness. Only the gleam of a moonbeam filtered through, providing limited illumination. Not that it was needed. He turned to the right and moved to his provided room.

"I heard."

Jack whirled toward the sound to find Micah stepping out of the shadows. "What?"

"And I know what you intend."

Swallowing against a thickness, Jack bade his heartbeat slow. "And what exactly is that?" Jack glanced back at the stairs. Would he see or hear if one of the men below followed him? He certainly hadn't seen Micah until he'd made himself known.

"You mean to take my sister from here. From the protection of her family."

Jack's brows came together. "You are suggesting I plan to misuse her?"

"I have seen how you look at her. Don't play me for a fool."

What was he to do? Assuage Micah's fears? But at what cost? He couldn't risk her father gaining a hint of Jack's true intentions. "I would not do such a thing. If you overheard, then you surely know I only seek my mother's blessing on the marriage."

Micah's eyes narrowed.

Jack sighed. "Regardless, I don't think it is any of your concern. I have secured your father's permission, and that is all I require." Turning, he focused on the door to his room. If he could but make it to that solace, he might not betray more than he wanted to.

"I see the way she looks at you." Micah's voice was pained. "She wants to believe you. Because she has a care for you. A care that could blind her."

Jack bit back his words, those that wanted to tell Micah the truth.

Micah groused. "I am not so trusting."

Letting out a breath, Jack faced Micah again. "I don't suppose it would do either of us any good for me to offer assurances of my character. But you play with my good name in what you suggest. I am willing to dismiss all as the overreaching worry of a brother."

Micah made a noise that sounded like a snort. "Am I to just accept this?"

Jack firmed his stance. He would not back down and would not show fear. "I don't think you have any other choice." Then he strode to the door. "And with that, I bid you good night." Pushing into the room, he closed the door behind himself and leaned against it.

His head ached with the efforts made this evening. Could he have managed anything further? Thankfully, he was certain it would not be needed.

He prayed that Laura was sleeping soundly by now. A passing thought gave him reason to wonder if Micah would risk his father's ire to wake Laura and share his worries. But that was less likely.

The important thing remained that Jack get Laura out of this place. For good.

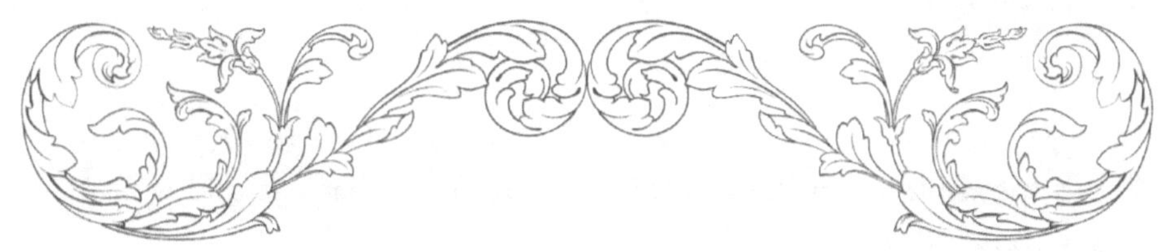

CHAPTER 20

Meetings

Memphis Central Station
Memphis, TN
May 17, 1900

Laura shifted uncomfortably next to Jack at the train station. This morning had been busy and quite surreal. First, Hattie awoke her and inform her they would be traveling that day. The packing and preparations that followed were all a blur of activity.

It ended with her being hustled out the door. None of her family members talked to her, no one seemed to care...except Micah. He stood across the hall, watching her depart, a glower about his features. He was not pleased with this arrangement. In truth, she wasn't sure what Jack's angle was, but she wouldn't risk speaking up. Still, she prayed he had a plan.

Not that he shared anything. Hattie came along, as Laura's companion and chaperone. It was for the best. Though it prevented her and Jack from open communication. And she was rather desperate to talk with him openly—about this travel to Chicago, about what she had overheard, about so many things.

A whistle and rumbling chug foretold the train's imminent arrival.

Right on time. As the engineers often pushed them to be. What part had speed played in the accident in Vaughan? What part did it play in any accident?

She remembered the words she had heard about the time of the accident—engineers often pushed for speed as the consequences for being late were greater than the minor infraction of pressing the train faster than was generally permissible. Working in the engine of a train was dangerous. Risky.

So was living under her father's thumb, she mused.

Jack glanced over. "Are you ready?" The way he lowered his voice made it feel as if his words were more intimately intended for her, yet they could have been spoken to anyone.

She nodded, still craving more of his gaze, his words, perhaps a moment alone with him.

But one look at her maidservant dashed that idea. The woman's sole responsibility was to keep track of Laura and, secondarily, report back to her father and mother. Neither of these merited Laura stepping out of the societal boundaries—or her father's—and sharing a private conversation with Jack.

She sighed, drawing Jack's attention once more. With an eyebrow arched, he watched her.

Setting a hand to his arm, she offered a small smile. "I am simply tired."

His features softened and his gaze warmed. "I shall ensure you have time to rest once we arrive."

She nodded, not terribly confident in that prospect. The little she did know of their trip was more anxiety-inducing than anything. Meeting Jack's mother and sister...could anything worry her more? What if they didn't approve of her any more than her own family? Would she be forever ostracized in both circles?

Perhaps, then, there would be room for her to believe something was inherently wrong with her. Maybe it wasn't her father's hard edges or her mother's sharp personality. But her.

That stung. Could she bear it?

Jack stood and offered his arm.

She rose and gripped it, perhaps more firmly than was necessary.

He set his opposite hand over hers, heat permeating her travel gloves. If only she could soak in that warmth or press further into him. Memories of last evening in the carriage filled her. Not just the images, but the pleasantness of being close to him and allowing his strength to cover her.

Perhaps she might trust in it. In him. Not only did she have limited options to the contrary, but she had decided to trust the story God was telling in her life. No matter how grim everything may seem. His word promised that He would work all things together for good for those who love Him and are called according to His purposes. She sent up a silent prayer for God to help her trust in that...and to help her unbelief.

Hattie cleared her throat.

Laura's face heated. How long had they been standing there staring at each other?

Jack shifted his focus, breaking eye contact. He led her toward the platform, her lady's maid trailing behind them.

Laura had little doubt this trip would feel a hundred times longer than it was. But if she was going to trust God—and trust Jack—she had to start somewhere in giving herself over to God's plan.

In the next several moments, they loaded into the car and found seats. She leaned back—Hattie perched across from her, and Jack securing the seat beside her.

Though that might seem a bit forward, Hattie did not appear the least bit concerned. Again, however, Laura did not doubt she was taking mental notes for a full report.

The first part of the journey went by without incident, even if it passed entirely too slowly.

Laura tried to read but found herself rereading the same page over and over. Jack's nearness was distracting enough, but the worries that flitted across the edges of her mind did a fine job of it as well.

After some time, she felt heat from Jack as he leaned closer.

Laura jerked to attention, her gaze shooting to Hattie.

The woman had drifted to sleep. For how long, Laura was not certain.

Diverting her focus to Jack, she held herself back from leaning into him. There were still plenty of wagging tongues about the car for them to risk unseemly behavior.

"Are you truly well? You seem distant." His soothing baritone warmed her all the more.

She drew in a breath and pushed it out. "It all happened so fast. I only know that I am going to Chicago to meet your family and for you to take care of some business."

He nodded. "That is the short of it. But I couldn't stand one more minute in that house. Not with the way they talked around you and about you." There was iron in his voice.

Her heart melted. He did care. Perhaps what she had overheard was, in fact, him doing his part to appear aloof. Her father needed to believe Jack was under his control. For now.

She slid a hand over his.

He flipped his palm up and intertwined their fingers. "I didn't trust them with your wellbeing."

A thought occurred to her—getting out of Memphis was only part of Jack's plan. She whispered, "What are your intentions?"

The corners of his mouth tipped upward. "To marry you."

Her breath caught. She had known that was his aim, but to have him speak those words in such an intimate moment filled her heart.

"And..." His gaze became more serious. "To protect you from your father."

She delved into his eyes. Their blue depths refreshed her soul. Did he truly plan to put himself at risk of her father's ire?

Laura couldn't stand back. "I can't let you do that."

His features jerked a bit. "What?"

"You cannot put yourself in such a position with my father. It would not go well for you, for your career." And he did care so for his work...and his future. She couldn't let him sacrifice that for her.

"Laura..." His voice dipped into a lower octave. "I would do that— and more—for you." He squeezed her hand.

Is this what it was like to be held in high regard? To be cherished? Treasured? It was both elating and rather unsettling. She didn't want him to risk losing so much.

He leaned closer. "I...care for you. So very much."

It was all she could do to steady her breaths. She had felt his regard for her, but the words spoken aloud meant much. "And I you." Dare she profess the depths of her feelings? This didn't seem to be the right moment.

"If it is your wish, darling, you never have to see your father again. At least, not as long as I can help it."

She swallowed. His words were too wonderful to take in. "That means more than you can know." She bit at her lip. "But it wouldn't end there. Not if you defy him. He will come after you with all that he has. And he is quite powerful."

His mouth became a thin line. As his lips parted, movement across the space dragged Laura's attention.

Hattie stirred and shifted. Now her eyes were on the pair. Even more, her gaze fell to their joined hands. And she frowned.

Jack tried not to stare at the lady's maid. Were the staff—her included—under strict orders from Mr. Millington? What had she seen? What had she heard? Could he realistically keep her from sending a telegram to Memphis?

He would do whatever it took to protect Laura, but not without boundaries. They would have to be watchful and mindful of their interactions and shared words.

Releasing Laura's hand and remaining aloof seemed his best option. It felt cowardly, but it was the best course. So, he let go of Laura and looked out the window.

She shifted beside him, but likewise said nothing.

It was weak, but what could they do short of creating a scene? Maybe it *was* the best course.

As he watched the scenery, grassy fields giving way to the city, he noted many increasingly familiar sights. They neared Chicago. In a matter of minutes, the conductor moved through the car declaring that very thing.

Jack chanced a glance at Laura to find her features tight. Was she concerned about meeting his family? Why? She was everything anyone could want for him. Every day, he discovered all the more how she complemented him. She was the sureness to his insecurity; he was the strength for her uncertainty. But at the core, they had much in common.

So he had with Clarise. Thoughts of the woman who jilted him tore at his heart.

This was not the same. *Laura* was not the same.

But underneath that layer, there was doubt. He'd never had a reason to question Clarise's loyalty until she left him. By then, it was too late. She had broken his heart and, as he realized, perhaps his ability to trust in love.

It wasn't something that added up. No matter how one attempted to calculate it, love was beyond reason. And beyond sense.

That wasn't the question though...would he be able to sacrifice all for Laura? For his love of her? He wanted to believe he would, but the still open wound made him question that.

Fingers landed on his arm. He jerked in that direction.

Laura drew back as if fearful what he might do.

That pained him. "Sorry. Did you need something?" He glanced at the maidservant to find her staring at him as well.

"We've arrived." Her words were simple, almost curt.

Indeed, the train had stopped. How had he missed it?

He stood and reached for their travel cases overhead. Then stuck out a hand toward Laura. She, however, was already on her feet and looked at his hand quizzically. He needed to snap out of it.

"I am eager to see my mother and sister," he said, as if that were explanation enough. But he couldn't share what truly weighed on him. Not here, not now...perhaps not ever.

He waved an arm down the aisle, ushering first Laura, then the maidservant toward the exit. Had he ever heard the younger woman's name? Should he have? Pushing that to the side, he worked to get Laura and the lady's maid settled in a hired carriage and have their things loaded. Then they were off through the packed streets of Chicago.

The short trip to his mother's home was entirely too long and too brief at the same time. He struggled under the maidservant's constant scrutiny and found reason to hope that a conversation with his sister would bring some clarity. It usually did.

Soon enough, they were parked outside the simple townhouse. He thought to be embarrassed in the humble home. Compared to the grand estate that Laura lived in, it was beyond humble. It occurred that she may not be willing to live so simply. His thoughts of bringing her here were of protecting her. But what if she preferred the less ideal treatment of her father if it allowed the luxury she had always known? Might she be as comfortable as a tradesman's wife?

He ached to look at her and gauge her reaction to the sight but couldn't quite make himself do so.

The door of the house opened, and Annie rushed through it before he was fully out of the carriage.

She embraced her brother. "It is so good to have you back. Mother has been beside herself." Annie's gaze wandered over his shoulder and into the carriage. "Oh my."

He turned to see that Laura had moved closer to the door. And she exchanged a look with Annie. There was likely much to be discerned in the exchange between the full-hearted women, but he could read very little in their affects.

"Welcome," Annie blurted at last, setting a smile firmly on her features. "Miss Laura Millington, I presume?"

Laura nodded and waited within the carriage.

It then occurred to him that he should assist her down.

Shaking his head, he reached for her. "My apologies, Miss Millington. This is my sister, Anne Patterson."

Laura's hand closed around his as she made her way out. Then she focused on Annie. "It is my pleasure to meet you." Laura's voice was almost hesitant. Was that due to her disappointment with their circumstances?

"The pleasure is mine." Annie smiled. "Jack has told me so much about you."

Laura's eyes widened and she closed her mouth. "I can't imagine that all of it is good."

Annie laughed. "You know my brother very well then."

Laura's face lit up and the lines of her features softened.

And Jack could breathe fully again. All would be well.

He assisted the maidservant out of the carriage and stepped closer to Laura and Annie. "Let's get everyone inside and your trunks unloaded. There is someone else I'd like you to meet."

Annie looped an arm through Laura's and shuffled her inside, all but forgetting about Jack.

He kept up with them, determined that he would be present at the meeting of his mother and future bride. What was Annie thinking?

Rushing through the front door, he caught his sister and Laura as they stepped into the meager front parlor.

His mother sat in her favorite chair, taking it all in as Laura entered the room. Mother did not look altogether pleased.

He grimaced. Did she, too, think of the past and how he was injured by Clarise? Maybe he wasn't the only one leery of another wedding.

Annie tugged Laura forward. "Mother, this is—"

"I would like to introduce Laura Millington." Jack brushed past Annie and spoke loud enough to cut her off.

Mother looked from Jack to Annie rather oddly. But only for a moment, then she settled her gaze on Laura. And tried to stand, leaning heavily on her cane.

But Laura leaned down and took the woman's hand. "It is such an honor, Mrs. Patterson. Your son is a fine man, and it is a privilege to meet you."

Jack didn't know quite what to say. He was touched that Laura met his mother where she was rather than watch her struggle to her feet. As well, her words honored him. He couldn't help but grin. His gaze latched onto Laura. The genuine warmth and excitement in her features moved him to greater affection.

He set a hand to Laura's back as she stood. "Mother, this is the woman I will wed. As soon as possible."

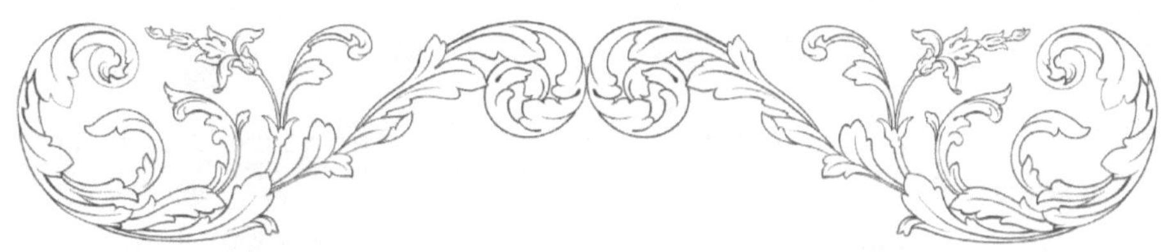

CHAPTER 21

Confession

Patterson Home
Chicago, IL
May 17, 1900

Laura was certain her eyes had widened. Did her jaw slacken as well? For Jack's words had not only taken his mother by surprise, but her as well. Laura had not imagined he would make such a declaration so soon after arrival.

Mrs. Patterson took in Laura and Jack, now side by side. There was a light in her eyes, but the hint of a frown upon her face. What was that about? "Wed? As soon as possible?" The woman blinked as she settled her gaze on Jack. "Why the rush?"

Jack stiffened and shifted his weight from one foot to the other. "There are...extenuating circumstances that bid we take vows sooner rather than later."

The woman gasped and glanced at Laura's midsection. "John Patterson, you haven't—"

"No, Mother!" Jack was quick to interject. "Nothing so untoward. Miss Millington is a lady and I have been an honorable gentleman."

There was a stricken look about his features as if he were injured by her insinuation.

Laura could not fault the woman's suspicion with how Jack behaved. Had he not spoken with his mother about this before he went to Memphis to seek her hand? That was odd.

Jack glanced at Hattie. Would he tell his mother the whole of it if not for the maidservant's presence? Did he, too, suspect that anything spoken in the woman's presence would make its way to Father?

"Let's get you settled," Annie said, stepping to Hattie. "I'm afraid I didn't ask for your name."

"Harriet. But everyone calls me Hattie."

Annie steered her from the parlor as Hattie looked over her shoulder at Laura. There was something in her regard that Laura couldn't discern. And that unsettled her.

Though Laura could not deny that she breathed a bit easier with Hattie's watchful eyes gone from the room.

Jack, too, eased his stance. "There are...challenges...with Laura's family."

Mrs. Patterson looked between the two of them. "Challenges?"

Jack tugged at his collar. His temporary easing had been short lived. Would he feel free to speak with his mother were Laura not here? Did Laura want them talking about her with her in another room?

"I may need to see to the bags," Laura offered, hoping it was clear that she did not necessarily wish to remove herself, but did so for Jack's sake. It wouldn't do to have Mrs. Patterson think that Laura was unwilling to converse with her. "I must excuse myself for a bit. It has been a long day."

Mrs. Patterson met her gaze. "Yes. You must be tired after such a trip."

Laura exchanged a look with Jack, then moved to the door.

"Let me show you to your room," Mrs. Patterson said, again trying to stand.

"That isn't necessary." Jack set a hand to his mother's arm. "I am quite capable of showing her to the upstairs bedroom."

Mrs. Patterson opened her mouth. Then closed it. What was it she wanted to say but held back? That wasn't a comforting thought. Did she think Jack's escorting her to her room was inappropriate?

"I'm certain Annie will be about in the hall." He spoke as if that were all that was necessary to protect Laura's reputation. Should Laura naysay him? Could she do so without appearing disrespectful?

He took Laura's arm and moved to the doorway, turning briefly to his mother. "I will be back in a few minutes."

Then they stepped into the small hallway...alone.

Jack tugged her closer. "I apologize for my mother's suggestion that we would have..." He didn't seem able to finish the sentence.

Indeed, Laura's face burned at what had been implied. "I understand."

Jack glanced at her. "Thank you."

Then they started up the stairs.

"Your mother seems...rather reserved. Perhaps I am not what she expected for you."

Jack kept his attention on the steps. "It is not that."

Why wouldn't he look at her? Was there more to this? What did he hide? Her drive for truth and openness would not allow him to dodge her questions for long.

She halted, bringing him to pause as well. "What is it then?"

He met her gaze and there was regret in his eyes. Which confused her all the more.

"Jack," she said softly. "Please tell me. I cannot bear the idea of secrets between us."

He swallowed and resumed his climb, urging her to come with him.

Annie and Hattie's voices became more audible as they went farther up.

"You know the whole of my sordid situation. Why can you not trust me with yours?" A very real ache grew in the center of her chest. What did he hide?

He seamed his lips. Why would he not share?

She wanted to stop again and insist he tell her the whole of it. But what would she do? No matter what it was, he was her only hope of salvation from Mr. Higgins...or the asylum. So, she pushed out a long breath and prayed.

They reached the top of the simple staircase and Jack turned to the room on the right. He made short work of opening the door and ushering her within.

"Jack! We cannot be in here alone."

He grimaced at her tone. "I will leave the door open." Then he released her arm.

They stood in a rather awkward silence for some moments before he strolled to the room's only window. "You are not the first woman to be offered my name."

What? Had he been married before? That didn't seem likely. He was so young. Perhaps he had been widowered soon after the marriage. "I... am sorry."

He looked at the floor. "It was not meant to be. She certainly didn't think so."

That only intensified Laura's confusion. "Who?"

He glanced at Laura, naked hurt in his eyes. It pained Laura to imagine how much he must have loved this woman. "Clarise." Jack spoke her name reverently.

It pained Laura all the more. She licked her lips and wished she might sit upon the bed. Her knees felt weak. "What happened?"

"She decided to take another man's name."

Oh goodness. He had been jilted. She prayed it had happened soon after the engagement. Not that it would lessen his hurt, but she hoped beyond hope that he wasn't at the altar.

"On..." He cleared his throat and gazed out the window again. "... our wedding day."

Laura closed her eyes. How horrible.

"We knew each other well, had been friends and schoolmates since youth. But I couldn't see...what was right in front of me. She cared more deeply for my cousin."

Each detail he revealed was worse than the last. What must that do to a man? How that must make him slow to trust again. Memories of their interactions rushed through her mind. And it clicked into place. He had been hesitant to risk his heart again.

She stepped closer, but not quite near enough to touch him. That was best. "Jack, I am so very sorry."

He shrugged and kept his focus to the world beyond the room. "As I said, it wasn't meant to be."

"Jack..." She ached to comfort him. But her better judgement froze her to the spot.

Shaking his shoulders, he turned back to her. "I had better let you get settled." He moved across the room.

She reached out and caught his arm. "Jack, I'm sorry." Her eyes watered. "For not understanding before."

He nodded and looked to the floor again. When he glanced up, the lines of anger and pain were gone. In their place, a mask of indifference had slid into place. "You didn't know."

That didn't excuse it.

Jerking the hem of his jacket, he settled his eyes on the open doorway. "I have some business to attend to. Should you need anything, my sister will be more than happy to oblige."

She held firm to his arm. And leaned in, brushing her lips across the side of his face.

He drew in a ragged breath. But then pulled away and left her alone with her thoughts.

City Streets
Chicago, IL
May 18, 1900

JACK TRUDGED THROUGH THE SIDEWALKS OF DOWNTOWN Chicago. He had asked the coachman to drop him several blocks from the Pullman Company headquarters. For certain, he needed some space and time to think...and to calm his worries.

His telegram from Memphis after his conversations with Mr. Millington had alluded to his leaving the company, but he hadn't said it outright. How would his superiors view what he had written? Would they feel at all confident enough to let him remain? Either way, they deserved a face-to-face conversation...and an explanation. Even if they wouldn't permit him to remain employed.

What would he do if that were the case? He needed gainful employment to move forward with his plans for himself and Laura. They couldn't rely on her father. And his mother and sister were in no way able to help him financially.

He neared the familiar building and his heart raced. As well, his stomach churned. If only he could share his worries. Would unburdening himself have been helpful?

Sharing with Laura about Clarise had not improved matters. He still ached from that betrayal. Even more, he wished he had not created distance between himself and Laura. Maybe it wasn't that he had told all, but that he had rushed out. She *had* pressed a kiss to his face. What if he had lingered in that moment? Pulled her closer? Let the moment be what it was?

The door in front of him opened and a couple of men stepped out. Men he knew in passing from Pullman's offices. He had arrived.

Looking up at the expansive facility, he sucked in a breath and pushed it out. He could do this. He would make it through this next hour whatever it may bring, because he had to.

Jack reached for the door and, taking one more cleansing breath, stepped within.

From there, it was a short trip up the stairs to the main offices. The receptionist greeted him warmly. He doubted she had any reason to suspect the purpose of his meeting. All seemed as it should be on any other day.

She slipped into the adjacent office and returned shortly. "Mr. Jones is ready for you."

He offered her a simple nod and moved in that direction.

The secretary watched him rather curiously. Why?

Only then did he realize he had started to crush his hat.

He loosened his grip and, as he entered the office, set the hat to the side before extending his hand. "Charles, thank you for taking the time to see me."

The man rose from his seat behind a large desk and took Jack's hand. "John."

Jack sat in an available chair in front of the desk. But found it diffi-cult to get comfortable. Strange, he had never noticed that before. Maybe it was more than a physical discomfort.

"I must say, your telegram had us quite confused," the man said pointedly.

One of the things Jack always liked about Charles Jones was that he didn't meander through conversation or make small talk. He was always right to the point.

"I have no doubt of that." Jack shifted yet again, fighting the urge to bounce a knee or fidget with his shirt cuffs. "I apologize for not being more forward."

Charles's brow lifted. "So then, what did you need to speak with me about?"

Here it was—the moment of truth. There was no more hiding, no more putting it off.

"My...situation has been altered since wiring you."

"Oh?" Charles leaned back in his chair.

Jack nodded. Why was he stringing this out? "I wanted to clear up any misunderstandings from those ill-timed words."

"There is a bit of that. I tell you, John, it almost seemed as if you wished to end your employment with the company." The man's gaze was not hard, but his features were tight.

"I understand. And, at the time, honestly, I thought that may be the case."

One of the man's eyebrows shot up. "Thought that may be the case? So, you *did* intend to resign?"

Jack swallowed against the tightness in his throat. "I did."

"But no more?"

"No. That is, not if the company will still have me."

Charles sighed and leaned forward, setting his arms on the desk. "I admit, I was more than a little surprised. We all were. I think you have a great future here. Do you not think so?"

"I do." Jack wanted to sink into the chair and disappear, but he had to face up to this. "It was a horrible mistake."

"Mr. Pullman was certainly not pleased. And even less so at the mention of Mr. Richard Millington."

"Why is that?"

"He wouldn't say exactly, but I should warn you to be careful in your dealings with the man."

Was Charles being intentionally vague? What was he not saying?

"I have learned that to be true. And that is why I am prepared to do whatever it takes to assure you of my loyalty. I never wanted to give up my position here." He stopped himself from sharing further. It may not be needed, and certainly would only complicate things.

Charles was silent for several moments. He watched Jack, as if trying to gauge the truth of his words.

Jack itched to pull out his handkerchief and wipe his brow. He had started to perspire. Would the man not put him out of his misery—one way or the other? He slid a hand over his vest, assuring himself that his pocket watch was still there.

Charles dragged in a breath. "I have been given leeway to decide."

Jack chewed on his lip. This was impossible. "And?"

"I don't want to lose you. Not only are you a hard worker, but you are also very capable."

Jack let out the air that had pent up. He couldn't speak for the overwhelming relief that flowed through him. His body melted into the seat.

"That is...if you are certain this is still the place for you."

"Oh, yes, sir. It is. Undoubtedly."

Charles nodded and stood.

Jack did as well. "Thank you, sir."

Charles came around the desk and motioned toward the door. "I do have another meeting in a few minutes. Do you mind showing yourself out?"

"Not at all." Jack reached for the knob.

"And I expect you back in the office next week."

Jack paused. Was that possible? Would Laura be well with a quick wedding and no manner of honeymoon?

"Something wrong?" Charles's tone was flat.

Jack turned. "I may be getting married this weekend."

The man's eyebrows arched. "You *may* be getting married this weekend?"

Jack shifted his weight. "Yes."

The air in the room seemed to be sucked out in that moment. Jack struggled to take in a full breath.

"But I promise, I will be here regardless."

Charles folded his arms across his chest. "I don't think Mr. Pullman will be pleased to hear this."

Jack held his breath.

"But I want you to take the week to get everything sorted out. And return fully present the week after." The man's gaze was stern.

How could Jack thank him for such leniency?

"I appreciate the time. I won't give you any reason to doubt me again."

Charles nodded and returned to his chair. "I truly hope so."

Jack exited the office, nodded at the receptionist, and left as quickly as humanly possible. And thanked God for His mercy.

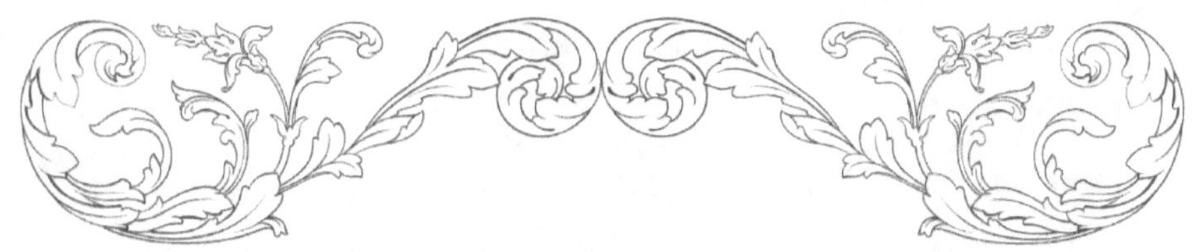

CHAPTER 22

Intentions

Patterson Home
Chicago, IL
May 18, 1900

Laura came down the stairs, no more certain about things than she was yesterday. Her last interaction with Jack had been rather discouraging. How could he not respond to her attempt at soothing him? He simply walked out the door and left for the rest of the day. Though Annie and Mrs. Patterson had been wonderfully pleasant. Still, it made her ache. For something more than she had known only with Micah. Could a family truly be as connected as Jack's seemed?

She stepped off the bottom stair.

Annie's voice filtered through the wall to the parlor. These walls were quite thin after all. "Do you have any idea what she thinks?"

Who did she speak with?

"I...am not certain. I just know that this has to work."

Jack. Did he have a plan? Something he intended, but hadn't told her? That felt familiar and uncomfortable. Too much of her life had been directed by her father. Rarely had she ever been informed or asked for her permission. His words left an uneasiness in her midsection.

"You need to talk to her," Annie insisted.

"I will." Jack's words were rushed and exasperated. "I will."

Footfalls came closer. One of the two siblings headed this way. And there was nowhere to go.

Jack appeared in the doorway. His gaze landed on her immediately. "Laura."

She pulled in a long breath. What could she say? Should she apologize for eavesdropping? "Jack."

He glanced back into the parlor and then to the floor. Did he suspect she had heard?

Annie came around Jack. "How was your rest?"

"It was...refreshing." Laura looked between the two. "I hoped to take a walk and get some air."

Annie gave her brother a pointed look.

Jack ignored her. "I shall escort you." He stepped forward as if to intercept Laura.

How could she deny him? Still, she needed space to consider all that had happened, and what her options might be. The last thing she wanted was to be alone with him.

Annie smiled. "I'll let Hattie know you've gone out for a bit."

Laura attempted to return her smile, but it felt stifled.

Jack opened the front door and waited.

Could she just tell him no? That didn't seem likely. So, she moved toward the door, nodding at Annie. "Tell Mrs. Patterson we won't be long."

There. At least she could preemptively put a limit on their outing.

Annie glanced at her brother. There was more behind that look than Laura could discern.

It didn't matter. Jack stepped forward, ushering Laura outside, and closed the door.

She rushed down the front stairs before Jack could offer his arm. It may be best if they had some distance between them.

When he did join her, it was not with an arm outstretched. Had he sensed her reluctance?

"Which way shall we go?" he said, finally looking at her.

She glanced one way and then the other, as if she could gauge which.

As if she had any idea what lay in either direction. Though he had given her some autonomy, and she would take it.

Turning right, she noted a strikingly similar view to what appeared on the left—sidewalks filled with passers-by and tall buildings. The townhouse was nestled in the midst of the large city. She opened her mouth to ask him which way he would prefer but then sealed her lips. These moments of choice were so few in her life. It wasn't a big thing, but it was something.

Looking both directions once more, she opted for the right. Perhaps this could be an adventure of sorts. Still, she wished for Hattie's unassuming company over Jack's. Even if she couldn't trust the woman completely. At least then she wouldn't feel pressured to make conversation.

"How was your evening?" Jack spoke into the silence punctuated by the clip-clop of her boots on the sidewalk.

She frowned. Why must he remind her that he had all but abandoned her yesterday after his confession? Sure, he may have needed time to think, but that didn't make it fair. Shouldn't she be able to ask him questions?

Trust. There was that word again. More and more, she hated the reminder. Probably because of the truth of it.

"I enjoyed your mother and sister's company. They are quite amiable. And welcoming."

He smiled but looked down.

"And the meal was simple, but filling."

His step stuttered. Had she said something wrong?

"I only meant that it wasn't a production. It was exactly what it needed to be."

He lifted his gaze and glanced over at her. There was a vulnerability in his eyes that she had not seen. Did he regret his small beginnings? She hated that for him. His family was free of pretention. And that was worth more than all the finery in all the world.

Instead of scrounging up the courage to say so, she let silence fall over them again.

As it stretched out, it became rather uncomfortable. Why had she allowed that? It didn't seem right that this man whom she had shared closeness with would be thusly put off.

"Laura…"

"Jack, I…"

Their eyes met again, and she grinned. "You first."

One of his eyebrows arched. Would he insist she speak instead?

He drew in a full breath. "There is something I wanted to discuss with you." His words came out measured. Was he so uneasy with it? What could he say that would bring out such trepidation?

She wanted to clear her throat but resisted. "Yes?"

"I hope you know that I care for you." His gaze darted ahead. "Very much."

Why wouldn't he look at her when making such a confession? Was he ashamed?

"And I have become rather…concerned…about how things are for you in your father's house."

Was it *her* turn to feel shamed? He had seen and heard things that she greatly regretted.

"And I don't think that I can offer a better life, necessarily, but I…"

What was he not saying? Would he put her aside now? Send her back to that fine dungeon? It may be luxurious, but prison it was all the same. Dare she speak into the moment?

"I would like to make an offer."

An offer? She glared at him. Did he have some motive, some plan here to preserve his career and save face?

"Jack," she said, coming to a stop and facing him. "I don't want you to feel responsible for me. You aren't."

He looked away, gritting his teeth. "I'm not doing this right."

"Doing what?" Her heart raced. What prospect would she be facing when he answered?

He shifted his focus back to her and took her hand. "I want to marry you."

She had heard him say as much. Was this the product of as much a struggle as it seemed? She didn't trust herself to respond but bit at the inside of her mouth to keep from tearing up.

He looked up and down the street. Several people passed by. Jack gripped her arm and steered her to the side of the walkway, closer to the buildings. "It is my most earnest wish to have courted you properly. To treat you every bit the way you deserve. But there isn't time. I cannot send you back to your father. I won't."

She couldn't make sense of his words. "What are you saying?" Her voice was timid, hesitant.

"I know it's not fair, but I..." His gaze dropped again, but he straightened his shoulders and lifted his regard to her.

She opened her mouth, but something caught her eye to the right. A dark-skinned man passed. As she watched him, it was as if she knew him.

Laura followed his progress. It was Mr. Sim Webb! The woman he walked with looked oddly familiar as well...could it be the Bradys' daughter, Janie? The one who had been married to Casey Jones? Why were they about the streets of Chicago?

"Laura?" Jack's uneasy timbre pulled at her.

But she was focused on Sim and Janie. What were they doing here? They settled themselves at the front of a nearby building and, after exchanging a few words with a young man, stood front and center of the building's entrance. Would they be doing something soon?

"Excuse me." Laura pulled free of Jack and moved closer.

"Miss Millington," came Jack's desperate plea.

She couldn't help her fascination. Guilt had plagued her since last she saw Sim. She had to know what they were doing here. And what they might say.

And hope that Jack would understand.

City Streets
Chicago, IL
May 18, 1900

JACK COULD NOT FATHOM WHY LAURA PULLED AWAY. WAS she vexed? Was he being too rash? The buildings around him loomed even as the passers-by moved in and out of the businesses.

His gaze followed her as she approached a nearby structure. A dark-skinned man and familiar-looking woman positioned themselves as if to deliver a speech from the top step. This was not his first interaction with this man either. If only Jack could place him.

But there wasn't time for that. Laura picked up a rapid pace to approach the pair.

"Laura, wait," he called as he moved to follow. "What are you doing?"

That may not be a fair question. He didn't own her...or her actions. Still, the whole thing bothered. And, if he were being honest, he was hurt at how easily she'd brushed him aside.

At last, she paused just short of the stairs, and he caught up to her.

"Laura," he started, a tad put out.

She didn't look at him but kept her gaze on the man who yielded to the woman with him.

"I think I deserve an explanation." The sting of her rejection fueled the question he didn't truly believe.

"Shhh," Laura admonished him.

That did nothing to assuage his injured heart. What was it about these two individuals she found so captivating?

The woman at the stairs took a step closer to the edge of the top landing and spoke. "Hello. My name is Janie Jones. I am the widow of Casey Jones."

A couple of people stopped. Yes, the song about the famed engineer had spread far and wide...as well as the story of his tragic accident. But her mention of Casey brought to Jack's mind memories of that day, of how he tried to keep Laura from involving herself too deeply. And of how she turned from him. Just like she was now.

"I would like to tell you about my husband. As I can imagine, there are many questions about his heroic act that resulted in a tragedy. And, yes, it was a heroic act. This man here, Mr. Sim Webb, was there that day, right beside my late husband, just before the crash."

A small crowd had collected.

But Jack only noticed the gathering pedestrians in passing. For he realized why Laura was so fascinated—she had tried to intervene that horrible day, to support Sim's story. Would she be so thoughtless this day? If she did try to speak on Sim's behalf, on Casey's behalf, for certain her father would hear of it. Anything contrary to the decision of the railroad executives would not be tolerated by Mr. Millington.

"Laura," he whispered, tugging at her sleeve. "We cannot stay here."

She pulled free and made no move to follow him.

Mrs. Jones told about her husband's character, his reputation, and his care for others. The man seemed honorable enough. Indeed, Jack knew he was, sacrificing himself for the safety of others. Of him and Laura. And so many others. His chest ached all the more as the woman continued.

Then Mrs. Jones yielded to Sim.

Jack didn't have to scan the area to discern that the crowd was less enthused by the prospect of Sim speaking.

He spoke of that last train run, of how they had taken the ill-fated trip for another engineer who was unwell. And he was honest about how Casey pushed the train hard to make up for lost time. Something that the crowd likely did not understand was the industry, that the consequences for delayed arrival far exceeded the marks for driving at such speeds. And Casey was never late. People were able to set their clocks by his arrivals.

Yes, Jack had done some digging. He had wanted to know more about the man who'd sacrificed his life.

"What did the railroad company decide of the accident?" a dark-haired man who seemed rather unassuming asked. But it wasn't that simple. The man clearly intended to create an argument.

Sim and Janie admitted that the railroad determined it to be Casey's fault, but that there was more to the story. Things that had been ignored.

"According to who?" the man returned. "You?"

The crowd grew restless. Several of the intrigued onlookers outright gaffed at Sim's words. Others waved their hands as if to dismiss the two and moved on.

All the while, Jack's ire heated. He was not blind to the situation.

Nor were others. Their ease in writing them off was due to the color of Sim's skin. And Janie's gender. That their witness should mean any less was nothing short of appalling.

"I believe," the dark-haired man said, now speaking to the crowd, "that Mr. Jones is reported to have ignored flagmen warning of a train in the station."

"That's not true," Janie said, her voice surprisingly calm despite this man's challenge. "Sim was there. He saw no flagmen at their post."

"And we are to take the word of this man?" The man had the nerve to scoff. "I think not."

"I would not be so quick to reject his accounting," Laura shouted from her position.

Jack glanced over, praying it wasn't so. He grabbed for her arm to try and still her, but she pushed through to the front of the gathering.

"I was on that train."

It was as if the crowd gasped in unison.

Janie looked at Sim, who just stood and watched Laura.

"I, too, saw no flagmen. As well, I can vouch for Mr. Sim Webb. He was there—in the engine—until the last possible second."

The adversarial man muttered something.

"What?" Laura challenged. "I couldn't hear you."

"I only wondered why we should believe you, miss." The man's features hardened. He didn't like losing ground.

She glared at the man.

Don't do it, Jack silently pled. *Dear Lord, don't let her.*

"Why should you not set me aside as quickly as you are prepared to do with these fine folks? Is that what you are asking?"

She was going to do it. Jack wanted to rush forward and cover her, protect her...but he could not. Even as he pressed toward her in anticipation, he knew he couldn't make it in time.

"I am Laura Millington, the daughter of Mr. Richard Millington."

A rumble of chatter set into the crowd. And the man who had been so fiercely against Sim and Janie glowered but stood his ground.

At last, Jack pushed to the front and stood by Laura. The gathering became restless. This could become dangerous quickly.

He urged her closer, hoping he might slip her away before things got worse.

"Ah, the daughter of privilege, of a railroad tycoon...truly a woman of the people." The man dared to counter.

Laura narrowed her gaze. "At the very least, you listened to my testimony."

The man's face twisted all the more.

Jack leaned in. "It's not safe here."

Laura shook him off.

"What is it there, sir? Trying to calm the lady? Please, sir, put her in her place!"

Jack whirled toward the man, gritting his teeth. What was he to do? Perhaps nothing he could do would make matters worse. "I beg you, do not tempt me."

The crowd shifted.

And the dark-haired man turned to leave. "I've heard enough."

"I was there, too."

The man jerked around. "You?"

"Yes," Jack ground out. "And everything these people are saying is true."

"You saw the flagmen stations vacant?"

Jack dipped his head. "I did not."

The adversarial man's shoulders straightened.

Jack squared his own shoulders, standing his full six feet and two inches. "But I know that Miss Millington speaks honestly. My own eyewitness is not contradicted by hers. There is no reason for me to believe her to be anything less than truthful."

Laura gripped his arm. For support? He turned to face her. There was something gleaming in her eyes that was difficult to discern.

"I won't stand here and listen to such poppycock." The man threaded through the grumbling crowd and walked on.

It wasn't over. Jack was not so daft as to think it was. This would only deepen his and Laura's entanglement. Did she even understand how she had risked herself?

Several people pressed in toward Janie and Sim. And they answered a litany of questions.

Jack reached for Laura. "I think it's time we returned."

She did not pull away this time but looked at him with wide eyes. "Why?"

"You have done what you can. And I don't wish to worry my mother."

She glanced at Janie and Sim as if trying to discern if her voice was needed. Then she nodded. "I don't wish to cause your family any discomfort."

He closed his eyes briefly and thanked God. Tugging on her arm, he shielded her as he led her away.

Her breaths came in gasps. Was she struggling to keep up?

He paused once they were a fair distance away. "Are you all right?"

"Yes," she said, still fighting to draw air in it seemed.

Because of the rapid retreat? Or something else?

"You...you stood by my side. The things you said...I..." She floundered for a few moments. "Never has anyone supported me so publicly. You believe me. You really do!" Her arms came about his neck and embraced him.

He wanted to linger in the feel of her and that smell of lilacs, but he couldn't. So, after she settled, he pulled away. And did his best to hold down his anger.

Confusion filled her eyes.

"Laura, I can scarcely speak."

Her features softened and her eyes misted.

But he had to hold his ground. "Never..." He forced his features to maintain their neutrality. "Never have I been so afraid."

She pressed a gloved hand to the side of his face, her brow furrowed.

"Or so angry."

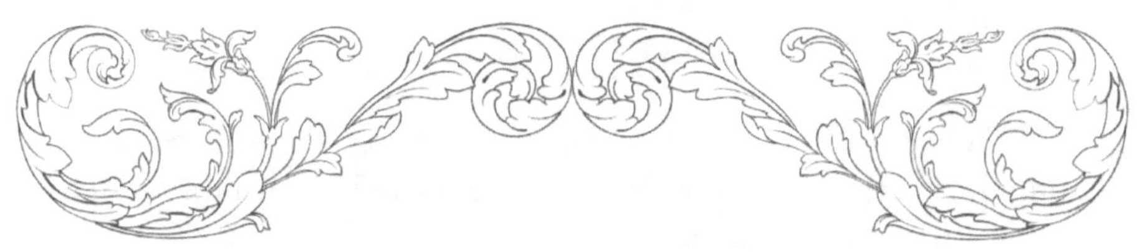

CHAPTER 23

Wisdom

"ngry?" Laura wasn't certain she had heard Jack correctly. She let her hand slide from his face. He had just said he was scared...that she understood. He had been worried about her, about what might have happened to her. That was endearing in a real, but troubled way. Then he'd revealed an equal depth of anger. That didn't make sense.

"Yes, Laura, *angry*." He searched her features. What was he looking for?

She drew back. "Why would you be angry?"

He looked off in the direction they had just come from. "Because what you did was reckless. It was thoughtless. And it was careless."

Had they been at the same gathering? Sure, the man that challenged Janie and Sim...and her...had been a mite unpredictable. But violent? He wasn't that bold. "Surely, you're exaggerating. There was no real danger with—"

"No real danger?" he huffed. His gaze was intense and his words sharp. "Have you any idea that your father will hear about what was said and done here today?"

His tone stung and his words flabbergasted.

"My father?" Could it be true?

195

"Yes, your *father*. The man who wants to play you for a pawn. Did you not realize you just gave him cause to rescind his permission? That he may very well find me incapable of...?"

"Of what?" Now her anger flared. What was Jack about to say?

"Nothing." He shoved his hands into his pockets and refused to meet her gaze.

She crossed her arms, equally determined. "I want to know what you were about to say."

He caught her gaze again. "You really want to know? All right." The harsh tone grated. "He may think I'm incapable of bringing you to heel and keeping you in your place."

It was as if he'd slapped her. Is that what he thought? That he needed to 'bring her to heel'? Keep her 'in her place'? How could she have been so blind? He was exactly like her father.

"Excuse me. I won't trouble you any longer." She gripped her skirts and started for the stairs.

He grabbed for her arm, his hold sure, but gentle. "That's not what I meant, and you know it."

"Do I, Jack?" She glared at him, hoping she could sustain her anger long enough that her wounded heart wouldn't expose itself. "From where I stand, it seems as if I'm trading one tyrant for another."

He tugged her toward himself.

She resisted at first but let him, wanting to believe he would say something to make all of this okay.

"I only meant that your father *expects* me to lord over you. I have no intention of doing so." His voice had quieted.

Even so, she could not escape her bruised feelings. "Except that right now, you're telling me what to do and what not to do." It was as if she saw red. Indeed, everything had a darkened tint to it. But there was a part of her that wanted to have reason for compassion and under-standing.

He released her. "That is not what's happening here." His words were measured. And something passed in his eyes.

"How can you not see that it is *exactly* what is happening here? My father always tells me what to do, where to go, how to speak, what to say...even what to think. As if my own thoughts are flawed. My own words. My ideas. Well...no more!" She moved up the stairs and reached for the door. "Please, tell your mother I must beg off dinner. I am not feeling well."

She waited a single breath to give him time to respond.

He said nothing.

She flung the door open and stomped into the house. Then she fled up the steps and toward her borrowed room. But Annie was in the hall as Laura topped the staircase.

"Laura?" Annie sounded surprised. She looked more closely at Laura. "Are you all right?"

Laura had no doubt that her face was red and her eyes watered. She had lost the battle with her heart. And her emotions now spilled down her face.

"I am." She moved around Annie.

"I don't know about that." Annie's words were gentle.

"Would everyone please just leave me be?" Laura pushed past and rushed into her room, slamming the door, and shutting out the world.

First Church of Avondale
Chicago, IL
May 19, 1900

JACK STEWED IN THE WELL-WORN AND RECENTLY OILED church pew. There were no two ways about it—he wanted to kick himself for not pursuing Laura yesterday after their spat. And even more he wished to not have to face her this day. A decision had to be made soon. If he were to protect her from her father and move her beyond the man's reach, they would need to marry. Quickly. Although, he was most certainly the last man she could be talked into to marrying at this time.

His heart had pulled back from the equation. There was much he did not trust in her regard for him. It smacked of indifference. How could she so assuredly turn her back on him at the first sign of trouble? Did she mistrust *him* so much? There wasn't much space, then—or desire—on his part to fully commit. Not when things were so uncertain.

It felt a bit too familiar. He'd had some misgivings about Clarise earlier in their courtship, but he had buried them all for the sake of his commitment to her. For the sake of his tender feelings toward her. And that had been a regrettable mistake. Had he been blind to Laura's true heart? Her intentions toward him?

He shuddered to think he might have to nurse a broken heart once again. Or his movement could be due to the church building having cooled somewhat. There was little to enhance this space with stark walls and wooden pews. But there was a warmth that came from something beyond the accoutrements. Something that the people and the humble Reverend Daniel Downs brought each and every Sunday.

Jack closed his eyes and settled into that peace, but his stomach churned. How could he find rest when his heart and mind were so torn?

He opened his eyes just in time to see his mother, Annie, and Laura enter the sanctuary. And his heart beat faster. How was it that even as he sat here so uncertain and so vexed, that she could have that effect on him? Yet one more assurance that he was in dangerous territory with her. Should he hunch down and hope that they wouldn't see him? He had taken a seat across the room from their normal spaces. Maybe they wouldn't notice.

Annie sent a small wave in his direction.

No chance of eluding them now.

His sister motioned Laura in that direction and steered Mother toward him. *Blast it all!* Annie was always meddling when she should leave well enough alone.

He straightened his shoulders and tugged on the bottom of his jacket, suddenly overheated, and wishing he might remove it for comfort's sake.

Annie settled Mother in the pew and indicated that Laura should take the seat beside Jack.

Laura appeared to feign ignorance and sat on the other side of Mother, the only space that remained for Annie was between Mother and him.

Could he survive the whole morning with Annie? There was little he could do about it now. She sat in the vacant space before setting a hand to his arm and offering a smile.

"We were…surprised…to not see you at supper." Annie was not one to flit about a subject. "Nor did we anticipate an evening with our guest absent. What happened to upset her?"

Was Laura still upset? Had she truly been so angered—or hurt—by his actions?

"It was not my preference either. There were…circumstances beyond my control." Hopefully, that would silence his sister.

"What circumstances were those?" She watched him, her eyes peering into his as if to see beyond what he wished her to.

"Must you interrogate me? Miss Millington and I had…a difficult discussion."

"Oh…she is Miss Millington to you now? That must have been some discussion indeed."

He had no desire to bring Annie into this. How was he then to stop her from pursuing him? "That is a perfectly acceptable way to refer to Laura. Even more appropriate, might I add, than by her Christian name."

"Is she no longer endeared by you?"

Why must Annie push? He hadn't the strength to continue like this.

Mother set a hand to Annie's arm and shushed her.

It could not have happened soon enough. But as he turned his gaze forward, he saw that Reverend Downs had stepped to the pulpit. That would keep Annie quiet. At least for now.

The reverend called for everyone's attention and welcomed the congregation.

Jack had always liked the man of God. He enjoyed Reverend Downs's open and honest manner. It seemed as if even hard truths were always delivered with compassion and humility. As if even the reverend did not view himself as above anyone, or above temptation. It was refreshing. Though Reverend Downs's church was limited in size—especially by comparison to the many much larger churches Chicago boasted—and his congregation small, Jack did not sense that it bothered the reverend one bit. He simply served where he had been called.

As the opening hymns quieted and everyone took their seats, Reverend Downs began his oration. All were directed to open their Bibles to Proverbs 3, verses 5 and 6, a passage Jack knew well. It had been his father's favorite passage. Jack and Annie had learned these verses early. Probably before they could even read or write.

Jack sighed. With such familiar words, would there be anything new for him?

But Reverend Downs spent the bulk of his time on the portion that spoke of not leaning on one's own understanding. The reverend reminded his listeners how tempting it could be to want to control their circumstances and rely on the information at it was presented. But Proverbs whispered that the human mind's understanding was finite, limited by one's perception and awareness. God was not so hemmed in. Thus, His plan was ultimate and able to be trusted.

Jack didn't like that at all. Was he working too hard to control the situation? Was he lacking trust in God's plan and God's design? Even as he watched Reverend Downs, he was reminded of how this man lived out God's calling and purpose. The reverend's living was small and carefully measured out. But he trusted. He served in this smaller church with less financial support, but no less provision.

His own circumstances were different, Jack argued within himself. He wasn't worried about his own life, but Laura's. He did what he did to protect her...and she turned away from him.

Even in that, however, God nudged Jack to see that his anger and hurt was because *his* plan had been upset. Was he so determined that everything go the way he wanted it to? Did he so limit God that he only believed to a certain point?

He beseeched the Lord. *God, help me. Help me trust. Help me move beyond my understanding...and lean on You. Even if that means I risk my heart.*

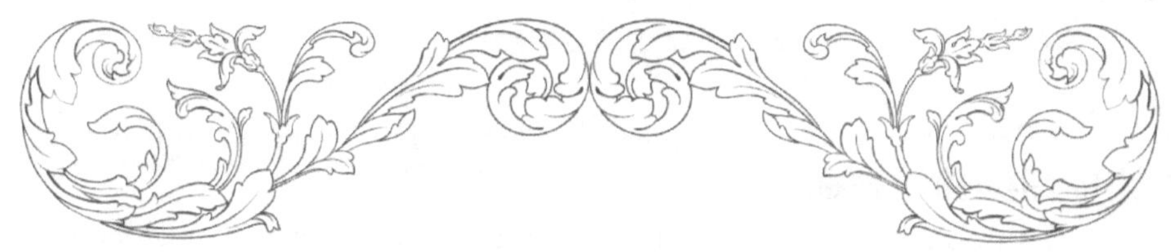

CHAPTER 24

Reconnecting

Patterson Home
Chicago, IL
May 19, 1900

Laura assisted Mrs. Patterson as the older woman settled into a chair. Turning briefly, she noticed that Jack had not followed them into the parlor. She let out a breath that also released some of her tension, yet her heart ached. For him? Or for the closeness they had shared?

"You are such a dear," Mrs. Patterson said as she shifted in the seat. "I must confess, I worried there might be airs about you." She watched Laura and motioned toward the nearby settee.

Laura sat, albeit on the edge of the piece. Should she linger? If she dared walk out of the room, would she find Jack waiting to pounce? Yes, it was best she stay put. "I appreciate your kind words. I've never been much of a Millington, I suppose."

Sealing her lips, she stopped herself before continuing. Might she say more than she wanted? Reveal just how out of place she was in her family?

"I'm not sure what you mean by that." Mrs. Patterson smiled as if she knew all too well.

Laura's experience at church this morning had been rather different. Her family went to a grand church, where they were known by reputation. She doubted that the reverend there knew anything beyond that. It was safer that way.

But Reverend Downs greeted each congregant by name as they exited. And asked deep questions about their lives. He took care with each person in word and affect. It was...refreshing. Was that how the body of Christ was supposed to be?

"Something wrong?" Mrs. Patterson leaned forward, a softness to her features.

"Just thinking back to the sermon." That wasn't fully the truth, but Laura didn't feel as free to share her wayward musings. She didn't want Mrs. Patterson to think ill of her. Why was that? Because she hoped she and Jack would mend their relationship and continue onward toward matrimony? Did Jack still want that?

"It was a good word. My husband loved that passage. I daresay it was his favorite in the whole of Scripture. That is saying much, because he loved the Bible and everything it had to say."

Laura offered a smile, but it was stilted. What would it be like to have such a father? One steeped in God's word? "Tell me about him."

"My husband?"

Laura nodded and settled more fully into the settee.

"He was a wonderful man. Caring, generous to a fault...even despite the fact that we didn't have much. A train engineer isn't often known for such qualities. They are valued more for their work ethic and capability...which he certainly had as well."

"A train engineer? I assumed he was a tradesman like Jack."

"No. Jack has done much with his start in life. We did not have the means to help him. It's a shame that in our society a man is valued more for his station than his finer character qualities."

"That is a shame." Laura had never heard it put so succinctly. But it was true. In society—especially in the lower classes—people were only worth what they could produce. Not that it was isolated to the lower class. Didn't she herself struggle with being valued for what she could gain for her father? Or how a connection to her could elevate a husband?

"My husband loved well. His peers and family were left with a large hole when he passed. Those who worked with him couldn't help but develop a friendship, I'm told. And it seemed as if the very heart of this family had been removed. It was, in a way. The grieving took its toll on Jack. I don't think he's ever been the same. Of course, the mishap with Miss Ellis didn't help matters."

Was there another woman Jack had become involved with after Clarise? "Miss Ellis?"

Mrs. Patterson's hand flew up and covered her mouth. "I shouldn't have brought it up."

Perhaps it wasn't someone else at all. "Do you mean Miss *Clarise* Ellis?"

"Yes." Mrs. Patterson's hand dropped to her chest. Her voice filled with relief. "Then Jack has told you of the ill-fated engagement?"

Laura nodded. "He has."

Mrs. Patterson watched Laura for a moment, her eyes soft. "I thought he might never love again. But then you turned his head." She reached for Laura's hand.

Laura took the proffered weathered, aged hand and squeezed gently. "That is kind of you." Were her eyes watering? She sniffed, an attempt to control a display of emotion.

"It's true. He hasn't been the same since he met you. A mother knows these things." Mrs. Patterson winked.

The door opened and Jack peered into the room. His gaze darted between his mother and Laura. What did he intend? Her heart fluttered. Did she want him to have come to speak with her?

"Ah...here you are." He slipped into the room more fully.

Had he not known where they were? That didn't seem likely.

"Did you need something?" Mrs. Patterson asked as she glanced at Laura before directing her focus back to her son.

"I...was hoping to speak with Miss Millington."

Mrs. Patterson looked at her companion. "I need to check on the meal anyway. You two stay and chat." She attempted to stand, leaning on her cane amidst her struggle.

Jack rushed forward as Laura rose, leaning in to assist.

Their hands brushed as each pressed in, assuring Mrs. Patterson got to her feet.

Laura pulled back, trusting that Jack was more than capable.

Soon enough, Mrs. Patterson was upright and shaking Jack off. "I may be old, but I am still able to walk about by myself." Her tone was not hard, rather teasing.

Jack did not so much as grin at the lightness, but watched his mother move to the door and step beyond. Would he need to speak privately? So much that he would close the door? Or would propriety win out and he leave it open?

Turning, Jack's gaze found her, and his eyes seemed to penetrate through her exterior. "Please, sit."

She shook her head. "I'd rather stand. I've been sitting for most of the morning."

He nodded, then shifted his weight as he wrung his hands. It seemed as if he were torn about what he needed to say. Would he dismiss their engagement altogether?

"Jack," she started. Could she make things right? She had to try.

He looked at her, his eyes softening in the same way his mother's had earlier.

She swallowed and, abandoning her pride, pressed on. "I'm sorry."

His eyebrows arched. "Sorry?"

"Yes. For my anger. For walking away like I did. You were absolutely right, and I just didn't want to admit it."

He stepped closer, but only by a couple of paces. "I went about it poorly. It is my desire to interact with you in a gentle and understanding way. And I let my emotions get the better of me."

Did that mean he intended for them to remain betrothed?

"I don't want to ever again give you cause to walk away like that." His features eased.

Her heart thudded so hard she was certain it could be heard in the moments of silence. "I don't want to give you cause to withhold your thoughts...or your feelings."

He took tentative steps to close the distance between them. "Laura, I..."

She lifted a hand and laid it on the side of his face, the scruff of his beard tickling her palm.

"I only want to honor and protect you."

A tear escaped, trailing down her face. "I know."

The moment between them heated. So much swirled in her that she feared she could not adequately express it all. His eyes deepened, and she felt as if she could see his very heart for her.

She leaned forward, their faces a breath apart. Would he close the gap?

After a few painstakingly long seconds, his lips found hers. It was different than their previous kiss. This was gentle and slow, as if they had all the time in the world. His arms came around her and held her with ease. She relished the feel of him so close.

But all too soon, he pulled back. Then he laid his forehead against hers. "Laura..." His voice was husky. "Marry me. Today."

"Today?" Could he be serious?

"Yes." His thumbs caressed her upper arms. "I don't want to give your father any chance to tear us apart."

She wanted that, too. But could she let him sacrifice his future for her? Her father would be vexed and may very well make it impossible for him to continue working in the railroad industry.

There was more to it though. She loved him. Completely. How could she deny him? "I..."

The front door burst open just within the hallway, and a man called out. "Where is she? If I must, I will have this house torn apart."

Before she could process a single thought, the intruder pushed into the parlor. Annie was on his heels, crying out for him to stop. But it wasn't enough.

Thomas had come for her. Jack's plan had just lost any chance of success.

Jack pulled Laura behind himself. He would not risk her. But how could he keep her from her family? There was no law he could think of that would permit him to do so.

"Laura," Thomas barked. "Come here. We're going home."

"What if I don't want to go with you?" Her voice rang in the space.

Annie grinned from just behind Thomas.

Jack was equally proud of his Laura.

Thomas took a step toward them, his tone intensified. "What did you say?"

Laura swallowed and held her ground, still behind Jack. "What if I'd prefer to stay right where I am?"

Thomas spit out a dark laugh. "It's not about what you'd prefer. You should know that. It's never been about what you want."

Laura shifted as if she would concede and step around Jack, but he sidestepped, effectively putting himself between her and Thomas once more. He wasn't backing down so easily.

Hattie raced into the room, coming to a stop just short of the small group. Had she betrayed them to Laura's family? She appeared as stunned as the rest of them.

Thomas straightened his jacket and lengthened his stance, rising to his full height. He emitted a calm demeanor, but there was thunder under the surface. "Come along, Laura, before you do something thoughtless."

"What do you mean?" Laura's words were just as sharp.

"I am telling you that marrying into this..." Thomas glanced about the house. "...level of society, would be far beneath you. And you would regret it for the rest of your life."

Annie gasped.

Jack puffed out his chest. How dare this man throw mud at his mother...at her home and her place in life. "How do you know we are not already married? Would you take a woman from her husband?"

Thomas's features slackened and then tightened, contorting into an angry glare. "Are you married?"

When no answer was forthcoming, Thomas looked to Hattie. "Are they?"

Hattie stared at the ground, gripping her hands at waist level. But she remained silent. That surprised.

Thomas growled and then set his heated gaze on Laura. "Are you?"

There was little sense in carrying this lie forward. So, she confessed, "We are not."

Thomas sealed his lips and swallowed. The relief on his face was evident. But his green eyes turned on Jack with a renewed ire. "Then are you sure you want to stand in my way?"

Jack took a measured breath. He *was* certain. He was prepared to defend Laura no matter what.

Thomas leveled his gaze and narrowed his eyes. "Let me ask this another way, Mr. Patterson." The man made Jack's proper address sound like a curse. "Are you certain you no longer wish to work in the train industry?"

Jack seethed. Thomas reached too far. While Mr. Millington may have his claws in most every part of the railroad industry, there was reason to doubt that the Pullman Company would bend to his bidding. Or would they? Either way, Richard Millington could make things very difficult for Jack, and, by extension, Mr. Pullman. What—and who—was Jack willing to risk?

It didn't matter. Jack had promised on his honor to protect Laura. And that's what he intended to do. After all, he loved her. Could he bear to part with her? To release her to her family's clutches? He opened his mouth to demand Thomas leave the premises.

Laura interjected before he could. "I will come with you."

Annie shook her head and made a sound that was indistinguishable but seemed like a whimper.

Laura pushed Jack's arm aside and moved around him, her fingers lingering a moment longer than necessary. "I will go, Thomas. Just leave Jack alone."

Would she give up her future—*their* future—for his sake? He couldn't allow it.

He stepped toward her. Could he hold her back? Talk sense to her? "Laura, I—"

She whirled toward him, effectively halting his progress. "I've made my decision." Her voice was rougher and firmer than he'd ever heard it.

Thomas held out a hand for her but looked at Hattie. "You are dismissed."

Jack silently pled for Laura to reconsider and come back to him.

But she slid a hand onto her brother's arm and let him lead her from the room.

Annie watched Jack. "Aren't you going after her?"

"It's done." And it was. If Laura was not ready to stand with him and fight for them, he had no grounds to do so either.

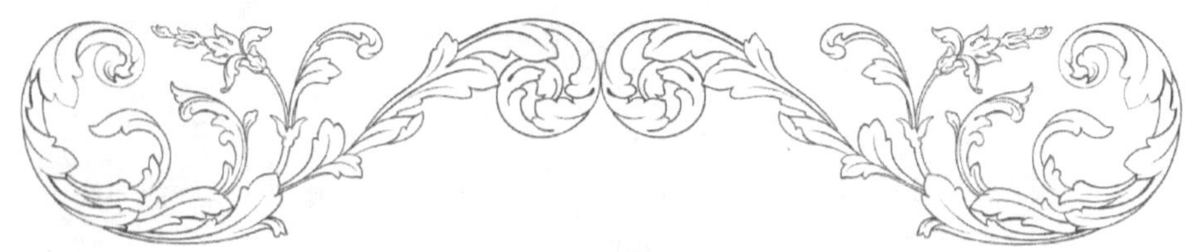

CHAPTER 25

Separation

Memphis Central Station
Memphis, TN
May 19, 1900

It was raining when the train pulled into Memphis. It was fitting. For Laura's outlook was just as dreary...if not more so. She was shuffled to a waiting carriage and then, minutes later, into the house. What had she done? Why had she left Jack? But she had to...for his sake.

She longed for the privacy and solace of her room. There she could spend her tears, and there she could collect herself. Shrugging out of her wet travel jacket, she moved toward the stairs.

But as she passed her wet things to the butler, Samuel caught her arm and stopped her. Where had he come from? Did it matter?

"Where are you going?" he demanded.

"To my room." Her words were simple and plain. All the fight had gone out of her, any that remained worked to tamp down her emotions until it was safe...well, *safer* to spill them.

Samuel exchanged a look with Thomas and shook his head. "Father wants to speak with you. Now."

"But we only just arrived home, I—"

"Now." His tone was insistent. There would be no escape from facing her father. Not in this moment.

Her shoulders fell as did everything within her. She no longer owned her future. Never again. "Of course."

Samuel waved Thomas off as he all but dragged her toward Father's study. Not that she resisted, but apparently, she didn't move nearly as quick as Samuel wanted her to.

"You're hurting me," she muttered. Not that he cared.

He scoffed. "Better you than what you have done to this family."

Why did he hate her so? Why was Micah her only ally in this place?

She considered the last twenty-four hours...and how Hattie had stood firm against Thomas's question, to her own detriment. Perhaps, then, she wasn't the spy Laura had pegged her for. Were there others who would aid should she need it?

Samuel stopped in front of the door.

Laura watched him, waiting for the next direction.

"Go on in. He's waiting." Samuel gestured for her to push the door open. "And I don't need to tell you how impatience can cloud his mood."

As if Father could be angrier.

Still, she nodded and reached for the door's latch. Pressing into its solid surface, she pushed into the study.

Father sat behind his desk. As she appeared, he leaned forward and held out a hand toward the seat opposite. "Sit."

It wasn't a request. Nor did it seem the demand she knew it was. His expression and tone were even and measured. Not quite what she expected.

She obeyed, and, as she sat, she heard the door click closed behind her. Again, what did it matter? Her father would do as he pleased, and she had no recourse.

Father rose and walked around the desk. She noted that his hands were in fists. That was all that betrayed the anger he must be feeling. "I heard about your little speech."

Of course. Somehow that had made it back to him.

"I wasn't at all pleased to discover you are still doing these stunts."

"Yes, Father." It wasn't what she wanted, but it was best to comply. "I apologize."

"I was quite certain we had an arrangement."

Yes, they did. So, it would be the asylum for her. And who knew what they would do to her? If his mistress had earned shock treatments, isolation, and eventually a lobotomy, how could she expect any less? Was her life worth anything even to her at this point?

"So, as you see, it is imperative I bring you into line."

She had known that was coming. Maybe if she obeyed in the way he wanted, she would be spared such a dismal future. "Yes, Father."

He nodded. "I am pleased you seem to know your place again." Moving back around the desk, he took on a dismissive air. Perhaps he was almost done, then. "Mr. Higgins will take you to wife on the morrow."

That couldn't be. Surely even her father wouldn't risk losing face among his peers by going back on his word.

"You gave your word to John Patterson." Her voice sounded timid even to her.

He whirled on her. "It has been rescinded."

She flinched but was thankful that nothing more showed of her growing fear.

"It was never going to happen."

Her eyes widened. What game had he been playing? Did he still play at?

"You didn't honestly think I would give your hand to some nobody, did you?" His words were almost laughed out.

She had. For a time. What had he stood to gain from Jack, though?

"This was always about business, about advantage. Don't you realize that's all you are—a piece of a bigger puzzle?"

Yes, she had known. But it hurt to hear him spell it out just the same. If he held out the hope of marriage long enough for Jack to destroy his relationship with his employer, Father would have secured Jack's allegiance without having to marry her off. It all fell into place. Father had never intended to go through with it.

"You were always meant to seal a deal with Mr. Higgins. And you will. Tomorrow."

He sat and waved a hand as if she were to leave. No play of kindness, no words beyond the commands he gave her. What was her life if this was all it would be? Mr. Higgins would overlord in the same way. Only with him, her life may be as good as forfeit.

"I won't." She surprised herself in responding.

Father's head jerked up and his eyes widened. "What did you say?"

She swallowed and prayed for strength. "I won't do it."

"You will." His eyes darkened. "Unless you are prepared to go into the asylum. And believe you me, there will be no release from that nightmare."

She believed him. But would losing her mind be better than losing her life? It was an impossible choice.

"What will it be?" He rose and leaned over his desk. "It matters little to me. For either way, you will no longer be my problem."

She wanted to shrink back, to disappear. But nothing would free her from this decision. It was the last piece of autonomy left to her. How would she use it?

Patterson Home
Chicago, IL
May 21, 1900

JACK GRUMBLED AS HE LOOKED OUT THE WINDOW. THE gentle breeze moved the trees, bending the branches this way and that. It was a pleasant sight for his foul mood.

Turning his attention to the small desk and the paper stretched out before him, he dipped his pen in the inkwell. This correspondence was a much overdo update for Ernest. So much had happened since he was at his friend's home. Things that shouldn't have happened. Things that had to happen. He had given up much...and had more taken from him. It was a year of loss.

The parlor door opened, and he dropped his head over his letter once more. Would that keep the womenfolk in this home from disturbing him?

From the sound of even footfalls and the rustle of skirts, he guessed Annie came. A clunk on a nearby table told that she set something down. A vase of flowers perhaps? When he breathed in, the scent of fresh wildflowers filled his senses. Annie always did care more for the common blooms than the rarer ones. Such as lilacs.

"What are you about?" she finally asked.

He glanced over and found her rearranging the flowers in their bunch. Likely an unnecessary practice altogether. Surely, she but found an excuse to speak with him. Dropping his gaze to the paper once more, he sighed. "I am trying to write to Ernest."

"I do hope all is well with the newest addition to his family."

Annie's recall for these random details always amazed him.

"I am certain the little one is to blame for the lack of rested-ness Ernest spoke about in his last letter."

"I do not doubt it." Annie continued to make a show of setting the flowers to right. "What of you? Are you rested today?"

He peered at her from the farthest most stretches of his vision. It was clear she wanted to say something. Why didn't she just do so? Beating about the topic was not like her. "I am."

"Liar." She held her gaze solidly on him.

He jerked upright. "What?"

"You are no less weary than I, staying up all night worried about what will become of Laura." There was a challenge in Annie's eyes.

"You don't know what you are talking about." He bent over his letter again.

She moved closer and tugged the paper from him. "Then why haven't you found the wherewithal to write a full sentence?"

It was true. The paper she thrust back at him only had the greeting.

"All right." He jerked it back from her. "Maybe I am a bit tired."

Keeping his gaze out the window, he hoped she would leave him be. But there was little chance of that.

She *harrumphed* and crossed her arms. "I don't understand you."

He turned to catch her gaze again. "What?"

"You spout words of conviction and commitment to Laura, yet here you sit."

"What am I supposed to do?" He stood abruptly, nearly knocking over the chair.

Annie wasn't the least bit affected by his sudden movement. She altered her gaze to look up at him and said, "Go after her, you daft man."

He gritted his teeth. "You don't think I want to?"

She balked at the force of his words.

He shoved a hand through his hair. "I want to. Believe me, I do. But I have no basis for demanding anything from her father."

"You would let that..." She waved a hand as she hunted for the right word. "That *monster* intimidate you?"

He settled back on his heels, wishing that she wasn't right and wishing that he was wrong. "It's more than that. *She* relented. If she isn't prepared to stand with me, how can I fight this?"

"Poppycock," another voice said from the doorway.

He turned in that direction. Somehow his mother had slipped in. How did he not hear her uneven gait or the thud of her cane? "Mother, I don't think—"

She held up a hand as she moved farther into the room. "I have never seen you back down from a challenge. Especially when it came to something you really wanted."

That was true. He had fought tooth and nail to overcome his meager beginnings and rise to the level he had achieved. He hadn't let anyone dissuade him or tell him it was impossible.

She paused, catching her breath. But her eyes bored into him. "And I can't believe you have ever loved anything as much as you love her."

He looked to the floor. Was he such an open book? Were his feelings so easy to read?

Annie set a hand to his shoulder. "Go after her. Fight for her. You know she needs you to."

"Your sister is right," Mother said with a knowing smile. "As usual."

"But—"

Annie held up a hand. "No. Don't stop and think about it." She laid her hand over his chest. "Let your heart tell you what to do for once. And trust God to guide you."

He looked between his sister and his mother. Could he do this? Could he risk losing a piece of himself and return whole? There was no chance...if he didn't try.

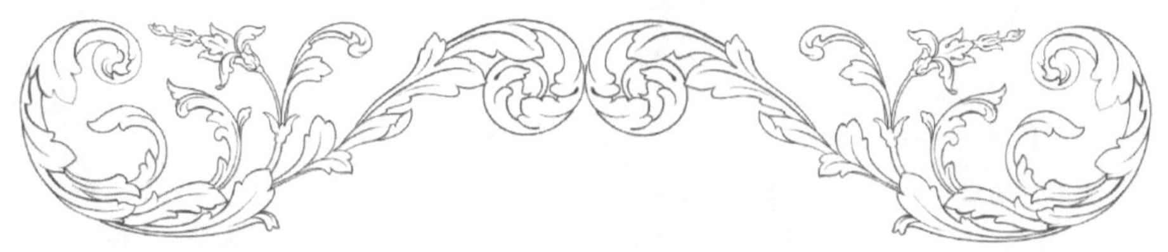

CHAPTER 26

Risk

Grand Central Station
Chicago, IL
May 22, 1900

What was he doing? Jack approached the train station with less confidence than he wished. He didn't have a plan. Not really. Not beyond getting on the train and going to Memphis. How was he to gain an audience with Mr. Millington? And, if he should, how was he to convince the man to give up his daughter?

But he had to do something. He had to try.

And he trusted that the right path would be laid out before him. He just knew that God would do so and would not abandon him...or Laura. What was it Reverend Downs always said? 'Pray and act in accordance with God's will such that if God doesn't come through in it, there will be nothing else to save the situation?' That never made sense to Jack. Until now.

He had to act. Had to go. And rely on God to come through. If not, he could lose the things he still had some hold on.

The train in the station chugged and whistled its departure. His train should be arriving soon.

He approached the manager's office to purchase a ticket. While the man counted his money and got his ticket ready, Jack's gaze wandered to the telegrapher in the back of the small room. The man was hard at work.

"John Patterson?" the manager said. How long had he been trying to get Jack's attention?

"Yes?" Jack shifted his focus.

"We've been hoping you would stop by."

That was curious. "You have?"

The manager turned to address his office mate. "William? Weren't you looking for Mr. John Patterson?"

The telegrapher looked up from his work. "I was."

As the manager moved a step to the side, he indicated Jack.

"Ah, Mr. Patterson, I have a telegram for you." He thumbed through the papers off to the side. "Came in yesterday. We tried to find you."

"Oh...I haven't been to my townhouse in a few days." Why had he decided to stay with his mother and sister? Did he think it brought them a sense of security and peace? Or him?

The man shrugged. "No worries. You're here now." William walked the single piece of paper over. He handed it to Jack and gave a mock salute. "Delivered."

"Thank you." Jack took his ticket and the telegram and moved to a nearby bench.

He opened the folded paper and read the typed-out words. And gasped.

It was from Micah. He told that Mr. Millington would be committing Laura. And gave him an address at which Micah could rendezvous with him.

Would Jack be too late? A wave of apprehension spread through him. What if it had already been done? Could he and Micah get Laura out? That was doubtful. Everyone in that town was under the power of Mr. Millington. Everyone, it seemed, but Micah.

No sooner had he finished reading than the pierce of a train whistle sounded. And soon after, the chugging of the wheels on the tracks. It couldn't be here fast enough.

Jack rushed to the window. "I need to send a reply."

Both the station manager and the telegrapher turned.

He must seem desperate...and he was. Pressing against the counter, he repeated, "I have a reply."

William exchanged a look with the manager and rose. As he neared the counter, Jack pulled out a few coins. "What does it need to say?"

Jack licked his lips. "I'll be there on the noon train."

The man arched a brow. "I will get it sent, but I can't guarantee the recipient will have possession of it before you arrive.

"I understand. But it's urgent." Jack forced himself to remain calm as he handed over the money. "Thank you."

The man nodded and walked back to the telegraph machine. Sure enough, he started tapping out Jack's message forthwith.

Please help me, God. Don't let me be too late.

Millington Home
Memphis, TN
May 21, 1900

THERE WAS NOTHING LEFT FOR LAURA. SHE GLANCED ABOUT her bedroom and realized how little the material things within mattered. None of it could she take with her. And none would survive her mother's hand on the room.

She sighed and whispered a farewell to the space that had been hers since she could remember. But she had made her choice and she would move forward with courage. After all, bravery was not about the lack of fear, but about moving forward despite it.

What the next days, months, maybe even years would bring, she couldn't fathom. She only prayed that whatever was to happen would be quick and painless. And that she might retain her mental faculties until the end.

It seemed odd to ask such things of God. Did it communicate a lack of faith? Perhaps. But did she have any place in her that believed there would be a deliverance from her fate?

Lord, I cannot continue without You. And I want to believe even if You choose not to set me free, that You will be with me. Help the places in me where I struggle to trust.

A sense of peace overshadowed her heart. Yes, it was God's gift. And that was the most she could ask for or expect. Hadn't she given herself over to this? First, in letting Thomas return her home for the sake of preserving Jack. And then, for the decision she made to let Father commit her. Yes, she would own her choices and lean into the Lord's grace for endurance.

There was a knock at her door.

"Come in." She fought to keep her voice even and free of the trembling that she felt throughout her core. She would be strong.

The door opened and Thomas stood there. Her brother had a tightness about his eyes. Was that evidence of regret? Sadness? She couldn't quite discern it.

"It's time." His words were quiet. Remorse perhaps?

She nodded. There was little sense in heaping guilt onto his shoulders. He had only done what he had to. As did she.

Crossing her room for the last time, she slipped into the hall.

"Laura," Thomas said, halting her. "Are you certain this is what you want? It's not too late to submit to—"

"I'm certain," she said firmly. While she wasn't eager for what was to come, it was preferable.

He nodded slowly. "Then I'll make sure you get to the carriage."

They spoke no other words as she followed him down the staircase and to the entry.

One of the maidservants helped Laura into a wrap. Strange, it wasn't cold, but she shivered all the same. And she was thankful for the kindness.

A door creaked down the hall, and solid footsteps told that Father drew near.

Laura looked around for Samuel, her mother, or, at the very least, Micah to see her off. There was no one. None but Thomas and the two staff members that attended them.

Soon enough, Father appeared, a grim look upon his features.

She had expected something more—what exactly, she wasn't certain. Just...more.

He nodded at Thomas, who took Laura by the elbow with a gentle grip and steered her to the door.

In short order, she and Father were loaded into the carriage. And off.

How long would it be until they arrived? She couldn't know. Her gaze latched on her hands in her lap. For there was little point in seeking out Father's. Would she see eagerness there? Determination? Relief? Not one of those emotions would make any of it better. And regret or remorse were altogether unlikely. So, she watched her hands.

The ride was as smooth as always, until the carriage turned suddenly. And they then bumped along. It became quite uncomfortable. Laura worked to keep her gaze on her hands. But it didn't stop her mind. Had they gone off the road for some reason?

Father shuffled as if agitated. Even from her periphery, she noted he looked out the window to the right, then to the left. And slammed the hood of the carriage.

"Harrison, why have we left the road?"

There was no answer.

That got Laura's attention. Her gaze darted between Father and the overly grassy scenery. Had they left the hub of Memphis? For what reason?

Father did appear put out. He leaned into the window opening. "Harrison!"

Again, no response.

"Harrison, where are you taking us? Turn this infernal thing around this instant!"

Laura had no idea where they might be. Or where they were headed. More...why?

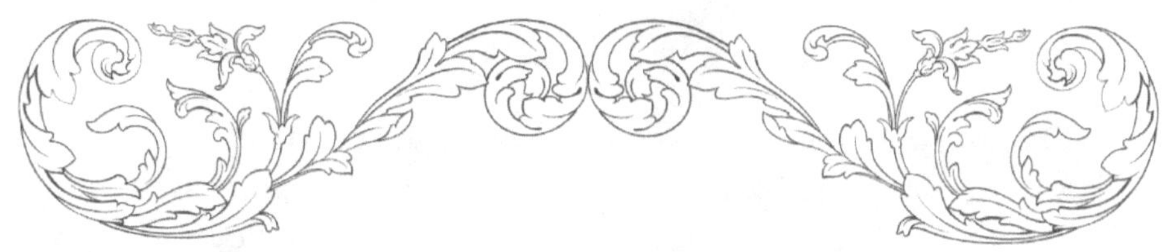

CHAPTER 27

Opening

Memphis Central Station
Memphis, TN
May 21, 1900

Jack was on his feet as the train came to a halt. The entire ride to Memphis had been dreadful. And long. Every second that ticked by his heart ached with worry. He needed to find Laura. He needed to get to her. And prayed it wouldn't be too late.

Once the whistle blasted and the conductor called for everyone to disembark, Jack was pushing through the aisle, wishing he could make the other passengers understand. Many hard looks were shot his way, but he didn't care. He couldn't.

Finally, he was down the few steps and onto the platform. He glanced this way and that. Would Micah have received his telegram? The chances, as the telegrapher in Chicago alluded to, were slim. Still, there was hope.

Micah seemed to have some sort of plan. What was it? And what part did he envision Jack playing?

Looking here and there, the seconds continued to tick. Then Jack gave up. He had to get to Laura. Now.

Pressing through the crowd of welcomes and reunions, he made his way to the livery nearby. He waited with bated breath and less patience than he'd have liked for his turn. As he reached the front of the line, he had to clasp his hands to keep them from shaking.

"I need to rent a horse."

"I think we just lent out our last one."

"No," Jack shot out. That couldn't be. How could God present him with such a challenge? *Help me!* he prayed...over and over. "Are you quite certain there are none left?"

The man leveled his gaze on Jack. "Quite."

"Just for surety's sake, might you check within one more time?"

The stableman's glare was hard, but some softening about his eyes came as he seemed to take in Jack's desperation.

Jack drew in a breath, praying he wouldn't have to take the time to explain.

At length, the man nodded. "I will do that, sir. But the ledger here does not have any horses available, so don't get your hopes up."

The few minutes that the stablemaster was gone dragged. Each moment, a lost opportunity.

After nearly ten minutes, the man reappeared with a sullen look about him. "I'm sorry, sir. There are none."

Jack gnashed his teeth. It couldn't be so. "Where can I find a carriage to take me?"

He shook his head. "That won't be any more fruitful."

Hands becoming fists, Jack pressed one to his mouth to keep his words in. They would not help him or the situation. But the angered fright tugging at him also stung his eyes.

"Listen," the stablemaster said as he leaned closer. "I don't have a horse to rent you, but my personal horse is here."

Jack's eyes widened. How much might he have to pay for the use of that animal? It didn't matter, he would pay whatever he must. "Yes?"

"I can see you are hard pressed to get somewhere. And I can lend you that horse."

Without charge? That seemed too good to be true. There were indeed still decent people in the world.

"But I cannot do so without some collateral."

There it was. Jack's heart fell, but a desperation rose within him that would not be doused. "I'm listening."

"Understand, sir, I don't know you. And I just want some insurance that my animal will be returned."

"I assure you, it will be."

"I want to believe you. How about that fine pocket watch?"

Jack set a hand over the precious heirloom. "This was my father's."

The man's brows lowered, and he nodded. "Then I know you'll be sure to come back for it."

Dare he trust this man to not sell his watch? It was far more valuable to him than a horse. But not more so than Laura.

Jack unclipped and extended it toward the man.

The stablemaster opened his palm below Jack's hand. And waited.

Jack took in one more steadying breath and dropped it, knowing full well it may be the last time he saw it.

The man opened the heirloom. "Does it even work?"

Jack shook his head. "Not for many years."

As the man tucked the watch into his trouser pocket, he waved Jack farther into the stable. "This way, sir."

The horse turned out to be older and more ambled than Jack anticipated, but it would get Jack to Laura faster than his own two legs. So he said nothing.

"This here is Freddy. He's not much to look at, but he is sure-footed and strong." The stablemaster seemed prouder than Jack would have been. Maybe the horse was important to him. That gave Jack some measure of confidence in the return of his father's watch.

The stablemaster saddled the horse quickly, much to Jack's relief. And Jack was mounted within a few minutes.

"Thank you, sir," Jack said, giving the man one more moment. "You cannot know how much."

The man nodded once more and gave Freddy a gentle slap.

And they were off. Without Micah. Without a plan. But with a glimmer of a chance.

City Streets
Memphis, TN
May 21, 1900

Laura blinked as her Father became even more irate. As if he had a tenuous hold on the situation when, in fact, he still held all the power.

"Harrison, you will do as I say," he commanded. "Move this carriage."

There was still no answer. Had the man had an attack of some sort and died in the driver's seat and the horses just led them astray?

Father glared at her and held up a finger. "Don't move."

She held herself stiffly to keep from drawing back. He was as angry as she had ever seen him.

Reaching for the door, he cursed as he pushed it. Once out, he slammed it shut. "Harrison!"

Laura watched as much as possible from the window.

Father swore again about the mud and how it would tarnish his shoes. If she weren't so downcast, it might be humorous.

Her father moved out of her line of sight, still calling to his ever-faithful driver.

What followed could only be described as an exchange of heat. What was happening here? Did the driver not wish to do Father's bidding? For what reason? For her?

She thought back to Hattie and how she stood silently when Thomas questioned her. Not an eye batted when he dismissed her from service. Would the same, or worse, happen to Harrison? Did he risk so much on her behalf? It didn't seem possible, but so it was. Harrison had diverted the carriage and stalled out here.

Father yelled at the man.

Harrison made some comment about being stuck in the mud.

Father growled something about Harrison pushing it out.

At length, Father demanded that Harrison get out of the way so he might drive the team.

Laura could not remain any longer. She opened the door and set her foot on the first step.

"I told you to stay put." Father's ire turned on her.

Dare she push on? What more could Father do to her than he had already done?

Stepping down to the wet, muddy ground, her boots sank at least an inch. Perhaps Harrison was not exaggerating. The rain had slowed to a drizzle, but it would certainly ruin her hat. She didn't mind. She was beyond caring about such things.

Father glared at her. "Get back in the carriage this instant." His face was red and his words carried spittle with them. He steamed at the situation.

She looked at Harrison.

The older man's gaze eased as his eyes met hers. Perhaps all his gloominess had been for her situation...not *about* her. Could it be that the serving staff truly saw her? Cared about her?

Father marched to her and gripped her arm painfully. "If we have to walk there, we will."

She tried to tug free as he pulled her, but his hold was too strong. How was that so? But she would not give up. Not when there was a chance she might be free.

The carriage creaked as Harrison shuffled to get down. Would he challenge Father further?

Thundering hooves nearby warned that a rider came.

She turned in that direction. Indeed, a man rode toward them on a horse with an uneven gait. Would it be reinforcements for Father? Or— dare she hope—for her?

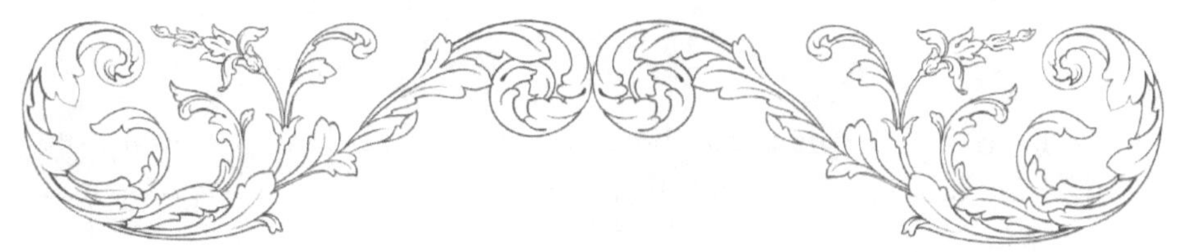

Way Out

There...in the distance...a fine carriage. A man pulled a woman in the direction of the road as another dropped from the driver's bench. To assist the man? Or the woman?

As he narrowed his gaze, they came into sharper focus. *Laura!*

He pushed the horse faster, though it was for naught. The more aged horse was already giving Jack all it had. Still, he thanked the Lord that it wasn't too late. For what, he didn't know. But he would not let Laura go without a fight.

Her captor—likely her father—looked in his direction. Then he pulled at her all the more. Did he know who came upon them? Jack was still some distance away.

Laura twisted her arm, likely working to free herself.

Jack's fear became iron in his veins. He would make sure her father could not hurt her again. In any way.

The ground beneath Freddy's hooves thickened and affected the horse's footfalls all the more. But to the animal—and the stable master's—credit, the horse's steps were sure and solid even in the thickened mire.

"Laura," he called. "I'm coming!"

She cried out for him. "Jack!"

Then her struggle against her father intensified. There was some sort of scuffle between them and she fell onto her backside, splattering mud everywhere.

Her father reached for her, but she scurried away as best she could.

By then, he was closer. Jack halted the horse and jumped down. Then he stumbled through the mud, racing to her aid.

"Stay back," her father threatened. "Or I will have you arrested for kidnapping."

Jack cared little for his threats and pushed on.

The man stepped between Jack and Laura as he approached. "I tell you, this is all for naught." Mr. Millington glared at the driver then at Jack. "Naught!"

"You cannot be so calloused," Jack said as he slowed, drinking in the sight of Laura and thanking God for His providence. "What is it to you if we marry? You will be free of us."

"How thoughtless can you be? I will not yield," Mr. Millington said with a wide-eyed, wild glare.

Jack watched Laura, so close, yet so far. And he wouldn't stop now. He stepped forward, prepared to do what he must.

Mr. Millington jerked a pistol from under his coat, aiming it well at Jack's head. "Don't come any closer."

"Don't," Laura cried, struggling to her feet. "You can't."

"I can. And I will."

"You can't be serious," Jack breathed. There was no way this man of some standing would risk everything to shoot an unarmed man. But there was something crazed and unstable about the way he sent menacing glares around the small group.

"I will *not* yield."

What was the way out of this? Jack calmed his racing heart. *God, make a way.*

This was impossible. And unimaginable. Father held a gun to Jack's head. What should she do? What *could* she do? Was there a way to stop this madness?

"Father," she pled. "Please, listen. I won't fight you anymore. Just let Jack and Harrison go."

"Laura," Jack warned, his voice rising even as he kept his gaze on her father.

Father pulled the hammer of the pistol and steadied his aim. "I do not say things I don't mean."

Harrison moved, shifting closer or struggling in the mud, it was difficult to discern.

Father turned the pistol in his direction and fired.

Harrison crumpled.

"No!" Laura screamed.

Jack rushed forward, but Father turned his gun around before Jack could overtake him.

"You still want to try my patience?" Father demanded.

Jack shook his head slowly. He made eye contact with Laura. There was something in the depths of his eyes, but what? What was he trying to communicate?

The ground rumbled again. Did someone else come? Dare she hope for another miracle?

"Do you hear that?" Jack said to Father. "Someone is coming. This might be your only opportunity to stop this."

Father kept his gaze leveled on Jack.

"Stop," another voice rang out. "For the love of all that's holy, stop!"

She knew that voice. Turning in the direction of the coming rider, her heart flew—Micah. Then her heart fell once more. What more could he do? Dragging her beloved brother into this standoff was the last thing she wanted to do.

Father cocked the gun again as he swung the revolver toward Laura. "Don't come any closer."

Jack gasped.

Micah pulled the horse to a halt.

Father glared between them. "There is only one way this can end."

What did he mean? What were his intentions here?

Father set his gaze on her.

"There *is* only one way this can end," Micah countered from atop the horse. "And it is not this."

Father seemed confused. He shifted his focus to Micah.

"There is only one way you can leave here unscathed."

Father laughed. It was a maniacal kind of sound.

Micah exchanged a look with Jack, then said, "What you don't know, is that Evelyn kept records."

That gave Father pause. He lowered the gun slightly as he turned to look at Micah. What could Father's long-gone mistress have to do with this?

"You lie." Father's voice shook the slightest bit. "Even if that were true, how would you know?"

"I don't know why, but she trusted me." Micah's voice, by contrast, was calm and steady. "And she ferreted everything to me before she was taken away. You cannot imagine what I found. Especially involving the Commissioner."

Father's arm fell a little more. "You are lying."

"Believe me," Micah said as he steadied the restless horse, "I wish I were."

Everything was silent but for some groaning noises coming from Harrison. Might he be alive?

Laura looked in that direction.

Harrison moved, a slow, pained motion.

"How was I to know to what lengths you would go to for your precious railroad?"

Father's eyes widened. "For us. For you. All of it to build a legacy."

"Stop it," Micah yelled. "It was all about money, wealth, and power. Nothing else."

Father's hand shook—the slightest tremor, but unsteady all the same.

Jack inched toward Laura. Would he risk himself?

She looked at him and shook her head. It did not stop his slow, but decidedly forward progress.

"Put the gun down now. Let Laura and Jack go." Micah's voice was steady and even again. "And I will not expose you for the monster you have become."

Father twitched.

Jack leapt forward, falling on the gun and pulling Father to the ground.

Micah dropped out of the saddle and rushed for Laura.

A shot rang out.

The two men stilled.

"Jack!" Laura cried. "Jack, no!"

His back was to her, but he moved. Thank heavens, he moved. And stood, gun in hand.

Her focus fell on her father. Was he...?

But he moved, too, gnashing his teeth. He tugged his leg closer, then she could see that the bullet had pierced Father's shoe. Still, she could not help being relieved.

Micah now stood over Father. "It's over."

Father's features slackened as if he realized for the first time he was beaten.

"And I don't want to see you ever again," Micah muttered. "Do you hear me?"

Father just stared.

Jack moved to Laura and pulled her into his arms. "Thank the Lord above...you're safe."

She relished the feel of his embrace for a moment, then turned to where Micah looked down on Father.

"This is what will happen: you will not chase Laura nor me. And you won't touch Jack in any way or I'll release what I have."

Father grimaced. But nodded.

Laura released Jack and rushed to Harrison.

He was breathing. And he rolled toward her, pressing a hand to his shoulder. "It is nothing, Miss Millington. I'll survive."

Micah joined Laura and helped lift Harrison to his feet.

Jack, too, moved closer to examine the wound.

Father's limped footsteps pounded through the mud.

Laura jerked her regard in that direction.

He ran for Micah's horse.

No one made any move to stop him as he mounted and pressed the horse onward. There was little he could do to harm them. Not anymore.

Micah tended to Harrison as Laura fell once more into Jack.

He wrapped an arm around her and pressed a kiss to her hair. "I was so afraid."

She nodded against him. "I know."

He pulled back and lifted hands to frame her face. "I cannot bear to be separated from you again. Not for a moment."

Tears filled her eyes. Partly from the intensity of the situation, partly because her heart overflowed with gratitude. God *had* worked all things out for their good.

Jack's mouth found hers and the kiss that sealed his declaration held equal measures of hope and love.

They had each other. And now they had the freedom to be together. For as long as they both should live.

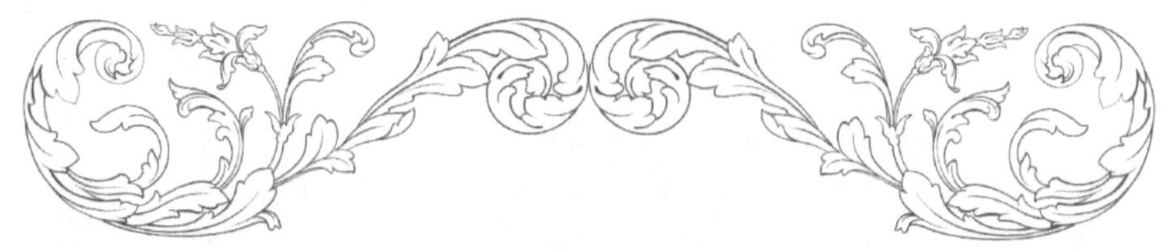

Epilogue

Laura settled into the parlor's settee with Annie to one side and Mrs. Patterson in a chair on her other side. And all was at rest. After the long journey, they were finally at peace.

"Where will you be headed then?" Annie's excited girlish voice begged for more details.

"I think we will have a short trip. Only a few nights. Then Jack will be back at work."

"It's a shame there won't be more time for your honeymoon trip," Mrs. Patterson said. "It doesn't matter, though, I know it will be wonderful. And then you'll have your whole lives."

Annie stuck out her lower lip. "Still, it is terrible Jack can't have more time. You just got married for goodness' sake!"

Laura set a hand to her arm. "It will be fine. Your mother is right, it doesn't matter where we go...or for how long. We have a lifetime to cherish each other."

"That is so romantic," Annie crooned.

They fell into a companionable silence.

And Mrs. Patterson seemed to remember something. "I read something in the paper. Something about that Casey Jones you mentioned."

"Oh?" Laura turned her full attention to her mother-in-law. "What is it?"

"The railroad company has decided to absolve him of any and all blame. Something about more evidence coming to light."

Laura smiled to herself. Janie and Sim had done it. Her eyes watered.

Footfalls beyond the parlor gave Laura's heart reason to race. Had Jack come to collect her?

But when a figure appeared in the doorway, it was Micah. He looked every bit as worn and weary as he had been since the encounter in Memphis. It still weighed on him. Heavily.

Annie straightened next to Laura. So much so that Laura sensed it without looking. "Hello, Mr. Millington. How are you this afternoon?"

Micah smiled. "I told you...Mr. Millington is my father." Though his voice was light, there was a depth to his tone that spoke volumes. "It's just Micah."

Annie twitched. "Very well. Micah."

Why did she say his name so carefully? Was there more to that?

Laura spared but a thought on it before turning back to Micah. "Did you need something?"

He shuffled his feet. "I was hoping to speak with you. Alone."

Alarm bolted through Laura. What could he need to talk with her about that required privacy?

"Of course," Annie said, so very accommodating. She rose and leaned toward Mrs. Patterson.

"Don't trouble yourself," Micah said, holding out a hand. "Laura, can we step into the dining room?"

Laura offered Annie, then Mrs. Patterson her brightest smile. "Excuse me, ladies. I will be back shortly."

She stepped into the hall, Micah behind her, and walked to the dining room. Then she whirled on him. "What is the matter?"

He ran a hand across the back of his neck. "Who says anything is wrong?"

She arched an eyebrow. "I do. I know something is amiss."

He pushed out a breath. "I can't stay here."

"What?" They had agreed he would stay put in Chicago for a time. Try to find something to sustain himself.

"I can't let Jack take care of me. I won't be beholden to anyone. Ever again."

Laura swallowed. She could understand his feelings. But she dreaded what was to come. "Where will you go?"

"Farther west. Texas maybe. Or perhaps Arizona."

"But...that's not who you are. You've never known anything so wild."

His gaze darkened. "I'm not sure I know who I am anymore. Or that I ever did."

She dropped her regard to the floor. Could she keep him from seeing the pain in her eyes?

He set his hands on her shoulders. "Don't worry so. I'll write. I promise."

She looked to the side as a tear slid down her face. Could she stand to lose her brother? For a time of self-discovery? Or perhaps forever if he found a life out there as he hoped?

"Laura?" His voice was warm, but tight. "I don't know if I can do this if you are so against it."

She shook her head. "I want what's best for you. Always."

He nodded, a smile breaking across his face. "I believe that." Leaning forward, he wrapped his arms around her.

As he released her, she wiped at her eyes. "When will you go?"

"Tonight."

She wanted to beg him to stay at least a few more days, but she knew he had to do it now or he might never be able. "I understand."

"I wish you every happiness with Jack." His smile was genuine.

"Did I hear my name?" Jack stepped into the small room from the direction of the front door.

"When did you get home?" Laura beamed as she moved to his side.

He set an arm around her waist. "Just a moment ago." His gaze darted between Laura and Micah. "Everything all right?"

"Yes." Micah was quick to say. "I'll excuse myself and let you two lovebirds get out of here. You need to if you will catch your train."

Jack reached for his pocket watch, but instead looked at the hall clock. That was curious.

"Oh my. We are cutting it close."

Laura's gaze lingered on Micah as he stepped around her and Jack.

"Are you ready, darling?" Jack set a hand lightly to the side of her face.

"I am ready for anything. As long as you are with me."

He grinned and touched his lips to hers briefly. "Then let's find out what adventure lies ahead."

She leaned into him. "Right beside you."

Keep reading for a preview of the next book in the Railway Romance Series!

Thank you, dear reader, for for reading along with me! If you enjoyed this story, I would sincerely appreciate if you would submit a review. It would mean so much to me!

To read more about these characters, follow along with the Railway Romance Series. Find it at:

https://saraturnquist.com/railway-romance-series/

Author's Note

When I started dreaming up this series, the Tennessee folk hero Casey Jones was at the forefront of my mind. I knew I wanted to feature his heroic, yet fatal crash. The songs and stories about him are legendary... perhaps more so in Tennessee than anywhere else. The Casey Jones Home & Railroad Museum certainly keep his memory alive through all that they do.

It was this history that I wanted to honor. I did not know initially how much or how little of a role that Casey Jones would play. I did want to honor his sacrifice and open the eyes of my readers to the kind of man he was. But, as usual, I am hesitant to breathe life into historical figures on the page (for sensitivity reasons). That is perhaps why his role in the story is not what it might have been.

The events surrounding Casey Jones' appearances in the story are as accurate as possible with one exception. The banquet at the New Southern Hotel honoring Casey took place several years prior, in the early spring of 1896, some four years before his fatal run (in 1900). But I didn't feel that a four-year gap for my characters would work. So, I changed the date of the banquet for this reason.

It is always my desire to handle historical events with grace, and it was difficult for me to alter the date for the purposes of the story, but in the end, it was what needed to happen. I am thankful, then for Author's Notes in which I can clear my conscience and properly inform my readers.

During the dinner party scene, the woman that distracted Jack was, in fact, an homage to Casey's sister, Emma Jones. She would later that year (in May 1896) drown in a tragic steamboat accident.

The songs about Casey indeed increased his fame and awareness of the accident. You can find several versions if you search "The Ballad of Casey Jones." My particular favorite is one featuring Johnny Cash.

July 9, 1905

Approaching the Patterson House

Chicago, Illinois

A fine carriage bore Annie Patterson from the graveyard. It had been a dreary morning. Fog hovered thick over the city streets, making it difficult to view anything at a distance. That was irrelevant, however. Caught in the emotional grip of her loss, Annie couldn't see past her tears.

She had fought them these last few days…and lost. Miserably.

But what was she to do? Mother was gone. Forever. Annie would never again see her smile or hear her tender voice. How she wished she had appreciated those things more!

Mother had always been there, always nearby—whether to offer loving, caring advice or remind Annie to tend to her learning. It had quite nearly stifled her at times, but Mother's presence would now forever be sorely missed.

"Are you all right?" A gentle voice reached across the carriage.

Annie turned toward the woman. Her sister-in-law, Laura, watched Annie with soulful eyes, wide and shining with their own tears.

Her brother John—though no one called him anything but Jack—sat a bit straighter beside his wife and patted her arm before peering at Annie as well.

Annie sniffled and looked out the window again.

"Annie?" Jack's rich timbre filtered through the interior of the carriage. But the lowered tone told of his pain...and that struck her heart anew.

She bit her lip to keep from crying.

A hand settled on her knee. Even through her skirts, warmth pressed into Annie's cold skin.

Looking down, Annie found Laura's slender hand and perfect fingers lying on her lap. As she raised her chin, her gaze caught on Laura's enlarged midsection. It wouldn't be long.

Jack and his precious family would soon be four—the very young Casey, waiting for them at home, would have a brother or sister. That left the issue of her. Did she belong? Or was she just in the way?

"Annie?" Jack leaned forward as he repeated his entreaty.

She jerked her attention toward him, widening her eyes as she did so. Would he attempt to come across the carriage?

Releasing her lower lip, she nodded, the movement small but purposeful.

Jack's eyes glistened but swirled with concern.

"I am well enough," she managed to push out. "As much as can be expected."

He frowned.

Laura set her other hand to Jack's arm, coaxing him to ease back and settle once more.

He grasped her proffered hand and interlaced their fingers.

Laura pressed Annie's knee once more, then released her and rested back against the seat as well, rubbing her oversized abdomen. Had she pressed farther forward than she should? Had she injured herself or the baby?

Laura's clear eyes assured Annie that she was well. But there were shadows beneath them. She had been more fatigued of late. And with the preparations for Mother's funeral...

Annie's sister-in-law had been a great help. Perhaps Annie and Jack had relied on Laura more than they should. After all, it was Annie's responsibility, was it not?

"You must rest when we get to the house." Jack gazed at his wife. His voice not much more than a whisper. Yet in the small space, it was audible...and endearing.

Yes, Annie was quite out of place with them now. It was one thing when she had assisted in Mother's care. But now...what excuse did she have to burden her brother and his family?

Her face fell, as did her heart. The thought of separating from her brother left a heavy weight in her gut. Still, he would be appalled if he but dreamed she felt this way.

Maybe that was the problem. She loved him and cared for his wellbeing...just as she had for Father before his passing—had it been a decade ago?—and now Mother. And they both were gone. The hollowed cavern that remained within her overwhelmed everything else.

When would this ache stop? Perhaps it was that pain that drew Mother to her grave. For the older woman had spent the intervening years mourning Annie's late father.

It had truly been a heavy weight on her mother's rather frail body. And that depth of despair was something Annie refused to succumb to.

But how was she to rid herself of this immense burden? For if she remained with her brother's family, there would be naught but emptiness and grief.

Jack shifted, drawing Annie's gaze. He watched the fog-covered landscape beyond the carriage as his wife leaned into his side.

Such a great love was shared between her brother and Laura. Might Annie ever be loved that way? Would she feel so deeply for another? More...could she bear the risk of that loss?

A drizzle of water tapped on the roof of the fine vehicle, making streams down the windows. As if the whole of the sky mourned with her. Such nonsense, a silly notion indeed. Still, it gave some measure of comfort to her mind, whereas her reflections gave way to a twisting in her gut.

She sighed. And relented. Thoughts of the future would have to wait for tomorrow. For this day, she must surrender to the overpowering swell of sadness in her heart. To find some solace amidst the despair. In her own way. In her own time.

But her musings were interrupted as the carriage slowed to a halt.

Annie, more than ready to be free of the confined space, reached for the latch.

"Annie," came Laura's soft admonishment. "The rain."

Annie blinked at her sister-in-law. What did Laura intend with those words?

As if sensing Annie's confusion, she continued, "Wait for the footman. He will supply an umbrella." She tilted her head in the direction of the house.

Sure enough, a pair of footmen approached with dark umbrellas. What had she been thinking? Indeed, the truth was that she had not been. This new way of being waited on remained uncomfortable. No more so than the chaffing from Laura's instructions and reminders. Perhaps her kindly sister-in-law was right to do so. Annie just didn't measure up to the expectations of such a fine life. Maybe she never would.

She dipped her head as the carriage door opened.

And collided with Jack, who had apparently moved to exit first.

One eyebrow rose while his mouth tightened—an expression of his mildly amused frustration.

Why had he forced himself forward?

Oh yes, he would need to hand them down out of the carriage. Could she not remember anything?

After stepping into the rather drenched exterior, he lifted his hand back into the enclosed space, reaching for Laura first, then Annie. That was the proper way of it.

Then, taking Jack's arm, it was Laura who enjoyed his accompaniment into the house. Not so long ago, Annie would have been his main concern. But no longer. She had dropped in his priorities. As well it should be, she supposed.

Was there a place for her anymore?

As she was ushered into the house, Laura allowed her lady's maid, who met them at the door, to lead her up the stairs, presumably to change out of her wet attire.

Annie's own maid came forth, eyeing Annie's appearance, which had likely become rather haggard. Yet, before the woman could intercept her, she turned to her brother.

"May I have a word?"

Jack's gaze landed on her, his eyes intently darker under a single lifted brow. Did he wish to put on drier clothes as well? He glanced at his valet and, after a moment, waved the man off. "Of course."

At least she was more important than the drenched legs of his pants.

He indicated for her to precede him into the front parlor.

Her face warmed. Why had she beseeched him to speak now? They had just moments ago laid Mother to rest. And then endured the damp walk into the house. Surely, there would be a better time.

But her heart raced at that thought. It had to be now.

She stepped into the smaller space as Jack requested a tea service. What did he think this was? A pleasant afternoon chat? Would that it were only such.

She paused in the center of the room. Dare she sit on the fine furniture with her water-splattered skirt?

Jack stepped behind her and urged Annie toward the settee—the finest piece of furniture here. Why that?

Hesitating, she settled on the cushioned surface, keeping her wet hems carefully away from the fine fabric.

Jack sat on an upholstered chair opposite.

Then he turned his full attention on her. His blue eyes could be piercing. More so than hers...or so her mother had often said.

"What is bothering you?" Jack's voice was soft, but abrupt all the same. Was he eager to don dry clothes? Or did he long to see to his wife or small child upstairs? The fast-growing little one was no longer an infant and would be walking soon. Just thinking about her nephew brought a slight upturn to her lips. Casey's angelic face and wide dark blue eyes could steal anyone's heart.

But that was part of the reason she needed to speak with Jack. And there was no cause to tarry.

"I...have been thinking..."

"Sounds dangerous." He managed a grin, likely for her benefit.

Though there was no levity about her need, she offered a brief, small smile. "I know."

"What is it?" He leaned forward with elbows on his knees, quickly wiping at the fabric of his jacket as if that would remove the lingering wetness.

"You and Laura have been so kind, taking Mother in...and me. But I can no longer take advantage of your generous nature."

"What?" His eyes widened and his eyebrows arched so high she was certain they would infringe on his hairline.

She pushed out a breath and found she couldn't meet his gaze. So, staring at the floor she continued, "I...don't want to be a burden."

"How could you think that you—?"

Annie rushed to explain, "You only just married a couple of years ago. You and Laura are still settling into the house and life here. You have Casey...and soon another little one. I would just be in the way."

He gave her a sideways glare. "That is not true."

"But it is," she insisted. How to make him understand? "What, then, can I do to be of service? To earn my keep? I want to make my own way in this world."

"First, you have been listening to that progressive suffrage talk too much. Second, you don't have to do anything. You're my sister."

"That doesn't mean you need to provide for me."

He looked toward the door as footfalls sounded outside.

The door opened and a maidservant brought the tea service and waited upon them. But after the woman exited, Jack eyed Annie again.

"What makes now different? You've been here for some years now. And Laura and I have enjoyed your presence in our home. There is no reason that needs to change."

She dropped her head, staring at her lap. "I was here to care for Mother. It was my duty. I couldn't put that on you. Still, you brought us into your home so we'd be more comfortable. That was good of you."

He shook his head. "I'm sorry, Annie, but I don't see it that way. *You* were gracious to care for Mother as she ailed. It took a load off me. I was just as responsible for her as you were. Yet you took it upon yourself...and with grace."

Annie chose to ignore his compliments. "But I had a purpose here, a way to help." She met his gaze then. "Can't you understand? I cannot simply sit by and let others take care of me. I have to be useful." Her words were harsher than she'd intended. She softened her tone. "Please understand, it's part of who I am."

His lips thinned as he considered her words, looking at the rug as if he examined the pattern. "I don't like it. It is not a burden to accommodate my sister. My job and Laura's stipend has allowed for a very generous home. More than we need."

"I'm not exactly thrilled either." She lowered her voice, ignoring his reasoning. "I care about you a great deal. And your family. I don't want to leave. But I *have* to."

He peered at her, his eyes seemingly tormented. Then something sparked in their depths. "What if you didn't have to?"

"Jack, I appreciate your kindness, but I—"

He held up a hand. "Hear me out." Sitting upright, he licked his lips as if they had dried. "What if...what if you had a purpose here?"

What could he mean by that? Her features must have betrayed her because he continued.

"Laura has been...uncomfortable with the nanny we hired. We planned to tell her today that she needed to find a different situation. And with the baby coming, I don't like the idea of Laura trying to keep up with Casey."

Annie began to discern his intention. "You want me to nanny?"

He flinched as if pained. "Well, we wouldn't refer to you that way. I would rather you not feel the need to take something on. But, if you are so insistent, it would be helpful if you...helped with Casey." Jack squirmed.

Annie hated putting him in such an awkward position. Was he simply pitying her? "I don't know..."

"You were so good with Mother. Besides, Casey adores you. *And* we trust you implicitly. I don't want to insist upon it, though." He threw her a meaningful look. "We'll only move forward with this if you think it will work for you."

Annie chewed on her bottom lip. As her closest living male relative, he very well could force this. But if she could believe he was earnest about trusting her, this might be a fine arrangement. Perhaps she could give it a try.

"Will you?" His wide blue eyes, so like Father's, tore at her.

It was futile to resist him. She had never been able to say no to her big brother. At least, not to his face. And so, on a sigh, she said, "I will."

A smile spread across his worn features, and he stood. "Laura will be so pleased."

Annie rose as she offered what she hoped was a decent grin. "Good."

Would she truly be providing for Laura's comfort? Would she be offering something of value or was this merely a way for Jack to keep her under his roof?

She'd been in someone's care her whole life. But, as the suffragists often pointed out, options for women, while broadening, were limited. Especially at her somewhat elevated station.

As with anything, she mused, only time would tell.

To read more, find

***Annie, The Engineer's Daughter* here:**

https://saraturnquist.com/annie-the-engineers-daughter/

Read the rest of the **RAILWAY ROMANCE SERIES!**

Laura, The Tycoon's Daughter (Book 1)

She is in a hopeless situation. He has sworn off love. Can they find hope in each other and, possibly, a way out of their personal prisons?

Laura Millington's curious nature and desire for justice finds her caught up in the middle of a train run gone wrong. Can she stand for the truth even if it places her in opposition to her powerful father?

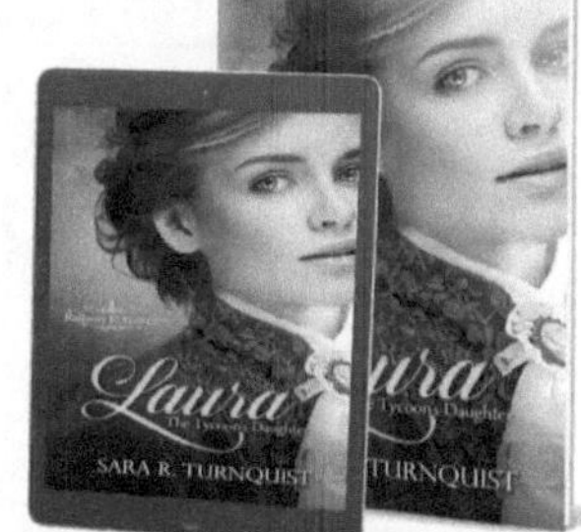

Jack Patterson is determined to never risk his heart again. The vulnerable, strong-willed Laura intrigues him more than he's allowed since his heartbreak. Can he overcome his reluctance? Moreover, will he be able to protect her from the man who would see her future dashed?

Will Laura and Jack find a way to stand side by side against the overwhelming forces keeping them apart?

Annie, The Engineer's Daughter (Book 2)

His life is forfeit. Until she gives him something to live for.

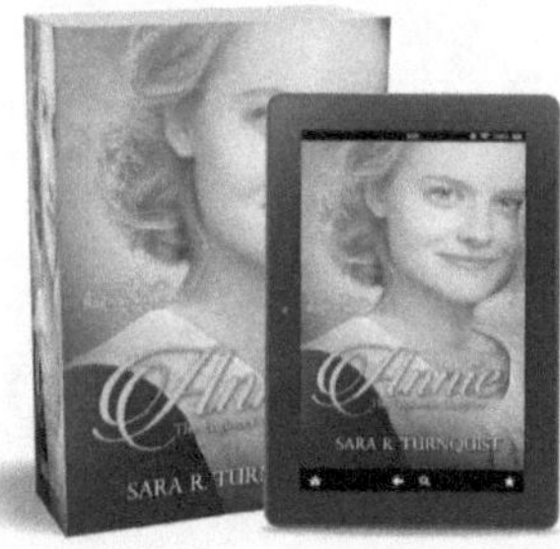

Annie Patterson rebuffs love and longs for independence. When her actions cause her to leave the safety and comfort of her brother's protection, she sets out to find a life farther West.

Micah Millington holds damaging information on his father. He only has as long as it takes for his father to find him. So he lives in anonymity. Then a woman from his past who stirred his heart comes back into his life...and challenges everything.

Can Annie and Micah evade his father long enough for their attraction to blossom into romance? Or will they find their very lives in peril?

Acknowledgments

I always resist writing this section. It's just hard. But I have so much respect and appreciation for the many people that make my books so great!

I have to thank Laura Beaver, the main character's namesake and the woman who helped us with so much history for this book. Your time and the resources you shared have been instrumental in this book. As well, I want to thank the Casey Jones Home & Railroad Museum for putting up with me invading your space and asking my crazy questions.

Cindy Smith and Kelly Hollman, you are so kind and gracious as the book is coming together, reading each chapter and giving me feedback and reactions as they come.

For my Novel Academy Huddle, your prayers and ongoing support are priceless. Thank you ladies for all you say and do.

VerBull Photography, I look better in my headshot thanks to you and your ability to get my "good side."

Julie Sherwood, my books truly shine because of your input. I trust your instincts and expertise. Thanks so much for the hard work and dedication.

Becky Brabham, I am always eager to hear my books come to life with your extraordinary talents.

Cora Graphics, this is just one more example of your gift with cover art. You are amazing!

My family, thank you for loving me and supporting me tirelessly. Even through deadlines.

My readers, you keep me going.

About the Author

Sara is a coffee lovin', word slinging, Historical Romance author whose super power is converting caffeine into novels. She loves those odd little tidbits of history that are stranger than fiction. That's what inspires her. Well, that and a good love story.

But of all the love stories she knows, hers is her favorite. She lives happily with her own Prince Charming and their gaggle of minions. Three to be exact. They sure know how to distract a writer! But, alas, the stories must be written, even if it must happen in the wee hours of the morning.

Sara is an avid reader and enjoys reading and writing clean Historical Romance when she's not traveling.

Please follow along with her journey through her newsletter at: http://saraturnquist.com/list

Happy Reading!

Also by Sara R. Turnquist

CONVENIENT RISK SERIES

A Convenient Risk

An Inconvenient Christmas

A Less Convenient Path

A Convenient Escape

An Inconvenient Acquaintance

These Golden Years

A Less Convenient Arrangement

Ranch Hands Collection (ebook only)

CRIPPLE CREEK SERIES

Hope in Cripple Creek

Christmas in Cripple Creek

Faith in Cripple Creek

Love in Cripple Creek

~Prequels~

Leaving Waverly

Leaving Stoneybrook

LADY OF BOHEMIA SERIES

The Lady Bornekova

The Lady and the Hussites

The Lady and Her Champion

The Lady and Her Secret

ACROSS THE YEARS SERIES

Among the Pages